Praise for

'Hilarious . . . Lansdale is a terrifically gifted storyteller with a sharp country boy wit.' *The Washington Post Book World*

'The most consistently original and originally visceral writer the great state of Texas (or any other state for that matter) has seen in a score of flashpoint summers.' *Austin Chronicle*

'The pace never slackens, the writing is elegance personified, and the story tugs at the heartstrings.' *Daily Mail*

'Lansdale has an unsettling sensibility. Be thankful he crafts such wild tall tales.' *Chicago Sun-Times*

'Throughout *Paradise Sky*, Lansdale the master storyteller gives lessons in corralling point-of-view, tone, plot, irony, character development and just plain old good writing . . . may well prove to be Lansdale's best.' *Dallas News*

'Enough guns, glory and goofiness to keep you entertained.' *LitReactor*

'Lansdale is one of those very rare authors who can have his readers howling with laughter during one sentence while bringing a tear to their eyes with the next.' *BookReporter*

'Lansdale has the delight in language of the best raconteur; he also delivers some wince-inducing violence and can crank up the tension to screaming point.' *Metro*

'Joe Lansdale has long been one of our finest and most difficult to classify writers . . . In *Edge Of Dark Water* he offers a beautifully spun tale of life in the sticks, friendship and mortality, and tells it with the wit, humor and pure-deep power we've come to expect of him.' Daniel Woodrell

'A

Also by Joe R. Lansdale

The Magic Wagon
The Drive In
The Nightrunners
Cold in July
The Boar
Waltz of Shadows
The Bottoms
A Fine Dark Line
Sunset and Sawdust
Lost Echoes
Leather Maiden
All the Earth, Thrown to the Sky
Edge of Dark Water
The Thicket
Paradise Sky

THE HAP AND LEONARD NOVELS
Savage Season
Mucho Mojo
Bad Chili
Rumble Tumble
Captains Outrageous
Vanilla Ride
Devil Red
Honky Tonk Samurai

SELECTED SHORT STORY COLLECTIONS
By Bizarre Hands
Sanctified and Chicken Fried
The Best of Joe R. Lansdale

JOE R. LANSDALE

The Two-Bear Mambo

A Hap and Leonard novel

MULHOLLAND
BOOKS
HODDER

First published in the United States of America in 1995 by Vintage Books
A division of Random House, Inc

First published in Great Britain in 2016 by Mulholland Books
An imprint of Hodder & Stoughton
An Hachette UK company

1

A CIP catalogue record for this title is available from the British Library

Paperback ISBN 978 1 473 63352 0
eBook ISBN 978 1 473 63353 7

Typeset in Plantin Light by Palimpsest Book Production Limited,
Falkirk, Stirlingshire

Printed and bound by CPI Group (UK) Ltd, Croydon, CR0 4YY

Hodder & Stoughton policy is to use papers that are natural, renewable and
recyclable products and made from wood grown in sustainable forests.
The logging and manufacturing processes are expected to conform to the
environmental regulations of the country of origin.

Hodder & Stoughton Ltd
Carmelite House
50 Victoria Embankment
London EC4Y 0DZ

www.hodder.co.uk

This one is for my family, Karen, Kasey and Keith.
Thanks for putting up with me.

The rising world of waters dark and deep.

John Milton: *Paradise Lost*

I

When I got over to Leonard's Christmas Eve night, he had the Kentucky Headhunters turned way up over at his place, and they were singing "The Ballad of Davy Crockett," and Leonard, in a kind of Christmas celebration, was once again setting fire to the house next door.

I wished he'd quit doing that. I'd helped him the first time, he'd done it the second time on his own, and now here I was third time out, driving up. It was going to look damn suspicious when the cops got here. Someone had already called in. Most likely the assholes in the house. I knew that because I could hear sirens.

Leonard's boyfriend, Raul, was on the front porch of Leonard's house, his hands in his coat pockets, looking over at the burning and the ass-whipping that was taking place, and he was frantic, like a visiting Methodist preacher who'd just realized the head of the household had scooped up the last fried chicken leg.

I pulled my pickup into Leonard's drive, got out, went over and stood on the porch with Raul. It was cold out and our breath was frosty white. "What got this started?" I asked.

"Oh, hell, Hap, I don't know. You got to stop him before they haul his black ass to the calaboose."

"It's too late for that, they got him. Those sirens aren't for jay-walkers."

"Shit, shit, shit," Raul said. "I shouldn't never come to live with a macho queer. I should have stayed in Houston."

Raul was normally a pretty good-looking kid, but out here in the night, the house fire flickering orange lights across his face, he looked desiccated, like the victim of a giant spider. He was sort of wobbling back and forth, like a bowling pin that hadn't quite got nailed solid enough by the ball, watching Leonard drag a big black guy out of the burning house and onto the front porch over there. The guy's shirt and pants were on fire, and Leonard was kicking him off the porch and across the front yard.

I recognized the guy. Mohawk they called him, 'cause of his haircut, though, after this night, they might just call him Smoky. Mohawk and a friend of his had once jumped on me and Leonard and we'd whipped their asses. I still dreamed about it at nights when I needed something to cheer me up.

Other folks were coming out of the house through the windows and the back door, scrambling for the woods out back. None of them seemed securely on fire, but a few had been touched by flames. A short stocky woman was in the lead. She wore only a brown bathrobe and some floppy house shoes and had a wig in her right hand. Her short legs flashed when she ran and the house coat moved and her breath went out and whiffed back in cool, white bursts. The wig was slightly on fire. She and her smoking hair hat and flopping bathrobe disappeared into the woods at a run and the others followed suit, melting into the timber with her, leaving in their wake a trail of scorched clothing smoke. A moment later they had vanished as handily as a covey of quail gone to nest.

The fire truck screamed into sight, and damn near hit Mohawk after Leonard swiveled a hip into him and twisted and tossed him into the street. The fella rolled on across, banged the curbing on the other side, and the fire truck swerved and ran up on the lawn of the burning house, and Leonard had to jump for it.

One good thing, though, all that rolling had put Mohawk's fire out. You know how it goes, that old advice the fire department gives you, "stop, drop, and roll," and that's what Mohawk was doing. Thanks to Leonard.

If you took the rose-colored view, you might say Leonard was doing nothing more than saving Mohawk's worthless life.

'Course now, Leonard had gone back into the house and a short black guy with his hair on fire came out on the end of Leonard's foot, and when he hit the lawn he got up running toward Leonard's house, Leonard yelling at his back, "Run, you goddamn little nigger."

I tell you, Leonard standing on the front porch, smoke boiling out behind him, fire licking out the windows, the roof peaked with a hat of flame, it caused Leonard's face to appear as if it had been chipped from obsidian. He was like some kind of backwoods honky nightmare vision of the Devil—a nigger with a bad attitude and the power of fire. Come to think of it, the black folks in that house probably saw him as pretty devilish as well. Leonard can be irritating to most anybody when he wants to be.

I left Raul standing on the porch about the time the little guy came out on the end of Leonard's foot, walked over and into the yard where Leonard was practicing arson and ass-whipping, put my leg out and tripped the little guy as he ran by.

He got up and I slapped him down with the side of my hand and put my foot on the back of his neck and reached down and scooped up some loose dirt in the driveway and dumped it on top of his head.

It put the fire out, except for the patch of hair burning low on the back of his head, like a spark in steel wool. The rest of his skull was smoking like a dry cabbage with a cinder in it. His body gave off quite a bit of heat, and he was wiggling as if he were being cooked alive. He was making a kind of bothersome noise that was so shrill it made my buttocks crawl up my back.

"I'm burning here," he said. "I'm burning."

"It's okay," I said. "There's not much hair left."

The cops got there then. Couple of cruisers and Sergeant Charlie Blank in his unmarked job. Charlie—wearing some of Kmart's finest, including high-gloss, black genuine plastic shoes that shone brightly in the light of the house fire—got out slowly, like his pants might rip.

He paused long enough to watch one of the blue-suit cops nab Mohawk, cuff him, and slam him in the back of a cruiser, after "accidentally" bumping his head into the car door while helping him inside.

Charlie came over to me, gave me a sad look, sighed, pulled out a cigarette, stooped, lit it off the little guy's head, and said, "I'm fucking tired of this, Hap. Leonard's giving me gray hairs. What with the Chief in cahoots with the bad guys and Lieutenant Hanson acting like he's got a weight tied to his dick all the time, I can't think straight. Get your foot off that fucker's neck."

I did, and the little guy, who hadn't yet stopped whimpering, came up on his knees and slapped at the back of his neck with a yell. The fire had already gone out, giving itself up to Charlie's cigarette, but I think the slapping bit made that dude feel better.

Charlie looked at him, said, "Lay down, buddy, and stay there."

The guy lay down. His head was smoking a lot less now.

"You know I got to run Leonard in?" Charlie said.

"I know. I thought you didn't smoke?"

"I started. I start two or three times a year. I like to quit so I can really enjoy it when I start back. I got to run you in too."

"I didn't do anything. I was just puttin' this guy out. I threw dirt on his head."

"You got a point. The dirt could make things all right." He said to the guy on the ground, "You think he was putting the fire out, sir?"

"Shit, man, that motherfucker tripped my black ass and knocked the dog shit out of me. I'm gonna file on his ass. I'm gonna file on everygoddamnbody."

"See there, Hap, got to run you in."

"Would it make any difference if I said when I hit him it hurt my hand?"

"I'll put that in my notes. You know, being this close to the fire, it's kinda warm. Toasty even. Very Christmas-like."

"That's Leonard," I said. "Always festive."

"The Ballad of Davy Crockett" was long gone and the Kentucky Headhunters were singing "Big Mexican Dinner."

"I keep trying to figure that song is offensive to Hispanics or not," Charlie said, "way the guy does that corny Meskin accent. You think it's offensive?"

"I don't know, ask Leonard's boyfriend, Raul. He could tell you. He's Mexican. But I can let you in on this, Leonard was using some bad language a while ago."

"Uh oh. I'll put that in my notes too."

"He called the young man on the ground here the N word."

"That's right," said the young man on the ground. "And in the house, he called me a motherfucker too."

"Wait a minute," Charlie said. "I got a problem here. Being how Leonard's black, is that racist? I mean, me or you said it, it's racist, but it's okay a black guy uses the N word, ain't it?"

"Changing times," I said. "It's hard to keep up. If it's not racist, I think it may be politically incorrect."

"There you are," Charlie said. "That's it. Politically incorrect. I think there's some kind of fine for that."

"Man, this is some shit," said the guy on the ground. "Let me up. Someone sees me layin' here, it ain't gonna look good."

"You think we got you out here to style?" Charlie said. "Shut the fuck up." Then to me: "Think Leonard's finished?"

"Well, the house is lit up good."

And it was. The fire peaked and popped and rose up into the night sky like a red demon, roiled and licked around the blackened frame of the house. Lumber screeched and sagged. The heat was not quite as pleasant as before. I said, "It was nice of you to stand here and wait."

"Hey," Charlie said, his face popping sweat in the firelight, "Christmas Eve."

Charlie looked at the firemen who were standing by with their hoses, and gave them a wave. They didn't exactly rush, but they went over to wash the place down, get it ready for the dozer to come in and push the burnt lumber around, make room for the dopers to bring in a new crack house.

And they would. Rumor was, the Police Chief had friends who had connections to the LaBorde dope traffic, and he liked to help them out for a little slice of the pie. Rumors like that could make a man cynical, even one of my naive and trusting nature.

When I was growing up, guy with a badge was just assumed to be honest, and the Lone Ranger didn't shoot bad guys in the head either. These days, Jesus would carry a gun, and the disciples would hold down and corn-hole their enemies.

"You think Leonard will do time for this one?" I asked.

"So far he hasn't, and I'll do what I can. A night in jail, maybe. But I keep him out of bad stuff this time, you got to make him understand he needs a new hobby. I know a hobby has done wonders for me. I used to be tense, then I got a hobby. You know, I don't get Leonard. I thought queers were into passive stuff. Like knitting and bridge."

"Don't even let him hear you say that," I said. "The passive part, I mean."

"You can bet I won't."

"I'll tell him," said the guy on the ground.

"You do," Charlie said, "and I'll stomp a mud hole in your head."

"I'm cool," said the guy on the ground.

Leonard strolled over to us then. He looked a little bushed.

"Charlie," he said.

"Howdy," Charlie said. "Okay, Leonard, you and Hap get in the cruiser . . . wait a minute. I'm gonna handcuff you together."

"Come on, Charlie," I said. "I didn't do anything, really."

"You hit this young gentleman. Put your hands out, both of you. Supposed to handcuff you with separate handcuffs, behind your back, but like I said, it's fuckin' Christmas Eve."

We were about to be handcuffed when Raul came over and took Leonard by the arm and started to cry. "Don't," Leonard said. "I can't stand all that cryin'. You're always cryin'."

"I'm fucking emotional," Raul said.

"Well, cut that cryin' shit. It makes me nervous."

"I'm crying, not you, so what are you embarrassed about?"

"It's got nothing to do with embarrassment."

"Hell," Raul said, and he tugged on Leonard's arm, but Leonard wouldn't look at him.

"Sorry, Raul," Charlie said. "You got to let him go. You want to see him, come down to the station. We got special times for asshole viewing."

"No," Raul said, letting go of Leonard's arm. "I won't be here when you get back, Leonard."

"Don't let the screen door hit you in the ass on the way out," Leonard said.

"You could ask me not to leave."

"I didn't ask you to leave in the first place."

Raul looked at Leonard for a moment, pushed his dark hair out of his eyes, turned and walked back to Leonard's house. He moved as if he were carrying a piano on his back.

"Shit, Leonard," I said, "Raul is just worried about you."

"Yeah, Leonard," Charlie said, "you don't always got to be an asshole."

"Man, you are one cold dude," said the guy on the ground. "I wouldn't talk to my woman that way, and she's stupid as a stick. You homos, man, y'all are chill motherfuckers."

"Shut up," said Charlie. "This ain't your business."

"Man," said the guy on the ground, "Merry fucking Christmas."

"Here," Charlie said, "hold out a hand."

He handcuffed me and Leonard together and sent us over to the unmarked. Part of the neighborhood was standing out on the curb watching the crack house burn. One old man, Mr. Trotter, stood there with his arms crossed inside a coat a grizzly bear might have worn. He was smoking a cigar. He said, "Of them three fires, this one's the best, Leonard."

"Thanks," Leonard said. "It's the practice makes the difference."

We got in the unmarked. We watched through the window as Charlie got the little guy off the ground and into an armlock and walked him toward a blue suit who came over and put the guy in handcuffs and shoved him into the back of the cruiser with Mohawk.

A handful of blue suits were combing the woods out back, and we could see one cop coming out with the bathrobed woman in tow. She was cuffed and had on her wig, which was giving off a faint trail of light gray smoke in the moonlight. She was cussing a blue streak. We could hear her with the windows rolled up. She was good at including "you fuckin' pale-dicked ass licker" into all her sentences without it sounding strained or overworked.

Leonard settled back in his seat and sighed slowly. "Shit," he said. "Raul's right. I always got to be the tough guy. I really like that fag. Really. Why have I always got to play it tough?"

"You're black and gay and inadequate sexually, and therefore find yourself doubly oppressed by white society, as well as being ill-suited emotionally for adjusting to the macho, black community that is your birthright."

"Oh yeah. That's right. I forgot."

"You also smell like a smoked ham."

Charlie slid in behind the wheel and closed the door, sharply. "We're leaving a couple of cops here to watch your house, Leonard. Make sure Raul's okay too. Least till he gets packed up and out. He said he's, and I quote, 'gone like the fucking wind,' unquote."

"All right," Leonard said. "Thanks."

"Will he really go?" I asked.

"Who's to say?" Leonard said.

Charlie cranked the car. Leonard said, "Could we stop for ice cream before we go in?"

"It's cold for ice cream," Charlie said.

"I like it anyway," Leonard said. "So, what do you say? I'm kinda depressed."

"I don't see why not," Charlie said. "Frozen yogurt all right? I'm on a diet."

"Suits me," Leonard said. "You're paying though. I don't have my wallet on me."

"I'm not paying shit," Charlie said. "You brought it up, you treat. Damn, Leonard, you're making my eyes burn."

"It's that cheap paneling in the house," Leonard said. "It goes up quick and stinks and the stink gets on you. Fucking walls are like they're made out of starter logs, which I guess is okay, seeing how I'm lighting the fire."

"I didn't hear you say that," said Charlie.

"I got money," I said. "My treat all around."

Charlie eased away from the curb. I took a last look at the burning house. Some timbers were sagging and crashing in with an explosion of sparks and smoke. Raul was standing on Leonard's porch watching us drive by. Leonard looked in Raul's direction. Neither of them waved.

I said, "Oh, Leonard, don't let me forget. We ever get back, I got your Christmas present in the pickup."

"Yeah, well," Leonard said, "I hope it ain't HIS and HIS towels."

2

We were in Lieutenant Hanson's office finishing off what was left of our yogurt cones, but the Lieutenant wasn't there. Considering we hadn't bought him anything, I guess that was best.

Charlie was sitting behind Hanson's desk. I was in a chair against one wall, and Leonard was in a chair against the other. We were supposed to be in a cell like Mohawk and the little guy with the burned head and the others, but we weren't. You might say we were getting special treatment. We were also getting a shadow show.

Charlie had the overhead light out and he had the desk lamp on, and he was using his fingers to throw shadows on the wall, make shapes. He did a pretty good dog and duck, but after that everything else looked like a spider.

"How about that?" Charlie said. "How's that?"

"It still looks like a spider," I said.

"I got to practice some more," Charlie said. "I got me a book now. Wife says I ought to have a hobby, so I got this. It relaxes me, but the wife thinks it ain't much. She wants me to go to the gym and work out, but this way, I can stay home and sit in the easy chair with the big light out, use the end-table light to throw a few shadows. I get tired of it, I watch a little TV. Look here, this one looks like a pussy, don't it?"

"How in hell do you get a cat out of that?" I said.

"No, a pussy. You know, a vagina. Women have 'em."

"Oh, yeah," I said. "I faintly remember."

"Look here, it does, don't it? It's kind of a dark V, ain't it?"

"It looks like a spider with its legs pulled in," Leonard said. "And don't tell me that book of yours has a section on shadow vaginas."

Charlie stuck out his middle finger and wiggled it. "This one's for you, Leonard."

A blue suit opened the door and light flooded in and the blue suit came in with it. He stopped and looked at Charlie and Charlie's hand shadow.

"What's this look like to you?" Charlie asked him.

"What?"

"The shadow, Jake, the shadow."

"Oh. I don't know. It looks like a shadow."

"Swell," Charlie said.

"Hey, listen," Jake said. "Chief ain't in—"

"Surprise, surprise," Charlie said.

"And Lieutenant Hanson's out."

"He's on his way."

"Well, we got a guy in cell three, he wants we should call his wife, tell her to tape a *National Geographic* special on bears. We got to do it now, he gets to catch it. It starts in fifteen minutes."

"What?" Charlie asked.

"He's gonna miss it," Jake said. "'Cause he's gonna be here tonight. Drunk and disorderly."

"What the hell does he think we're running here?" Charlie said, not looking at Jake, but wiggling his fingers in such a way that brought him back to his shadow shape standards. A dog, which he made a barking sound for, then a duck, which he quacked for.

"I'll tell him no," Jake said.

"I guess you will," Charlie said. "I can't believe you came to me with that shit. Wait a minute." Charlie swiveled in the chair and looked at the cop. "A *National Geographic* special?"

"On bears," Jake said.

"Hell, call her. I ought to be glad it's not *Charlie's Angels*, some shit like that. Maybe we're getting a better class of criminal in here. Go on and do it."

"All right," Jake said, and closed the door.

"Can we go?" Leonard said.

Charlie was back to trying to make a pussy. I think.

"Go?" Charlie said. "You fuckin' me? You burned your next-door neighbor's house down. That's three times, man. First time you and Hap did it, we worked it out. Second time you did it, we worked it out. But you're gonna have to take up shadow shapes or something,

Leonard. Quit this arson. We could put you behind bars so long, you got out, hair on your balls would be white."

"They're scum, Charlie," Leonard said, "and you know it."

"I went around burning houses belonged to scum, this town would mostly be a cinder."

"Bullshit," Leonard said.

In the middle of our examining another of Charlie's shadow shapes, the door opened again. It was Lieutenant Marvin Hanson this time. He was framed by the hall light behind him, and it made him look like the Golem. His black skin was all shadow and no features. He watched Charlie a second, then closed the door and turned on the light. I suddenly realized I preferred looking at him in the dark. That rugged face of his could be scary.

"Talent show's over," Hanson said. "And so's sitting behind my desk."

"Yassuh," Charlie said, and he eased out from behind the desk and took a chair and lit a cigarette.

Hanson went over and sat down behind his desk, swiveled his chair and looked at Leonard.

"Well, well," Hanson said. "If it isn't the Smartest Nigger in the World."

"Hi," Leonard said.

"That's the N word again," Charlie said to me.

"Yes," I said, "but it's two black guys talking to one another, so we've got the same problem as before. Is it racist, politically incorrect, or all in fun?"

"Ain't nothing fun about it," Hanson said. Then to Leonard: "You dumb motherfucker. I'm sick of your goddamn cavalier attitude."

"They killed a kid last year," Leonard said.

"He took the dope on his own," Hanson said.

"He was a kid," Leonard said.

"All right, all right, one house burning is okay," Hanson said. "But twice? Then three times? You got to respect my position here."

"Your goddamn Chief of Police has ties to the fucks who provide that house, and you know it," Leonard said.

"That's a point for Leonard," Charlie said. "He's right. You know it, I know it, the guys in the slammer know it. They know too they'll be out of here come morning. If it takes that long. They'll be suing Leonard, most likely."

"Shut up, Charlie," Hanson said.

"Yassuh, Massuh Marvin."

"That's kinda racist, isn't it?" I said to Charlie. "A white guy doing slave talk?"

"Think so?" Charlie said.

"Will you two assholes shut up?" Hanson said.

I could see "Yassuh" forming on Charlie's lips, but he decided to just wiggle them instead. Wise choice, I thought.

"What are these two fucks doing in here watching you and your fucking shadows?" Hanson said. "Why ain't they in a cell?"

"I figured they were kind of guests," Charlie said. "I mean, hell, I like 'em."

"Yeah, well, I don't," Hanson said. "Especially the Smartest Nigger in the World here. He's always doing what he wants. He doesn't think the law applies to him. He's some kind of crusader. Some kind of vigilante. Yes sir, he's the Smartest Nigger in the World."

"I don't know," said Leonard. "I hear great stuff about you and Jesse Jackson."

Hanson moved suddenly, and considering his size, it was a fast move. He grabbed the lamp on his desk and jerked it hard enough the plug came out. He threw it at Leonard, who slipped casually sideways in his chair, as if avoiding a punch. The lamp went by and hit the wall and exploded. Leonard and Hanson both stood up.

There was a beat of silence during which a lot of things could have happened, but didn't. Finally, Leonard smiled. Then Hanson smiled. Hanson and Leonard slowly sat back down. Hanson said, "Shit, my ex-wife gave me that desk lamp."

"And what a special little prize it was," I said.

"What I do when I lose a family heirloom," Charlie said, "is I go get drunk."

"That sounds about right," Hanson said. "Boys, get your coats."

3

Hanson said, "Can you believe that, two bears fuckin', right there on the television set?"

We were at Hanson's house watching the *National Geographic* special. Hanson and Charlie were drinking lots of beer. Leonard was nursing one, and I was having a Sharp's nonalcoholic beer. I'd given up drinking because I thought it was stupid and expensive and not very healthy.

Beer, however, didn't hurt Hanson's and Charlie's feelings.

Charlie said, "Actually, Marve, my man. Them bears are neither on, nor in, the set. Those bears fucking is recorded on videotape or something. Then they play it back so we can see it. You see those trees? That grass? It's spring there behind them. That means those bears could have done this fucking a year or two ago. Anytime really."

Hanson wasn't paying attention. He took another drink from his can of Schlitz, said, "Can you believe that shit? I was a kid, they wouldn't show two dogs one behind another for fear you might think one was gonna mount the other. And now, right there, in front of God and everybody, two bears doing the mambo."

"That's kind of a sexy angle too," Charlie said. "Only thing we're missing here is a diagram showing us the inside of the girl bear's ass, so we can see the boy bear's dick swell into a knot. They do that, I think. Like a dog."

Not being specialists on bear's dicks, none of us responded. We didn't want to look like fools.

The bears on the special finished up the mambo, as Hanson called it. Neither of them lit a cigarette, but they both looked fairly satiated. The camera cut to a guy in khakis. He was talking about bears as he walked. The guy came across a pile of bear shit in the woods and you'd have thought he'd found a fifty-dollar bill. He whisked that shit around with a stick and told us about the health of the bear that had left it. In fact, he told us everything about that bear but its blood type and hat size. I was impressed. I know how to track in the woods, know most of the species of trees and bushes, and can tell some basic things about critters from their stool, provided I have the urge to stir their shit around with a stick. But this guy was remarkable. It just looked like a pile of bear shit to me, but here he was seeing all kinds of stuff in it.

I wondered if you went to college to learn about bear shit.

The bear show was pretty good, but I got to admit, I burned out on it. I think decoding bear shit was about as far as my interest in bears went, and I felt uncomfortable at Hanson's house. I kept fearing Florida would come in. It was bad enough there was plenty there to remind me of her.

It wasn't any specific thing, it was the way the house looked. I'd never been in Hanson's house before. We mainly insulted each other at the police station and bad hamburger joints, but it was apparent there had been a feminine hand at work here. And not Hanson's mother.

Florida might still have her apartment, might not stay here all the time, but from the well-decorated Christmas tree to the way objects were laid out on the shelves, the house spoke as much of her as it did Hanson.

And there were little clues. For instance, I seriously doubted the books in the shelf on aerobic dancing and how to make love to a man were Hanson's, though you can't be sure about something like that.

I did observe, however, that all around Hanson's chair it looked like the city dump, but a little less organized. It was littered with cigar butts, ashes, junk food wrappers, and beer cans. When we came in through the kitchen, I noticed, while kicking a plastic bag of spoiled celery out of my path, that it appeared as if the place had been blown about by a tornado. I know I don't keep a greasy frying pan full of molding scrambled eggs upside down on the floor or leave my refrigerator door open when I'm out of the house. And most everyone agrees the floor is a bad spot for celery.

I tried not to let old-fashioned ideas about women and kitchens get into my thinking, but they did. I knew Florida. She wasn't a classic housewife type any more than she was a classic women's lib type, but she wouldn't have let the joint get like this. Even if it was confined to the kitchen and around Hanson's chair.

I couldn't imagine Hanson, slob that he was, allowing the place to get this bad either, unless his head was somewhere sad and distant.

And earlier, hadn't Charlie made some crack about Hanson going around as if a weight was tied to his dick? Then there was that lamp-throwing business. That seemed a little intense even for Hanson.

And inviting us over to his place to watch a *National Geographic* special? That was too nice. That wasn't the Hanson I knew. And why hadn't he mentioned Florida? Was she visiting relatives? Caroling?

I began to suspect he and Florida had broken up, and a sense of warm well-being flowed over me before it was replaced by a warmer sense of shame, because secretly, I had been hoping me and her might get back together. This was a somewhat bitter and wistful sort of thought that came and went from time to time, and truthfully, I was glad to feel it go. Hanson was an all-right guy, and Florida and I had taken our shot and it hadn't hit target. She had decided on Hanson, and I reckoned it was best all around. I knew it was over for me and her, and always would be. But I couldn't help remembering her soft honey-brown skin and the way she moaned when I gave her pleasure, the way her legs moved, the smell of her. I couldn't forget her smile and the razor sharpness of her thinking. And, of course, I couldn't forget she was kind of an asshole.

I asked about the bathroom, and Hanson pointed it out. I had to go through the bedroom to get there, and as I went, I looked at the bed. It was unmade and the covers were thrown back and it smelled of sweat and perfume. Chanel No. 5. Not Hanson's brand. He was an Old Spice man. The rest of the room looked in good shape, except there was a pile of Hanson's clothes on the floor at the right-hand side of the bed.

The bathroom was clean and orderly except for toothpaste and whisker hair in the sink. Hanson had made a kind of pig trail from the kitchen to his chair to the bed to the bathroom, leaving the rest of the joint neat and clean.

When I got back from the bathroom, Leonard was still on the

couch, but he had the book that told how to make love to a man. He was turning it at an odd angle.

He said, "I didn't know you could do that."

"Maybe you can't," Charlie said. "That's man and woman stuff."

"Homosexuals are pretty smart," Leonard said. "Sometimes we improvise." He put the book in his lap. "Figures. Me and Raul are broke up, and here's something nifty we could have tried."

"Leonard," I said, finding my Sharp's and my place on the couch. "You got to quit watching bears fuck. It gets you worked up."

Hanson cranked back his easy chair, laid his catcher's mitt hands on his chest and looked at the ceiling light. We looked with him. Nothing really important seemed to be going on up there.

"Guess I need to figure what to do with you boys," Hanson said.

"How about paper hats and whistles and we all go home?" I said.

"I don't think so," Hanson said.

"Well, how bad could it be?" Charlie said. "You got them over at your house drinking beer and watching TV."

"What I'm gonna do," Hanson said, "is make you boys a little deal. You two go over to Grovetown and do me a little favor, and I'll find a way not to press charges. You don't, I'll find a special way to press charges."

"Hey," Leonard said, "that's blackmail. And what the hell would you want us to do in Grovetown anyway? Look for antiques?"

"No," Hanson said, "I want you to check on Florida."

"I was wondering about her," I said.

"Figured you were," Hanson said. "Deal is, she went over there to do a little lawyering, kind of. You fellas hear about that Bobby Joe Soothe problem?"

"Nope," Leonard said. "I have enough problems of my own. Me and Raul, we've had hell trying to get a lubricant we like. K-Y is highly overrated. I bet we been through twenty-five tubes of this and that."

"I don't want to hear about it," Charlie said. "But you might check Kmart. They got all kinds of lubricant stuff there, at reasonable prices. From Vaseline to forty-weight lube oil."

"I don't think I'll be needing it now," Leonard said. "Unless I'm just gonna use a little bit of it in the palm of my hand."

"Bobby Joe Soothe," Hanson said, "was a black man had him a little accident."

"I did hear about that," I said. "On the news. Hung himself in Grovetown jail with his shoelaces. Something like that."

"Something like that," Hanson said. "There's a back story though. You see, this Bobby Joe Soothe, he was the grandson of L.C. Soothe. Heard of L.C.?"

"Hell yeah," Leonard said. "Country blues guitar. I got some of his stuff. One of those boxed set things. One of the greats. East Texas legend of the late twenties, early thirties. Kind of like Robert Johnson. Had the same story about him. That he sold his soul to the devil to play way he did. Some kind of deal where he took a piss in a fruit jar and took it to the crossroads and the devil came and drank it, then the devil peed in a jar, and L.C. drank it, then L.C. had the devil in him and the devil had his soul. After that, L.C. could play that old standard guitar like a sonofabitch. Used a pocket-knife or a bottle neck for a slide."

"I can't think of nothing I'd want so bad I'd drink wee-wee out of a fruit jar," Charlie said.

"L.C. only made a few records," Leonard said, "but he was a big influence on East Texas blues men. The records are rare. I think he made some recordings on 78s, whatever the method was then, and they were never released, or lost. I don't remember the details. It's just the general stuff I know about, and I got that out of the booklet in the collection box."

"All I know," Hanson said, "is a fella from up North read an article in some music magazine about this Bobby Joe Soothe who was tryin' to build a name on his grandfather's name, and Bobby Joe said he had in his possession this recorded, but unreleased record L.C. had made. Said too he was singing some songs L.C. had left written down, but never recorded. This Bobby Joe had a bit of reputation for good blues himself, see. So this Northern fella made contact with him, made some promises of money for the record, came down here to check it out, and supposedly, Bobby Joe cut that white boy's throat, took his money, then got hauled into jail where he decided he couldn't go on and hung himself with his shoe strings."

"I thought they didn't let prisoners keep stuff like shoe strings and belts," I said.

"Not supposed to," Hanson said. "Interesting thing is, there's been more hangings and accidents and suicides of this kind in that jail in the past forty-five years than there's been accidental prisoner deaths in all the state of Texas since nineteen sixty-five. And that includes goddamn Huntsville Prison. Guess I ought to give the cracker runs the place now some credit, though. Only one hanging, the Soothe hanging, has happened in the twelve years he's been Chief in Grovetown."

"What happened to the recordings?" Leonard asked.

"No one knows," Hanson said.

"How does Florida come into this?" I asked.

"I'm gettin' to that," Hanson said. "Florida, as you know, is an ambitious gal. She decided lawyering wasn't enough. She wanted to go out and do some investigative work. Go to Grovetown, ask some questions, use her law credentials, maybe get some kind of article out of this, move herself into investigative journalism. I think she wants to be on television. She's got the looks, the voice, the brains, and the personality, so it's not a far-fetched kind of idea. She's been sort of looking around for something to tie her to a bigger gig. A journalism career. Thought if she cowgirl'd this one, she could write her own ticket."

"In other words," I said. "Florida was looking for a rat to ride, and smelled one in Grovetown?"

"Yep," Hanson said. "She went down there couple weeks ago. I told her not to, that it was dangerous. She didn't listen, and that didn't surprise me. We hadn't been doing that good anyway. We were supposed to get married, but didn't."

"Kind of thought the date for that had come and passed," I said.

"Figured you were marking your calendar," Hanson said. "Thing is though, me and her had a fight. She thought I was being a male chauvinist jerk. If being worried about someone you care about, being realistic about what can happen to them is being a jerk, then I'm a jerk. Grovetown is a scary place for black folk to go hang around and try to pry into stuff, but she went anyway."

"Florida doesn't strike me as that brave," I said. "Least not in that way. Considering my own experiences with her, I'd say she's been cautious in the past."

"She's cautious till she wants something," Hanson said.

"True," I said. "Selfishness is one of her major traits."

"She got to Grovetown," Hanson said, "cooled some, called to say she was okay, and that things between me and her had reached a wall. She called again a few days later to say she was okay, and things were going good, but she didn't give details, and she said she'd have someone come for her stuff when she gets back."

"So you're split up?" Leonard said. "Like me and Raul. It's like a disease going around."

"Guess that means you don't get to keep the aerobic book and the one on making love to a man," I said.

"Looks that way," Hanson said. "I gotta tell you. I like that gal. Really. But I gotta tell you too, and this will sound like some horse-shit since I've been fuckin' her, but it was getting so our relationship was more like father and daughter, her being so much younger. Thinking so different and all."

"I don't think I like the sound of that father and daughter stuff," Charlie said. "Not with you throwing the pork to her."

"You know what I mean," Hanson said. "I think I was gonna cut it off between us. I didn't feel right. Maybe it's not just because she's so young, but because I still love my ex-wife, goddammit. You know, like that's gonna go somewhere."

This was a new wrinkle. I said, "So if you were developing a more father-daughter relationship than a romantic one, and she cut the romance off, why are you so moony? And why does your kitchen look like a tornado blew through it?"

"She spent the night with me morning before she left," Hanson said. "We had an argument. It got out of hand. I grabbed her. I'm ashamed of that, but I did. But she got right up in my face, see, and it was just reflex. I grabbed her and hurt her arm a little. It wasn't on purpose, guys, really. I'm no woman beater."

"We're all human," I said. "Everybody fucks up now and then."

"Really, I never hit a woman in my life, and I didn't hit her, but I grabbed her. She could be so infuriating. She was standing in there with the refrigerator open, looking for something for breakfast, and that's when the argument started and the door got left open. She pulled some celery out of there, hit me with it, and I grabbed her. When I realized what I'd done and let her go, she snatched up the frying pan and hit me on the shoulder with it and burned me, dropped it on the floor. I still got the egg on my pajamas. She left five minutes later and I haven't changed a thing in there since."

"Kind of a shrine, huh?" Leonard said.

"I keep telling him she'll get over it," Charlie said. "Hell, she called from Grovetown, didn't she? She knows Marve just lost his cool, and she had something to do with it. They're both to blame. A lesson was learned."

"It's not the getting back together that's bothering me," Hanson said. "I mean, not that way, you know. I'm just worried about her down there, and if I go check on her, that's just more male chauvinist stuff, and there's no reason she should report to me, and theoretically, she's out of my life, but . . ."

"Why don't you go there anyway?" Leonard said. "You could see she's all right, and if you're telling it straight, it's not like the relationship is coming back together anyway. Or that you want it to. So what's it matter she gets mad at this point?"

"I'd like to end this on a note of respect," Hanson said. "Not like I'm spying on her."

"And you think these two dimwits showing up down there ain't gonna make her suspicious?" Charlie said. "Hell, she knows them. She knows Hap biblically."

"Thanks, Charlie," I said, "you certainly know how to defuse a tense or worrisome moment."

"It's different," Hanson said. "She sees you two, you could say Charlie told you about her, and you thought you might go down and check on her. Old times' sake."

"Oh, now I told them about her," Charlie said.

"Maybe you could act like you'd like to take her on a date, Hap. Something like that."

"That sounds convincing," Charlie said. "I can see why you been so tired all week. All the heavy thinking it took to come up with that, I'd be strained too."

"Yeah, you're right, Charlie," Hanson said. "It won't work. It was a major stupid idea. It's like I been having a sack of shit for a head lately. Idea like that sucks big time."

"I can feel a draft from it over here," Charlie said.

"Yeah," Hanson said. "Let's have some eggnog, then, Hap, Leonard, we'll take y'all back to the hoosegow."

"Grovetown," I said, "it's a place I been wanting to visit. I'd just like to go by the house, get a change of clothes, maybe a paperback to go."

"Unless, of course," Leonard said, "you'd prefer we leave tonight. Right now."

4

It was after midnight, Christmas Day, when I took the wheel of Charlie's car and drove him over to Leonard's. Idea was, Leonard was going to get his car and follow me to Charlie's place. I'd drop Charlie and his car off, then we'd leave in Leonard's heap. Charlie was just too drunk to drive.

It had grown quite cold and it was a clear night. Kind of night I relished when I was a kid. My dad, who worked as a mechanic, or at the foundry from time to time, would go out in the yard with me and we'd throw a blanket over our shoulders and sit on the porch stoop and look at the stars. We were well out in the country then, and there were no streetlights, and with the house lights off the stars glowed in the black satin heavens like white dots of neon.

Dad was a heavy man and very tired and we didn't play ball together or do any of the classic stuff fathers and sons are supposed to do. He put in twelve-hour days and did hard manual labor, so he wasn't up for much ball chasing when he came home. But he did his best. He taught me about the woods when he had time, went to my school plays, made sure I had money for comic books, and found the time, now and then, when he should have been sleeping, to sit on the porch and point out the Big Dipper and the Little Dipper, and he had names for some of the other stars I've forgotten, but they weren't the names you normally hear. They were names given the constellations by his father or grandfather, and they had known the stars as well as a seasoned truck driver knows a road map.

Dad told me stories while we looked at the stars. He had known Bonnie and Clyde. He had driven around Gladewater, Texas, with them one Fourth of July and tossed firecrackers out the windows of their automobile. At the time, he didn't know they were being pursued by every law enforcement agency in Texas.

Late one night during the depths of the Great Depression, down by the railroad track where he was hoboing, he and his friends had met Pretty Boy Floyd. He had fought bareknuckle and wrestled at county fairs for money. He knew handed-down stories of Billy the Kid, Belle Starr, Sam Bass, and Jessie James, and when he was a child, he'd seen Frank James giving a talk in a Sears store on the ills of crime. He may have yarned a little, but I liked it all anyway.

Now, the stories I heard were off the late-night news. Rapes and serial murders and child molestations. Children with guns and no imagination and less ambition. It wasn't a world my father would have understood. Last time I had seen him was a Christmas many years ago. He looked as if he'd just viewed the new world he was living in for the very first time and didn't like it and didn't want to stay. He was dead in two weeks. A heart attack and he was out of there.

When we got to Leonard's, I knew he was hoping Raul hadn't left, but Raul's Ford station wagon was gone. There were a couple of cops there, watching the place. Leonard thanked them, shooed them off, and Charlie let him.

Leonard went inside while we sat in Charlie's car with the engine running and the heater turned high. It was quite cozy. Charlie was pretty drunk, but when he spoke his words were clear, so I figured he still had a few brain cells left.

"Here's y'all's Christmas present," Charlie said. "Some advice. Don't do this thing for Hanson."

"It beats jail," I said.

"You ain't goin' to jail. You know that. Hanson ain't gonna do shit. He'll get Leonard out of this. He knows the Chief knows he knows about the crack house. Chief knows Hanson is gonna nail him one day, somehow, if he don't get rid of him first. They're just playing some kind of cat-and-mouse shit. Chief fires him, Hanson can make a big enough stink all the fumigators in LaBorde couldn't get rid of it. Chief knows he's got to get rid of Hanson, but he hasn't figured how. Gives him every shit job there is, hoping he'll get killed. But Hanson, he takes a lickin' and keeps on tickin'. So, what I'm saying is, Hanson decides to get Leonard off, he'll get him off. He knows enough about where the bodies are buried to handle that."

Charlie turned to look at what was left of the house next door. A charred frame, a pile of gray ash, and a few wisps of smoke. "You know," Charlie said, "that is Leonard's best job yet."

"He likes his work. And Charlie, thanks for the advice, but odd as this sounds, Hanson's kind of a friend. Considering Florida and I once had this thing going, I think he's pretty much in need or he wouldn't ask me to get involved."

"All right," Charlie said, cracking the passenger window and getting out a cigarette. "I give you that." He pushed in the car lighter. "But this is his problem. Not yours. He feels there's something really wrong, he ought to take care of it himself. He ought not send citizens down there to do his dirty work."

"I think he's just a little concerned is all and doesn't feel it's a legal matter."

"Grovetown is a shithole, Hap. You ought not go down there with Leonard. They don't like black folks unless they're swabbing out a toilet or sweeping a floor. That's the main reason Hanson didn't want Florida going down there. He thought it was dumb some little black gal like her going down to Honkyland. He told her so. She thought it was some kind of male chauvinist bullshit. He was just talking good sense. There's people down there don't believe civil rights is a real law. They still think everyone ought to own 'em a nigger. Let me tell you something. I spent a week in that armpit on account of my sister's husband, Arnold—may he grow like an onion with his head in the ground. He left her. He was working the lumber mill there, had this thing going with a secretary, decided one day this chippie's pussy was all he wanted to smell, so he and her got out of Grovetown and left Sis sittin' on her ass with two kids, both of 'em in diapers. I had to go over there and get her. There were arrangements to be made. Old bills. Some things to sell. Usual shit. I sent her home and stayed to do the stuff she wasn't emotionally fit to do. I went into that town three, four times a week, and I tell you, man, it's like a time warp. Hardly any blacks come into town if they haven't got some kind of business—like buying groceries. Getting gas. Necessary stuff. And they see a white man coming they step off the sidewalk and assume a Rastus position. All teeth and bent heads. It's what's expected of them. It's what they know. They don't do that, Klan over there—or rather some offshoot of it, calls itself the Supreme Knights of the Caucasian Order, or some ridiculous handle like that—decides some black is uppity, they'll come down on 'em. Blacks in Grovetown are outflanked. Whites have all the power there. All the power."

"Lot of blacks would argue it's that way everywhere."

"And they'd be wrong. Everywhere ain't like Grovetown. They go to Grovetown, they're gonna find out things are a lot better elsewhere than they think. They're gonna find what it's like to be back in the sixties, before that Civil Rights Act. They're gonna realize things aren't near as bad as they've been. Except in Grovetown. Late as four, five years ago, a black woman was tarred and feathered by some of those Klan ass wipes. She was raped too, ten, fifteen times. Guys did that are the kind of creeps would stand up and tell you how whites and blacks ought not to be together, and whites and blacks shouldn't date, but they don't mind stealing some black pussy from some poor woman, tarring and feathering her. Hot tar, Hap. That shit is intense. That's not something anyone wants on them. She damn near died 'cause most of her pores were closed up. And then there was one other little touch. They sewed up her snatch. Sewed it up with a leather-craft needle and baling wire."

"Good God. What the hell did she do to get them down on her?"

"You'll like this. They didn't like the way she dressed. She was some young gal, nineteen, twenty at the oldest. Grew up in Grovetown, went off to the university here, went back to Grovetown for spring break, forgot how to play the game. Maybe thought times had changed. Year or two to someone that young is an eternity. Maybe she took an Afro-American course and bought a dashiki. Thought 'cause of that the whole world changed. She developed some pride, like anyone ought to. But then she went home and got that knocked out of her. Word was—and this was based on a couple of unsigned, unaddressed letters the editors of the university paper got from Grovetown—this all happened because this Klan offshoot thought she wore, as they put it, 'provocative clothing of an indecent nature,' and that the university wasn't for 'colored,' and such things as education were wasted on them. It was signed the Grand Exalted Cyclops of the Supreme Knights of the Caucasian Assholes, or whatever the fuck they are."

"They certainly sound like a progressive bunch."

"The letter denied she'd been raped, said if anything she'd been cavorting with her 'colored friends' before she was tarred and feathered, and then there was some bullshit about women in general and how they ought to stay home and raise kids and not venture into the world of men, and so forth, and that she had gotten sewn up to suggest, symbolically, that the world didn't need any more black babies."

"Sometimes you got to wonder if we're all part of the same human race."

"We aren't. Those motherfuckers are evil aliens. Got to be. Way I figure, one of those crackers came on to that gal, figured he had him a little nigger sweetie just couldn't wait to give a big white man some pussy, and when she turned him down, it pissed him off. He and some of the boys got together, caught her off some place, and he got what he wanted. And so did his friends. Used the Assholes of the Caucasian Knights as a blind. It's just plain old rape and brutality, justified with bullshit rhetoric."

"Anyone ever arrested for that?"

The cigarette lighter had popped out long ago and cooled. Charlie pushed it back in. "Nope. No one over in Grovetown seemed to know anyone in any kind of Klan-like organization. No one had seen a thing. They got away with rape and brutality. No telling what it done to that young woman. Not just physically, but emotionally."

"Do you know any nicer bedtime stories than this one, Charlie?"

"Nope. All I know is them kind. It's all I see. It's all I hear about. Don't go, Hap. It ain't for you."

"I guess Hanson figures we can take care of ourselves."

"Hell, yeah. He knows you can. You guys are dumb asses, but ain't no one ever said you were cowards. Hell, man, Leonard, that motherfucker would wade through the fires of hell with a hand bucket half full of creek water if he thought he was doing the right thing. And you, well, I ain't got you all figured out yet. But no one's so tough they can beat a town. You go over there and fuck around, don't come whining to me someone tars and feathers your ass and sews your dick to your leg. Or worse . . . Damn, I'm sick. My wife is gonna kill me I come in like this."

The lighter popped out and Charlie lit his cigarette. He turned and blew smoke through the crack in the window. He replaced the lighter and leaned back in the seat, held the cigarette tight between his knuckles.

After a moment he said, "I'm just telling you that you ought not do this thing. Hanson doesn't want to do it because he's a cop. Not his jurisdiction. And him being black, it'll look like he's stirring trouble with all this stuff going on down there about that guy hanging himself. Then you got the bit about he don't want Florida to know he's sniffing her ass. Add it up, it comes out two plus two equals shit."

"I appreciate your concern."

"You feel you just got to do it, leave Leonard here. Not only is he black, in case you haven't noticed, but he's got a smart mouth, same as you. He can't stand to let anyone think they're putting one over on him. Guys in Grovetown, they can't stand a smartass black guy. And it's not like Leonard is quiet about being queer, neither. He ain't bashful, you know what I mean?"

"I know what you mean."

"Man, you think a black guy will work their bowels, you add queer to that, toss in you and him together doing your stooge act, it's like throwing gasoline on a fire."

"Leonard wouldn't let me go by myself, even if I wanted him to. Not since Hanson asked him to go."

"That's where Hanson fucked up," Charlie said. "He ain't thought a clear thought in damn near two weeks. He's really messed up. A week from now. A month. He'd know better'n to ask something stupid like that of either of you."

"Leonard told Hanson he'd go. Leonard says he'll do something, he'll do it, Charlie. You know that."

Charlie sighed. "I'm too drunk to argue. Let me just sum up here, Hap. You and the Smartest Nigger in the World go to Grovetown, it's askin' for trouble. But if you're goin'—"

He eased his ass up, got his wallet out, unlimbered it, and gave me two hundred and fifty dollars. "You'll need this."

"I don't want to take it, Charlie, but I got to."

"I know."

I put the money in my wallet, said, "I been sitting here wondering how I was going to afford this little trip. I hate to keep sucking off Leonard, and it's not like he's rich either. He sunk a lot of his inheritance into this house. Fixing it up."

"Well, that ain't really enough money. You're gonna have to dip into Leonard's jack, but as for that two hundred and fifty, don't worry about it."

"That's good of you, Charlie."

"Naw it ain't. Ain't my money. Hanson gave that to me to give to you before we left his place."

I dropped Charlie and his car off at his house and Leonard followed. We wished Charlie a Merry Christmas when he got through puking off the side of his porch, then I drove Leonard's car back to his house while Leonard sat on the passenger side, looked out the window and brooded.

"Was Raul's stuff gone?" I asked.

"Yeah. There was one box of his things in there, packed with an address label on it. Had a note asking me to mail it to him at his parents'. Said he'd pay me back. My Christmas present for him was on top of the box. Unopened."

"This your first spat?"

"We had one every goddamn day, but I guess this is the worst. We were fighting right before I burned those assholes' house down. I don't even remember what me and him were arguing about. I think that's why I beat those fucks up and burned their place down. I mean, you know, I don't like 'em, and that's the biggest reason, but shit, these days, I get worked up, I burn whatever house is there down. It lets off some tension."

"What are you gonna do until they get a new house put up?"

"I don't know. Squeeze a rubber ball. Jerk off."

"And what if the house gets put in there isn't a crack house next time, but some old lady who just wants to putter around her flower garden?"

"I guess I could go over there nights and pull up her roses."

"I can see you've thought this through with options."

Leonard tapped his temple with a finger. "Thinking all the time."

He sat for a moment, said: "That goddamn Raul. I kinda thought I was ready for him to go, but you know, I miss him."

"Raul seemed okay to me, but it's not like I been around him much. Maybe him going away isn't so bad."

"That some kind of comment?"

"I haven't seen much of you lately either, Leonard. It's not like I know anything about y'all's relationship. See, I sort of thought you and me being like brothers, I'd get the inside scoop on things."

"Hey, you got to remember, I ain't had no loving in ages. You forget how you get when you have a woman. All you want to do is fuck."

"I guess that's normal at the beginning of any relationship. I just thought maybe you'd have brought him around. You and me, compadre, we're family. Besides, you can only screw so much, after a while, you got to maybe read a book, talk to friends."

"You got enough problems in your life doing crap work for a living, being mostly worthless without ambition, and being friends with me. Figured you didn't need me and my lover dropping by."

"You think it's like I got neighbors? And if I did, think they'd know just by looking at you? And if they did, think I'd give a fuck?"

"That's not what I mean, and you know it."

"What do you mean?"

"No matter how close we are, I think the whole thing jacks you around. You know, me fuckin' a guy."

"It's different is all. I'm not used to it. I see two guys hugging up, one of them my friend, guy I think of in a traditional way most of the time, well, I won't lie to you, it makes me uncomfortable. Not sick to my stomach or nothing, just uncomfortable. I don't visualize what you guys are doing in the privacy of your own home, not only because it's private, but shit, Leonard, I don't like to think about it. I know there isn't anything wrong with it. But I was taught one way all my life, that homos were perverts. I know now a pervert comes in hetero or homo, same as good people, but it still turns my crank backwards a little to know y'all got the same equipment to play with and you're willing to do it with each other."

"How do you think it makes me feel, see you kissin' on some old gal? That ain't natural to me, Hap. It don't matter what's supposed to be natural, my biology tells me one thing, yours tells you another."

"All right. Let's drop that. It's not like we're really in disagreement."

"You know what, Hap?"

"What?"

"I really thought this one was more than just sex. I thought me and Raul had a relationship. I thought me and him were gonna grow old together and come over to your place now and then for fried chicken and maybe borrow money, you ever got any. I really did mean to bring him around. Really. I just wanted to get stabilized. And, of course, I have. I'm by myself again."

"He could come back."

"I doubt it. I think I saw it coming for the last two weeks. We were just too different. I was confusing sex for loving 'cause I hadn't had either in so goddamn long. You know what? He liked *Gilligan's Island*. He wouldn't miss that fucker. Had books on that shit. Photos of the stars. Has a stack of videotapes full of *Gilligan's Island*. He thought Bob Denver was a good actor, and I think he had this thing for the Professor. Raul's big goal in life was to get a copy of the reunion episode."

"You're right," I said. "Mark Raul off your list. He's too dumb to live. Hey, one bright note. My Christmas present, I'm gonna cheer you up when I tell you what I got you. That 'Asleep at the Wheel' album you been wanting."

"The one where they get a bunch of folks together to redo Bob Wills's stuff?"

"Yep. Got that big-tittied singer you like on it."

"Dolly Parton."

"Yep. And it's got Willie 'Can't Pay His Taxes' Nelson too."

"No shit?"

"No shit."

"You said album, but you meant CD, right?"

"Yep."

"Great. Guess what? That was Raul's CD player. He took it with him."

5

That night I slept on Leonard's fold-out couch, which had acquired an assortment of potato chips, peanuts, and pretzel crumbs. I guess watching *Gilligan* gives you the munchies.

Leonard was up half the night, going to the bathroom, the kitchen, looking out windows, feeling blue over Raul. I lay there and watched him pad around, and thought about Grovetown. I'd heard about it being stuck in time before Charlie told me. Grovetown was like Vidor, Texas, another, and larger, and more infamous Klan stronghold. Vidor didn't even have a black in its town to hang. It was all white and proud of it. Leonard knew about Grovetown. Had some idea what he was getting into, but if he was overly concerned, neither his words or actions showed it.

I closed my eyes and remembered Florida. I could smell her hair. Feel her thigh on my finger tips. The first time we made love was in this house. In Leonard's bedroom. My God, it hadn't really been that long ago. I knew that hot summer night, when we lay in bed together, even before we made love, that I adored her. And just as surely, I knew she would break my heart. And she had.

She couldn't cope with my being white. Not having a career. Having little to no ambition. A man adrift. She said: "I like someone who gets up in the morning and has a purpose. A real purpose. I have one. I want whoever I love to have one."

And she was right. What I was about was day-to-day survival, and that was it. When I was young, I could look around corners. Now, I did well to see six inches beyond my nose.

Jesus Christ, how in hell, why in hell, do all my romances go wrong?

Next morning, not long after the sun came up and coffee had

boiled, Leonard called a couple fellas he knew and asked if they could stay over at his place for a while, watch it to make sure his former neighbors didn't drop by to return the favor to his house.

An hour later, the fellas dropped in with two paper sacks full of clothes and accessories. I hadn't met these guys before. They lived in the neighborhood. They were both black and huge and appeared to be in their mid-thirties. Their heads looked as if they had been boiled and all the hair scraped off. You could have put your fingers in their eye sockets and used their noggins to bowl a few sets.

Their faces were as warm and friendly as a switchblade knife. One of them had an eye with scuz all around it, like the crusty lips of an active volcano. They looked as if on their days off they liked to sit around and wring the necks of puppies, maybe stick coat hangers up cats' asses and toast them over a fire.

I was put in the position of entertaining the fellas while Leonard filled a suitcase. They didn't strike up a discussion with me concerning Melville's flawed masterpiece *Moby-Dick*, nor did they have anything to say about *Billy Budd*.

We mostly sat in silence, said a few things about the weather. The one with the scuzzy eye finally hit a note of interest. He said, "You know, ants come out this time of year if they want to. Our house is full of the little fuckers. Goddamn Christmas ants."

"No shit?" I said. "Christmas ants?"

"Yeah, there's ants in my underwear drawer," said the other one.

"It's 'cause Clinton's underwear ain't clean," said Scum Eye.

"Yeah, well what you been doing in my underwear drawer?" said Clinton. "Sniffin'?"

I looked around for Leonard. Still in the back room. Probably sitting on the bed having a laugh at my expense.

"I'll tell you though," said Clinton. "Them ants are busy little shits. They ate my banana. I left it on the table, and next morning they was all over it." He smiled. "I stuck it in the sink and drowned them. An ant can't swim for shit."

"Leonard," I said. "Man, we got to go."

Leonard came out with his suitcase, and on our way out the door he paused and gave one of the big guys some money, said, "Here's for food. But there's stuff in the pantry. I get back when I get back, if that's okay with you two."

"We ain't doin' nothin' anyway," said Clinton. "Peckerwood we used to work for had a stroke. He can't do nothin' now but sit around and look wall-eyed, drip spit on his chin. His wife fired us and everyone else over at the aluminum chair plant. They say it may go out of business 'cause his family don't want nothing to do with runnin' it. They're gonna sell it and whoever buys it will bring in a whole new crew of niggers. That's if anyone wants it."

"It wasn't any kind of job anyway," said Scum Eye. "We worked there ten years or better and didn't never get a raise. That pecker-wood was so tight when he blinked his asshole turned inside out. I hope all he gets to do rest of his life is sit around in one of them lawn chairs we made, crap his pants and nest in it."

"They are not only without jobs," I said to Leonard, "but they have an ant problem at their house."

"Christmas ants, we call them," Clinton said. "I mean, they don't just come Christmas, but we call them that."

"Well, guys," Leonard said. "You're gonna like it here. No ant problem. Christmas or otherwise. Watch TV, hang out, whatever, but make sure those chumps lived next door don't drop by."

"You don't want us to kill 'em, do you?" This from Scum Eye.

"No, Leon," Leonard said, "but I want you to discourage them. You got to kill 'em, drag 'em in the house. Law likes it that way better. Looks like breaking and entering. More clearcut as self-defense. Frankly, I don't think they'll come around. My house got burned down, they'd know I knew who did it. And they wouldn't want me to know."

"I hear that," said Clinton.

"You guys like *Gilligan's Island*?" Leonard asked.

"Uh huh," said Leon, better known to me as Scum Eye. "That's a pretty funny show. I'd like to fuck that Ginger. I bet she don't fuck black guys, though."

"It's you she wouldn't fuck," Leonard said.

Leon and Clinton grinned. Leon said, "Yeah, uh huh. I get it."

"Anyway," Leonard said, "I got a stack of *Gilligan's Island* tapes, you want to see them. They're on the kitchen table."

"Raul left a treasure like that?" I said.

"It was in the box I was supposed to mail to him. Couldn't find the toaster this morning, so I opened his goddamn box. He loved that fucking toaster 'cause it could do four slices of bread at once. He liked shit like that. If it could have done six slices of bread, he'd have peed on himself. Anyway, no toaster. He must have took that in the car. But he had most of my spoon drawer in the box, and those tapes."

"That guy gone?" Leon asked.

"Raul?" Leonard said.

"One Clinton bounced around at the store," Leon said. "The other queer. No offense."

"None taken. Yeah, he's gone. He comes back, don't give him a rough time, though. I ain't mad at him. Just tell him I'll be back, if he cares. I don't figure he'll be around though."

"Can we have girls over?" Leon asked, scratching at the scum around his eye.

"As long as it doesn't get out of hand," Leonard said. "I don't want to come home to broken furniture. And guys, use a rubber, okay? And I don't mean share one between you. AIDS is goin' around."

"Using a rubber's like taking a shower in a raincoat," Clinton said. "It ain't no fun."

"Hey, it's your dick," Leonard said. "You're too stupid to take care of it, that's your problem. I hope the women are smarter. I'll call you later."

"You might start my pickup now and then, let it run awhile," I said. "This cold weather, it doesn't get run a bit, it'll freeze up. I like to circulate the antifreeze. If you'd rather just drain the radiator, go ahead. Key is on the kitchen table. Merry Christmas, guys."

Leonard got his suitcase and we went out to his car.

As Leonard was backing out of the driveway, I said, "That was goddamn surreal."

"Yep," Leonard said. "Leon and Clinton, they're André Breton kind of guys. They're proof positive you ought not let people shoot a few baskets with your head. Let's you and me go to Burger King and have breakfast. I feel expansive."

"Who the fuck are those guys anyway?"

"They tried to beat me up. I whupped those motherfuckers like I was dustin' a rug."

"Both of them!"

"Not at the same time. On different days. They got word I was queer, so they jumped Raul at the Community Store. Didn't really hurt him, but roughed him up. Broke his Dr Pepper bottle. Scrambled a couple of his moon pies. Just took them in their hands and twisted them up inside the plastic wrappers. Really made them hard to eat. I went down to the store after it happened and found one of them—one with the left eye looks like it's got a disease, Leon, and kicked his ass so bad they had to carry him off. Kicked that muscle in the back of his leg so hard it paralyzed it for a while."

"Old Thai boxing trick," I said.

"Yep. Later that day, his brother came over to the house with a baseball bat, started beating on the door. I went out the back way and cracked him over the head with the barrel of my shotgun. Knocked him on his black ass."

"Of course, you didn't hurt him while he was down."

"That wouldn't be right. I just kicked him a little. Until both his eyes closed. They got so they like me now. They want I should teach them some self-defense."

"Jesus," I said.

Couple hours later we were out at my house in the country. I didn't light the heaters, but I made sure the water in the faucets was still dripping, then I threw some clothes together. Leonard had brought his pipe and tobacco with him, and while I packed he filled the pipe and lit it.

"Bring a gun," he said.

"I don't like guns," I said. "Bringing one causes trouble. Guns lead to guns."

"And if the other guy brings one and you don't, it causes you trouble. It leads to you being dead."

"It's all right with you, I'll pass. I thought we were just going to find Florida. I didn't think we were planning a shootout at the O.K. Corral."

"You're a little short on reality sometimes, Hap."

"I guess you're right. I suppose you brought a gun?"

"Shotgun. Broke it down, wrapped it in plastic. Got a couple revolvers and a couple of Winchester thirty-thirtys, not dismantled. Ammunition. It's all in the trunk."

"How about the gyro copter?"

"Trunk."

6

On the way to Grovetown, Leonard put a Hank Williams cassette in the player and we listened to that. I never got to play what I liked. I wanted to bring some cassettes of my own, but Leonard said it was his car, so we'd listen to his music. He didn't care much for what I liked. Sixties rock and roll.

Even Hank Williams couldn't spoil the beauty of the day, however, and the truth of the matter was, I was really starting to like his music, though I wasn't willing to let Leonard know.

It was cold as an Eskimo's ass in an igloo outhouse, but it was clear and bright and the East Texas woods were dark and soothing. The pines, cold or not, held their green, except for the occasional streaks of rust-colored needles, and the oaks, though leafless, were thick and intertwining, like the bones of some unknown species stacked into an elaborate art arrangement.

We passed a gap in the woods where the pulp wooders had been. It looked like a war zone. The trees were gone for a patch of twenty to thirty acres, and there were deep ruts in the red clay, made by truck tires. Mounds of stumps and limbs had been piled up and burned, leaving ash and lumps, and in some cases huge chunks of wood that had not burned up, but had only been kissed black by fire.

One huge oak tree stump, old enough to have dated to the beginning of the century, had taken on the shape of a knotty skull, as if it were all that was left of some prehistoric animal struck by lightning. Clear cutting, gasoline, and kitchen matches had laid the dinosaurs low. Driven by greed and the need for a satellite dish, pulp wooders had turned beauty to shit, wood to paper, which in turn served to make the bills of money that paid the pulpers who slew the gods in the first place. There was sad irony in all that. Somewhere. May saplings sprout from their graves.

Just past mid-day Hank was singing, for about the fifteenth time, "Why don't you love me like you used to do," when we reached the outskirts of Grovetown. Here the trees were thick and dark and somber. Low rain clouds had formed, turning the bright cold day gray and sad as a widow's thoughts. The charcoal-colored clouds hung over the vast forest on either side of the narrow, cracked highway as if they were puffy cotton hats, leaving only a few rays of sunlight to penetrate them like polished hat pins.

I watched the woods speed by, and thought about what was out there. We were on the edge of the Big Thicket. One of the great forests of the United States, and everything opposite of what the TV and movie viewer thinks Texas is about. The pulp wooders and the lumber companies had certainly raped a lot of it, like most of East Texas, but here there was still plenty of it left. For now.

Out there, in the Thicket, there were swampy stretches, creeks and timber so compact a squirrel couldn't run through it without aid of a machete. The bottoms were brutal. Freezing black slush in the winter, steamy and mosquito-swarmed in the summer, full of fat, poisonous water moccasins, about the most unpleasant snakes in creation.

When I was a child, an uncle of mine, Benny, a man wise to the ways of the woods, had gotten lost in the Thicket for four days. He lived off puddled water and edible roots. He had been one of those contradictory fellas who loved the woods and wildlife, and yet shot everything that wasn't already stuffed, and if the light were to have glinted off the eye of a taxidermied critter, he might have shot that too. He was such a voracious hunter my dad used him as an example of how I ought not be. It was my father's contention, and it's certainly mine, that hunting is not a sport. If the animals could shoot back, then it would be a sport. It is justifiable only for food, and for no other reason. After that, it's just killing for the sake of putting a lid on what still simmers deep in our primitive hearts.

But my Uncle Benny, a big, laughing man who I liked very much, was out late one summer night hunting coons for their pelts. He followed the sounds of his dogs deep into the Thicket, then the sounds went away, and he found that the foliage overhead was so thick he could see neither moon nor stars.

Benny wore a kind of headlamp when he hunted. I don't remember what the stuff was called, carbide, I think, but there were these pellets you put in the headlamp and lit, and they made a little stinky flame that danced out from the headband and made a light. Lots of hunters used them back then.

This headlamp went out and Benny dropped his flashlight while trying to turn it on, and couldn't find it. He spent hours crawling along the ground, but he couldn't locate the flashlight, and he couldn't relight the lamp because he'd gotten his matches wet by stepping waist deep into a hole full of stagnant water.

He finally fell asleep resting against the base of a tree, and was awakened in the night by something huge crashing through the brush. Benny climbed the tree by feel, damn near putting out his eye on a thorn that was part of a wrist-thick crawling vine that was trying to choke the tree out.

In the morning, after a night of squatting on a limb, he came down and found bear tracks. This was before the black bear had been nearly exterminated from the Thicket. In fact, there were still plenty of them in those days, and wild hogs too.

The tracks circled the tree and there were scratch marks where the bear had risen up on its hind legs, perhaps hoping to bring down a treat from overhead. The bear had missed reaching Uncle Benny by less than a foot.

Benny found his flashlight, but it was useless. He had stepped on it in the night, busting out the bulb. Even though it was morning, he found there was no way to truly see the sun because the limbs tangled together overhead and the leaves and pine needles spread out like camouflaging, tinting the daylight brown and green.

All day, as he trekked blindly about, the mosquitoes rose up and over him in black kamikaze squadrons so compact they looked as if they were sheets of close-weave netting. They feasted so often on the thorn scratch over his eye, that eye eventually closed. His lips swelled up thick and tight and his face ballooned. Everywhere he went he wore those mosquitoes like a coat of chain mail.

As the day slogged on, he discovered he had also gotten into poison ivy, and it was spreading over his body, popping up pustules on his feet and hands and face, and the more he scratched, the more it spread, until even his nuts were covered in the stuff. He used to say: "Poison ivy bumps were so thick, it pushed the hair out of my balls."

He told me he hurt so bad, was so lost, so scared, so hungry and thirsty, he actually considered putting the rifle in his mouth and ending it all. Later, that wasn't an option. Crossing through a low-lying area, he discovered what appeared to be a thick covering of leaves was nothing more than slushy swamp, and in the process of grabbing on to the exposed roots of a great willow tree to save himself from drowning, he lost his rifle in the muck.

Eventually he found his way out, but not by true woodcraft. By accident. Or in his words, "By miracle." Benny came upon a gaunt steer, a Hereford/Long Horn mix. It was staggering and its great head hung almost to the ground. It was covered in crusted mud from its hoofs to its massive horns. It had obviously been mired up somewhere, perhaps trying to escape the mosquitoes.

Uncle Benny watched it, and finally it began to move, slow but steady, and he followed the thorn-torn steer through the thicket, sometimes clinging to its mud- and shit-coated tail. He clung and followed until it arrived at the pasture it had escaped from, through a gap in the barbed wire. Uncle Benny said when that steer finally broke through the briars and limbs and the light came through the trees and showed him the bright green of the pasture, it was like the door to heaven had been opened.

When the steer reached the emerald pasture, it bellowed joyfully, staggered, fell, and never rose. Its back legs and hindquarters were swollen up as if they were made of soaked sponge, and there were wounds that gurgled pus the color of primeval sin and thick as shaving foam.

Uncle Benny figured the steer had gotten into a whole nest of moccasins, or timber rattlers, and they'd struck it repeatedly. Steer might have been out there in the Thicket for a week. The fact that it had survived as long as it had was evidence of the heartiness of the Long Horn strain that ran through it. It died where it fell.

From there Benny made his way to the highway and found his car. His hunting dogs never showed up. He went there for a week and called their names where they had gone in with him, and he drove the back roads searching, but never a sign. To the best of my knowledge, though he continued to hunt from time to time, Benny never went into the deep woods again, and the infected eye gave him trouble all his life, until at the age of sixty-five he had to have it removed and replaced with a cheap glass one.

You don't fuck with the Big Thicket.

Grovetown wasn't much. A few streets, some of them brick, and down on the square an ancient courthouse and jail, a filling station/grocery store, and the Grovetown Cafe, and a lot of antique and thrift shops. There were benches out front of most of the buildings, and you had to figure if it wasn't Christmas Day and most of those places weren't closed there'd be old men sitting there, bundled up, talking, smoking, and almost managing to spit Red Man off the curb.

The filling station/grocery was one of the few places open, and as we drove past, a tall, thirtyish, handsome, pale-faced guy in a gray shirt, heavy coat, and gimme cap stood out by one of the pumps with a water hose, washing down oil and grease in the center of one of the drives. He stared at us as we drove by, looking like a guy who might wash your windshield, check your tires and oil without having to be asked, just like in the old days. Then, on the other hand, looks could be deceiving. Guy like that might piss on your windshield and let the air out of your tires as soon as look at you.

Christ, I was beginning to think like Leonard. Everyone was a scumbag until proven otherwise.

We passed a washateria with a sign painted on the glass. It was faded, but it was defiantly readable. NO COLORED.

Leonard said, "Man, I ain't seen nothing like that since nineteen seventy. Jefferson, Texas, I think it was."

We decided we ought to get a room, least for the night until we could get the lay of the land. There were no motels in Grovetown, but there was one old hotel and a boarding house. We checked both for lodging, but they didn't have rooms for us. They claimed to be closed for Christmas. I found this hard to believe. Hotels and boarding houses don't close for holidays, and as for not having rooms, the Hotel Grovetown was so goddamn vacant of life you could almost hear rats farting behind the wainscoting.

At the boarding house, called the Grovetown Inn, there weren't more than three cars in the parking lot, but when we came in together, asked for a room, the proprietors looked at us like we were animated shit piles asking to lie down free on clean white sheets.

Outside the Grovetown Inn, Leonard filled his pipe, said, "No room at the inn, brother. Think it's that shirt you're wearin' they don't like? Personally, I've always felt blue makes you look a little scary."

We drove around awhile. Leonard said, "Have you noted there's no black section of town around here?"

"Yep. I have."

"They haven't even given us black folk a place out next to the city dump, like usual. Or maybe by a sewage plant or a nuclear reactor. I ain't even seen a black person walking around."

"Maybe it's because of the holidays. I haven't seen that many whites walking around. And guess what else? There aren't any more places to stay. We've seen it all."

"I'm hungry. Cafe's open. Let's get something to eat, then figure on what to do next."

"They'll be glad to see us there, Leonard. Why don't I keep things simple for now, get us a couple of sandwiches to go?"

"Hey, I'll tell you now, I'm not going to anyone's back door or stand in a separate line just because I got a better tan than someone else. Get that straight in your head, Hap."

"I'm just wanting things easy. What worries me about you, is I think you like confrontation too much."

"And what worries me about you, Hap, is you don't."

I pulled over in front of the cafe, started to get out. Leonard put a hand on my arm. "You're right. I'm acting like an asshole."

"No argument."

"We're here to find Florida, not have me prove what a badass I am."

"Still, no argument."

"Get us something. We'll eat in the car. I'll give a civil rights speech later. Provided I can get someone to accompany me on guitar."

"I'll just be a minute."

The Grovetown Cafe was not a place you would mistake for a French restaurant. It was overly warm and the walls were decorated with badly painted ceramic birds and squirrels, and there was some of that really bad hillbilly music you hear from time to time but can't quite believe it. It's not even AM radio pop. It only plays in ancient towns with jukeboxes that have glass cases coated gray by oily hands. It's like generic heavy metal and rap. Who listens to this stuff on purpose? It sounds like some kind of joke. The sharp little notes clung to the air and stuck to my head like prickly pear thorns. They went well with the stench of old grease from the kitchen.

I waded through grease and music and found a stool and sat down and waited. From a back booth a couple of guys stared at me. They were in their thirties, healthy-looking, but they had the attitude of men with "back problems" on workdays. It's a mysterious ailment that seems to descend on a large percentage of the redneck population. I couldn't help but think they were drawing a check from somewhere. Some kind of compensation. Maybe they were watching me nervously because they thought I was an insurance man that had caught them without their back braces.

I figured, at night, after a hard day of smoking cigarettes, swigging coffee, and cussin' the niggers and liberals, they'd buy a couple of six-packs, go home and pass out in front of the TV set after beating the wife and kids, a half-eaten bag of generic-brand potato chips clutched to their chests.

Then again, here I was judging people I didn't even know. I was starting to be just like the people I despised. They were probably a couple of nuclear physicists on vacation, stopping in here to soak up the homey atmosphere.

I had to quit judging. Quit being unfair. And I had to face what I was really worked up about. Knowing I'd probably see Florida and have all the old feelings again. And it was cold, and I didn't like it. And I had fewer future prospects than the smallpox virus. In final analysis, I had a hard-on for the world and no place to put it.

I noticed one of the physicists had turned in the booth and the other was leaning out on his side, looking not just at me, but past me. I looked where they were looking, and I could see through the plate glass window, between the fly specks, Leonard's car. He was visible behind the wheel, his head back on the seat dozing.

I began to have those prejudgment thoughts again.

I took a deep breath and let it slide. I tried to remember and paraphrase a comforting Bible verse. "Judge not others, lest ye be judged." Something like that. I also remembered a verse my daddy told me. "You end up havin' to hit some sonofabitch, don't just hit him once, and don't just hit to get his attention."

A fiftyish lady who might have been pretty if she'd had enough energy to hold herself straighter and her hair wasn't oily and stuck to her cheeks, came out of the back wiping wet flour on her apron. "What can I get you?"

"Couple hamburgers and large coffees to go. Some potato chips."

"It's early for hamburgers," she said.

"I missed breakfast. Got any fried pies?"

"No. We sell some candy at the register. Peanut patties, Tootsie Rolls, Mounds, Snickers, Milky Way. That's it."

"All right. Couple of peanut patties."

"That nigger out there will want more'n a couple of them patties," said one of the men in the back. "A nigger likes a peanut pattie. Next to what a woman's got, and a watermelon, ain't much they like better."

"And loose shoes," said the other fella. "And a warm place to shit."

"Boys," said the woman, "you watch your language in here."

I looked at them and smiled sadly. I began to understand why so many clichés persist. Too much truth in them. I gave them a real looksee for the first time.

Big motherfuckers. Not physicists. They looked like human book-ends for the Adult Western Novel shelf. Both rednecked and stupid. The one talking almost had a mustache, or maybe he just hadn't quite got shaving down yet. I wished, just once in a while, the guys wanted to harass me or whip my ass would be short. Kind of small. Weak even. In business suits. Yankees. That would make things a little more all right.

Better yet, I wished those dudes would just leave me alone. What was it about me that I was the one always stepped in the doo-doo?

If I walked ten miles around a cow lot to keep the manure off my shoes, I'd manage to find a fresh heap of dog shit to put my foot in.

"Better give me a couple creams to go with that coffee," I told the lady.

"Nigger working for you?" said the other man. This one was not a bad-looking guy, but he had a tavern tumor that was threatening the buttons on his paisley shirt, and a kind of smirk like he'd been corn-holing your wife and she'd told him to tell you so.

The lady said, "Boys, y'all ought to go hang out somewhere else." Then to me: "I'll just be a minute. You want those well-done, don't you?"

I spoke so only she could hear. "Actually, I'd like them about as quick as I can get them."

She smiled. "They don't mean no harm. They just don't like niggers."

"Ah."

Now I felt better.

I glanced out at Leonard. He was really snoozing. In fact, he might have been hibernating. Great. Here I was with the hippo twins, and the Smartest Nigger in the World was tucked in for the winter.

The boys came over and sat on stools on either side of me.

"I ain't seen you before," said Paisley Shirt.

"Well," I said, "I don't get through here much. Buy you fellas some coffee?"

"Naw," said the other one. "We've had coffee."

"Lots of it," said Paisley Shirt.

"I don't know about you," I said, "but lots of coffee makes me nervous. In fact, maybe I shouldn't have got coffee with my lunch. I've had too much this morning already."

"You look a little nervous," said Paisley Shirt. "Maybe you ought to give up coffee altogether."

"I just might," I said.

"Me and my brother," said Paisley Shirt, "we don't have trouble with coffee. We don't have trouble with beer, wine, or whiskey."

"What about Christmas ants?" I said. "You got Christmas ant trouble, I know two guys you ought to meet."

"Christmas ants?" said Bad Mustache.

The woman called from the back then. Her voice was a little halfhearted, like she was calling a dog she figured had gotten run over. "Y'all go back and sit down, now."

"We're all right, Mama," said Paisley Shirt.

"Mama?" I said.

"Uh huh," said Bad Mustache. "What's this about Christmas ants?"

"Little bastards are serious trouble where I come from," I said. "You think fire ants are hell, you get into some of them Christmas ants, well, those buggers won't never let go."

"I ain't never heard of no Christmas ants," said Paisley Shirt.

"Neither had most anybody else in LaBorde until yesterday," I said. "But you'll read about it in the papers today or tomorrow, see it on the news. They're epidemic there. Brought in from Mexico, they think. In a crate of bananas. Or a shipment of cigars. They're deadly dudes, these Christmas ants."

"Wait a minute," said Bad Mustache. "Is that like them ants in that movie where they take over this plantation and this guy—"

"Charlton Heston," I said.

"Yeah, I guess . . . you've seen it?"

"Yep," I said. "And that's exactly what I'm talking about. But that was only a picture. They couldn't show it the way it is. I tell you, LaBorde's a mess. I think the loss of life is in the hundreds. Maybe the thousands by now. The guy in the car, Doctor Pine. He's from the government. World's expert on Christmas ants. One reason he's passed out is he's been up all night battling them. He lost."

"A nigger expert?" said Paisley. "There's your goddamn problem."

"I don't know," I said. "He had some good ideas, but the ants were too entrenched. I'll be honest with you. I work for the city there. Water Department. We were the first to catch on to the epidemic. Lots of people don't give us credit. They don't think much of the Water Department, but they don't know the things we see. Alligators. Snakes. Christmas ants. You can't drown those little bastards. The Christmas ants, I mean. And you better not have a banana, or some kind of fruit in your house. They track to the stuff like a pig to corn. Anyway, what I was saying is this. I'm not going back. Dr. Pine out there wants to go back, and he can `if he wants, but not me. The ants have gotten too goddamn big for this cowboy."

"They grow?" said Paisley Shirt.

I smiled. "Look, it's not a science-fiction movie. It's not like they're ten feet tall. That's bullshit. They only get about the size of a rat. Some of them do, I mean. Most of them, they're more mouse or mole size."

"Naw," said Bad Mustache. "You're pulling our dicks."

"I wouldn't think of pulling your dick," I said. "Listen here, I wouldn't have believed it either had I not been there. These ants, they don't get that big in their own environment. But they thrive here. No one knew that until this week. What they've discovered, and it's something no one would have suspected, is that the tropical weather was keeping them small. They get a little cold snap, bam, they're big as rodents. It has something to do with the way they eat and the way their metabolism deals with the natural sugars and starches in human flesh."

"Human flesh?" Bad Mustache said.

"Uh huh," I said. "It's not a horror movie where they swarm someone and eat every inch of skin off of them. But they leave bad bites. And they can cause death, and have. Like I said, in the hundreds."

"They bite you to death?" said Bad Mustache.

"I'm a little sketchy on if it's the bite or the poisons in their system that kills humans. They do take a lot of meat with them, though. Actually, you'd have to get Dr. Pine to explain it to you."

"Wow!" said Paisley Shirt.

"Wow, indeed," I said.

"But why do you call them Christmas ants?" Bad Mustache asked.

"Again, you got me. I'm no ant expert. Maybe because they were discovered around Christmastime. That's what I figure."

The lady came out with my hamburgers.

"LaBorde," said Paisley Shirt. "That's not that far from here."

"No it isn't," I said. I got up, went over to the register, and called back to them. "I wouldn't alarm myself. I'd just be alert. Watch the ground. Especially at sunset and sunrise. That's when they like to travel."

The lady took my money at the register. She said, "Those boys are so dumb, I sometimes think maybe my kids were switched at birth, and they gave me these two jackasses. All they know is what they see on the TV."

"Maybe they ought to watch the educational channel. Last night they had a great *National Geographic* special on bears. I tell you, it tantalized me to the point I couldn't sleep afterwards."

"I like a good nature program myself," she said.

I got my change, and started out. Paisley Shirt said, "Hey, you said there were two guys we ought to meet."

"Well," I said, "I meant you would have liked them. They're back in LaBorde. Or were. But, you know . . . the ants."

"You been jacking with us, ain't you?" said Paisley Shirt.

"There's lots of people who've ignored the facts of scientific research," I said. "All of it to their detriment. Believe what you want, it's nothing to me. It's not my job to educate the masses. I work for the Water Department. But I will say this. I'm proud of that. I don't care what anyone else thinks about the Water Department. I'm proud."

I went out to the car and got in. I shook Leonard. He came around slowly and looked at me. "Man, I sort of passed out."

"Let's go."

Leonard started the car as the brothers came out of the cafe, stood on the sidewalk and looked at us. Leonard watched them a moment, backed out and drove off.

"Trouble?" he asked.

"No. But I will say this. It's not every day you can actually step into a science-fiction episode of *The Andy Griffith Show* by way of *Deliverance*."

7

We drove out the way we'd come, stopped off at a little roadside park we'd passed. We got out under the pearl gray sky and ate our hamburgers and drank our coffee and rested our elbows on the concrete table. It was cold and the air smelled wet. Blue-jays, bold as priests, came out of the woods and hopped around the table looking for crumbs. I don't think we left too many. We were starved.

"I could do that again," Leonard said. "Even if it did taste as if it was rubbed under someone's armpit first."

"Frankly, short of the meat being kneaded between the cheeks of a fat man's ass, I could have eaten it anyway."

"And how old were those peanut patties? Them peanuts were like gravel."

"The peanut patties aren't nearly as big a problem as the fact we still don't know where we're going to stay. Did you have an urge for two of those, by the way? The peanut patties, I mean?"

"What?"

"Nothing. Buddy, I tell you, the vibes from that town, from that cafe, it's like going back to the middle sixties, when I was marching for civil rights and getting my head cracked. Not only because I was for civil rights, but because I was white and marching for civil rights. You know, I don't know I'm brave enough to do what I did then. It was all going on now, I think I'd hide in the house."

"It is going on now, and you're not hiding in the house. You're back in the shit. You weren't special brave then, Hap. You were young and stupid and overly idealistic. You're still the last two, even if the idealistic part is slightly tainted."

"What amazes me, Leonard, is you're more of an optimist than I am. You even thought your time in Vietnam was well spent. If anyone should be bitching, it should be you. A black guy used up

49

and thrown out. You hadn't gone to war, man, no telling what you'd have made of yourself."

"I don't blame anyone or anything for who I am or what I do. I consider myself just fine, Hap. I make my own choices, my own decisions, I sail my own ship till it crashes. Thing with you, is you actually feel guilty you're not on the cover of *Time* magazine. Deep down, you believe that shit Florida used to tell you about how you weren't ever gonna amount to anything or do anything. You think to be important you got to be some kind of Wall Street stockbroker or Nobel Prize winner. Listen here. You're a good man and my friend, and we're true as we know how to be to what we think is right. I don't know what else there is that matters. All that other shit is just cake decoration."

"Thanks, Leonard."

"That's all right. I didn't mean any of it."

"Now that it's established we're good people and righteous friends, we still don't have a place to stay."

"We might try the black folks. I figure the other side of town is where they hang out. They got to be around, all this field work and lumbering has to be done. They got to be there so white folks can tell them what to do. And, of course, they need a nigger to hang now and then."

"Good thing you showed up, huh?"

Leonard looked at the sky. "You know, this weather is creepy. Last time I saw a sky like this it turned super-cold and full of ice, and bad things happened. I can still feel the pain in my leg now and then. And it was all your fault too."

"I remember. But the clouds look to me more like they're filled with rain. I think we're in for a hell of a soaking."

"We don't find a place, we could just go on back for tonight. Regroup, start over in the next day or two."

"I want to find Florida. It won't be any easier a day or two from now, even if the weather is better. And it could be worse. Seeing Grovetown, I'm a little nervous for her welfare. Florida has to be staying somewhere."

"It's logical that she'll be in the black section."

"Probably, but for protocol's sake, I think a good place to start is the Chief of Police. If she was doing research on this jail hanging, you know she talked to him. We might get something from the Chief that'll save us some steps."

And now, cruising back to Grovetown, eyes closed, listening to the tires humming, I tried to tell myself I wasn't really worried much. Tried to convince myself I didn't know Leonard so well that I could be certain he was worried too and didn't want to say anything to make me more uptight than I was. And maybe I was sensing nothing of the kind from Leonard. He had his own heartaches. Raul was gone.

But Raul wasn't dead.

Jesus. Don't let Florida be dead, and don't let that kind of bullshit get in your thinking, Hap, you jinx, you. Because if she's dead, that makes two, back to back. Then I was thinking about Florida, about her coffee-colored skin, soft as butter, the way she smiled, the white, near perfect teeth, the long smooth legs and the way she whispered to me when we made love. And there were the more primitive thoughts as well; the ones that are as real as any other. The way she took me inside her and moved her ass and made me feel strong and masculine, and loved me until the world went away and I was centered. A nirvana where all past and present and future moments were non-existent.

Shit, that was good. I got home, I had to write that down.

That's right, Hap, clown on out. Try not to think about the fact that you thought things between you and Florida were going to be wonderful and forever. And then she was gone.

But she hadn't married Hanson. I liked to think I was part of the reason. That she loved me still.

Yeah. And now and then, I liked to believe I would live forever too, and that I wouldn't age past where I was now and the meaning of life would soon come to me, and would not disappoint me when I knew it.

Sometimes I feared I knew the meaning of life. Simplicity itself. We're born to propagate, then we die. In my case, or so it seemed, I was merely born to die.

Clear the head, Hap, ole buddy, you loser times two. No bad

thoughts today. No letting a heavy gray sky hold you hostage. No memories you can't deal with. A step at a time. Keep an even heartbeat and roll on down the road.

But then I thought of Trudy, my ex-wife, dead now for . . . my God, what was it?

Four years.

Jesus.

It seemed like yesterday.

It seemed like a thousand years ago.

Blond, long-legged beauty with a smile like an angel and a misguided heart. And it had been winter then too. I nearly lost Leonard then as well, and that too had been my fault.

Okay, Trudy is dead and gone, Hap, I says to my ownself, but you don't know about Florida. You're overreacting. She's all right. You'll find her. If not today, tomorrow. Alive. She may not be happy to see you. Might think you're a meddling sonofabitch, and you are, but when you see her, and she's okay, that's all that will matter.

She's all right, Hap, my man.

She's fine.

Fit as a fiddle.

Ripe as a peach.

A roll of thunder. A crack of lightning.

I opened my eyes and turned and looked at Leonard in the cloud-suffocated light. He looked at me briefly with no expression, his fingers flexed on the steering wheel. He turned back to his driving.

The clouds were black now, with a little spoiled milk in them. They rolled down low and came in over the highway like hell's own tumbleweeds. The windshield turned dark as early evening.

Leonard pulled on the headlights and turned on the wipers as it started to rain.

8

Back in Grovetown, at the Chief of Police's office, a middle-aged lady with a sprayed, bleached blond hairdo high enough to house a colony of African wasps told us Chief Cantuck had gone out to investigate a fire, and she gave us directions. She eyed Leonard as if he might spring on her and rape her at any moment. She had a little aluminum Christmas tree on one corner of her desk and it was surrounded by a city of Christmas cards from well-wishers; she leaned in that direction, as if she might decide to hide behind them.

Back in the car, I said, "You made that lady nervous, Leonard. She thought you were going to try and take her on her desk."

"Wishful thinking. Actually, I wanted to fuck that hairdo she had, just in case there was something in it needed fucking. That little gap in it, right over her widow's peak, it reminded me of a butthole."

"Knowing you like I do," I said, "I hate it when someone says you aren't romantic."

We followed directions, drove out to where the Chief's car was parked beside the road, along with a rickety fire truck. The rain had temporarily subsided, but the sky was still ripe with it, and it didn't take a weatherman to see it would come again, and maybe harder.

The Chief, a fat man wearing a straw hat and boots with a khaki pants leg inside one and outside the other, watched the house burn, his hands behind his back. The rain hadn't slowed this baby down a bit. The firemen were all volunteers in regular clothing with a couple of fire hats and one Scott Pack between them—not that they needed it. They were on or around the truck and had a weak spew of water sputtering from a thick white hose. One of them got a brainstorm, got off the truck, turned on a leaky garden hose and started spewing that through a window that had been blown out by the hot pressure of the fire. He might as well have been pissing on an oil well blaze. Two other guys were eating Hostess Twinkies, one of them managing to chew with a cigarette in one corner of his mouth.

"We seem to have this thing about fire and the law lately," I said.

"That's the truth," Leonard said.

The house, which from the looks of things had never been any great shakes, was a lost cause. I'd had enough experience from Leonard's fires to know when a house was a goner, and this sonofabitch was a goner.

We got out of the car and walked over to the Chief. He noticed us out of the corner of his left eye. Rain was dripping off the brim of his hat. He had little pop eyes, like a Boston terrier, and his chin went back and low and reminded me of an iguana. He lifted his head slightly as if he was sighting us from a rock. As he did, rain splashed into his left eye and he blinked it out. Black goo, the source being the Red Man package poking out of his shirt pocket, oozed out of the corners of his mouth and slid into wrinkles that served as culverts on either side of his chin. His belly moved when he moved, and sometimes when he didn't. Like it had a mind of its own and places it wanted to go. Worse though, even if you didn't want to look, you couldn't help but notice the bulge in his pants. He'd obviously been ruptured and was in need of a truss. His right leg looked to be sprouting a grapefruit.

Near the grapefruit, riding in a long black holster, was a .44 Western-style revolver. Chief Cantuck appeared to be in his fifties. Maybe older. A face like that, a belly like that, it was hard to tell.

"Who are you?" he said, turning to give us a full view.

"Hap Collins," I said, and we shook hands.

Leonard stuck out his hand and the Chief hesitated, then took it the way you might take hold of something dead. Leonard grabbed Chief Cantuck's hand hard and shook briskly. "Leonard Pine, Smartest Nigger in the World."

"What?" said the Chief.

"It's just a little joke of his," I said.

"Well, all right. Look here, what do y'all want? This is law and fire department business. You ain't supposed to be hanging around here."

I said, "Lady at your office, with a hair cone on her head, said we'd find you here."

"Yeah, well, say what you want and get it over with," Chief Cantuck said. "And I don't know about you, but I think that cone of hair looks pretty good."

"Appears you've lost this one," Leonard said, nodding at the house.

"Yeah, guess it does," said Cantuck. "No big loss. White trash rental. Bill Spray owns it, rents it to anyone with thirty-five dollars a month or any gal wants to grease his rope. One or both of them things, and the place is yours on a monthly basis, long as he don't have to fix nothing."

"Guess it wasn't the sort of joint attracted the Rockefellers," I said.

"No, it wasn't. But a couple hundred dollars' worth of plywood, a few two-by-fours and some tin and cardboard, Bill can throw this buddy up again and start rentin'. Too bad the renters weren't inside. I'd have liked it all right had they gotten cooked with it. I been called out here half a dozen times by the neighbors. Always fightin'. Big ole fat gal and a couple of men lived here. Those two men fight over that sow like she was goddamn Marilyn Monroe.

"Last time I was in here they had all kinds of pornography strewn about. Them magazines with women with their hands up their holes, or their asses in the air with a carrot jammed in it. Stuff like that. And it wasn't just pussy magazines. They had'm some sex toys. Them little vibrating plastic dicks with knobs on 'em, like old cucumbers. Look here."

He pointed to something in the ashes: two large batteries lying in a flesh-colored puddle the shape of a large banana.

"That's one of them plastic dicks. Just me thinking about that thing being shoved up that old whore's hole makes me kinda woozy. There's some Elvis cards, though. I kicked them aside to let them smoke out."

"Beg pardon?" I said.

"Elvis cards." He walked over a ways and kicked at something. It was a charred deck of playing cards with Elvis's picture on the back.

"The heat gets off of 'em, I'll probably keep those."

"Why?" Leonard asked.

"Elvis is on them."

"Ah," Leonard said.

"It ain't the kind of music you people listen to," Cantuck told him. "My wife, she thinks Elvis is God. She'll like them cards, burned or not. Now what the fuck you want?"

"We're looking for a friend of ours," I said, "and we thought you might know something about her. Her name is Florida Grange."

"Colored gal?" Cantuck said.

"Could be her," Leonard said. "Depends on what color she was."

"You tryin' to be funny?" Cantuck said.

"I didn't say I was the Funniest Nigger in the World, I said I was the Smartest Nigger in the World."

"You're about to be the Most Ass-Whupped Nigger in the World."

Leonard got that look in his eye. The one he gets when he's burning the house next door or administering a serious head beating to some fool who has pushed too far.

"Come on, Leonard," I said. "Shut up, would you?"

Leonard studied Cantuck for a moment, turned and walked back to his car and got inside.

"He's just worried," I said. "You see, she's his sister."

"Yeah?" Cantuck said. "Well, I'll tell you something. I don't give a flying shit if she's his fucking Siamese twin and she left town with his left nut in her pocket. Ain't no nigger gonna be funny on me. And what the fuck you doin' hangin' around with a coon like that? We don't cotton to that shit here. I got nigger friends, but I don't associate with 'em."

"You certainly sound close, you and your nigger friends. Chief, anyone ever tell you guys you might be a little out of step? Behind the times?"

"Yeah, and we don't give a flying shit."

"You've heard of civil rights, of course?"

"Yeah, and I uphold them, they got to be upheld. That's what that gal was here about, some nigger's civil rights. Ain't my fault the stupid fuck hung himself."

"I don't care about any of that. I just want to know about Florida."

Cantuck paused, gave me a look I couldn't quite decipher. He said, "Comely nigger. I've always said I'd fuck a nigger, but wouldn't tell anybody, but that one I'd fuck and maybe brag on it a time or two. She had an ass on her."

Deep breath, Hap. He's just a stereotypical ignorant redneck. You've known them before. Nothing you say will alter their thinking. Nothing short of death will change them.

"You see," I said, "they work for me. Leonard and Florida. They're good workers, and now and then, well, me and her. Shit, Chief, after what you just said, you know what I mean."

I grinned in what I hoped was a lecherous manner.

Cantuck smiled. "My daddy used to tell me a nigger gal wasn't good for but one thing, and they were damn good at that. He was Chief here way back, and he dealt with a lot of niggers. Nigger gals paid him a lot of fines in a special manner. If you know what I mean. I take after my old man in that department. I'll fuck anything that ain't nailed down and has a hole. In fact, when I was a boy, I tore the ass out of a few chickens putting the dick to 'em. Got so every time my mama found a dead chicken she'd take the belt to me, whether I did it or not. Pigs squealed at night, Mom came in my room and beat me."

"No wonder you got a strained nut."

"Yeah. Well, maybe that's what happened. I do dearly love to fuck . . . My nut really look bad?"

"Well, I was you, I'd get a truss or something. Shit, man, don't that hurt?"

"Not if I turn kinda casual like."

"Not to dismiss a man's nuts too lightly, Chief, but where is Florida?"

"Hell, boy, it's gettin' cold out here. Let's you and me go sit in the car and talk."

I got in on the passenger side. There was a shotgun on a rack between myself and Cantuck. He cranked the car and turned on the heater. On the dash, and stuck all about the car, there was every kind of charity sticker you could imagine. Muscular dystrophy. Diabetes. Cancer.

"You give to all those charities?" I asked. "Or do you just collect stickers?"

"I give," he said. "A dollar or two here and there. It ain't like I'm raking in the big bucks here, so I don't give much, but I give. I think it's something you ought to do. Christian charity. I had a son had MD. He died of it just last year. Since then, and even before, I can't stand to see nobody crippled, not even a nigger."

He sat quietly for a moment, staring at the MD sticker. "That boy of mine," he said. "Jimmy. He got so bad, only way he could get around was me totin' him. He was eleven. My youngest. Damn good age for a boy, but for him it was hell. Spittin' image of me. Good boy. Never did nothing but try and be good. Made good grades until he got so bad he just couldn't study. His body turned to jelly. Just goddamn jelly."

"I'm sorry."

"He was a good boy. He was a good boy right to the end, trying to cheer me up. Trying to smile. He died with me holding his hand. It was so little, I closed mine, you couldn't even see his. He hadn't had that shit, hell, he'd gone to college and made something of himself. God bless him."

"I truly am sorry, Chief."

"Well, don't whine about it. You didn't know him. Wasn't nothing to you. I shouldn't even have said anything to you about it . . . now, this nigger gal."

"Florida."

"Yeah, Florida. She came to the jail, asked a few questions, left, and I didn't see her again, 'cept around town. Over at the filling station getting some gas in that little car of hers."

"A gray Toyota."

"That's the one. Real sporty."

"That's all you know about her?"

"That's it. I heard a few of the boys mention they'd seen her and that she dressed a little too rich, if you know what I mean, but had she been a couple shades paler, they might have taken her to church, and to a little social after."

I thought of Florida and her dresses. Mostly short. Mostly tight. I thought of the story Charlie told me. I had a sudden red-hot and angry vision of the Chief with an upholstery needle threaded with wire.

"Let me ask a couple of questions that don't have to do with Florida," I said. "This guy that hung himself in jail. Why?"

"Who's to know a nigger's mind? I wasn't even around. I was out of town."

"Lot of hangings in your little jail?"

Chief Cantuck studied me a moment. "You a reporter? The colored gal said she was doing some kind of article. Said she was a lawyer too, though I ain't sure about that."

"She was."

"If she was, then you just shit on yourself, pilgrim. She was a lawyer, then she didn't work for you, did she?"

"Well, she did law work."

"I think you're full of it, buddy."

I had been feeling superior and condescending to the old man, and he'd been baiting me all along. Dropping sugar in front of me until he got me close enough to whack with the swatter. His tone was different now. A lot less cracker. "You think you're so smart," he said. "Well, I got to tell you, you ain't that smart."

"I see that," I said.

He casually slipped the leather trigger guard off his revolver and shifted toward me in the seat, his hand resting on the butt of his pistol. A bead of sweat formed immediately on my upper lip and ran into my mouth.

"Listen here. I knew you and that smartass nigger were full of shit soon as I saw you. Ain't a word come out of your mouth that's even kin to the truth. There's nothing about you boys that fits, so I figure you're trouble. More do-gooders trying to come down here and check on our nigger trouble and make it into something it isn't. I haven't heard one do-gooder ask about the people this nigger killed. The white man this guitar plunker cut up for a few dollars."

"I didn't say anything about his guilt or innocence. I'm just asking about Florida."

"Don't take me for a fool 'cause I got swollen nuts and bad teeth and I eat too much. I'm on the dime much as you are, College Boy."

"Actually, I dropped out. And I'm way past being a boy."

"Well, you should have finished college, boy. Might have learned something. Let me tell you this, Swiftie. That little nigger came snooping around asking questions. She wanted to see if that boy was murdered. She figured the Caucasian Knights was in on it. Let me tell you something. The Knights are ripe in this town, and they're mostly nothing but a bunch of mean bastards, just like the Klan, which is really all they are, but now and then they do a good thing or two. There's folks need killin'."

"Then you're saying the Klan, or these Knights, killed the prisoner?"

"'Course I ain't. But I'm tellin' you this. The Knights take note of meddlers, and they don't worry much about a dead nigger, but they worry about the ones worry about a dead nigger. Understand me?"

"I believe I do. Your hand on that gun, is that some kind of threat?"

"Yeah," he said, taking the gun out of its holster and laying it on his knee. "It could be. And you see, sometimes, you wave one around like this . . ." He waved the revolver in my direction and placed it back on his knee, "and you got your mind on something else, a gun can go off, even if you was just showin' it to a fella wanted to see it."

"That would be murder, Chief. My friend in the car wouldn't like that."

"And I wouldn't care. He might have an accident too. You and him both might end up in the ashes of that fire there, and them firemen might be settin' you on fire instead of puttin' you out. I'm not saying they would, but it could happen. I mean, shit, boy, you two look to me to be the type would like them plastic dicks and stuff. You might even have been with the white trash lives here, and say the white trash went out for some beer and left you two in the house, and you were fucking around with some kind of electric dick or something. Started a fire. I even like the idea of us finding them rubber dicks up your butts, you know, just for looks . . . But however it's played, we come up with a cooked nigger in a house where white trash lives, we could pin damn near anything on the trash lives there.

"As it is, they're gonna be leaving town, just because I'm fed up with them. They don't know it yet, but when I find them, they're gonna be leaving. And right away. It ain't like they're gonna need to pack. And if they don't want to leave, I'm gonna persuade them.

I'm hoping I won't have to persuade you and maybe take them down with you to make things look nice and pretty."

"Me either," I said, and looked carefully at the gun on his knee. His fingers flexed against it, making me as nervous as a goat at a barbecue.

"Listen here, Swiftie. There's been folks worried about dead niggers before, and some of them ain't so worried now. About nothing. Get me?"

"You're coming across."

"Let me add something to that. Ain't a Klan member in this town or around it ever been convicted of shit. That sort of line your ducks up, Swiftie?"

"I believe it does."

It had started to rain again. The water ran in such thick rivulets on the windshield I couldn't see out. The car heater was too warm.

"One last thing," Cantuck said. "For the record. That gal. I didn't do a thing to her and have no reason to suspicion anyone I know did. Clear? But I wouldn't put anything past the Knights, and contrary to what you probably think, I found out they did something to someone didn't need it done, I'd come down on them."

"Sure."

"Now, you get in the car with your pet nigger, and you two go back to wherever you come from, where you and him can eat and sleep together, or whatever it is you want to do with niggers. But, fella, don't get in my way again, and don't ever let me hear you mention my balls again. It ain't polite. And lastly, I ain't never fucked a chicken in my life, but I thought it was the sort of thing you'd expect. You fuck with me, Swiftie, you better be thinking two and three moves ahead."

"What about the pigs? Did you fuck them?"

"Get out of the car, Swiftie."

When I closed Leonard's car door, Leonard said, "Learn anything?"

"Yeah, you wouldn't believe the stuff the Chief knows about the political situation in Albania."

"Yeah, but I bet that fucker don't know their major imports and exports."

"That cracker isn't as stupid as we thought, Leonard. Mean. Dangerous. Ignorant. But stupid he isn't. And subtle he isn't. In fact, his very nonsubtle statements about our temporary position in his community were so clearly stated, I'd like you to crank the car right now, and leave."

Leonard looked where I was looking. The firefighters were no longer fighting the fire. They were all turned in our direction, glaring. One of them was chewing a fresh Twinkie and the sticky white innards were covering his mouth like mad dog foam.

"I think maybe they ain't never seen anyone cute as us," Leonard said.

Chief Cantuck got out of his car and walked in our direction, stopped and waited. He had his gun in his hand, held by his side.

"He thinks we're cute too," Leonard said.

"Just start and go," I said.

"I hate being buffaloed," Leonard said. "And I hate a man thinks I don't appreciate Elvis."

"Yeah, but I hate more being dead."

Leonard fumed silently, fired up his junker and started to drive. Chief Cantuck leaned down and smiled tobacco at us through Leonard's rain-beaded car window as we went by.

When I looked back over my shoulder I saw him stooped by the remains of the house, working those wet, smoking Elvis cards toward him with a stick.

9

We drove back into town beneath a churning black sky kicked open and brightened now and then by cruel bursts of lightning. By the time we wheeled into downtown Grovetown, Leonard had on a rockin' zydeco tape even I could appreciate. Those dudes were blowing accordion music hot as devil farts through Leonard's cheap speakers, melting down the wires, making me hungry for gumbo.

We stopped at the filling station and I got out and got hold of one of the serve-yourself nozzles. Before I was allowed to put in the gas, Leonard had to finish hearing out a song on the tape player, and since his cheap system didn't play unless the motor was running, I stood outside willing and waiting with my gas nozzle cocked and ready, tapping my boot to the jump of the music.

Acquaintance of mine, Gerald Matter, who used to own a gas station in downtown LaBorde, told me once, you never load in the gas with the car motor running, or you might get a little spark, end up with your ass on the far side of the moon. "Safety first" was Gerald's motto.

'Course, Gerald lost the station for lack of payment back in nineteen seventy-eight, but he hadn't quite gotten the gas and oil business out of his blood. He did him a stretch in prison for trying to rob a filling station in Gilmer with a sharpened butter knife. Fat lady that ran the place came over the counter after him, got him by the throat, and beat the pure-dee dog shit out of him, took his knife away. She then proceeded to carve off part of his head before she could be subdued by a handful of shocked customers waiting on their free "crystal" dish with a fill-up.

Gerald has done his time and he's out now and he might even be a little smarter. But he's grown bashful, wears hats indoors and out to hide what's missing on top of his head, though except for a flap cap he wears now and then, it doesn't do a damn thing for his absent left ear. These days Gerald has abandoned gas and oil and has a little carpet-cleaning business and likes to go to bed early.

While I waited with the nozzle, the tall, pale-faced man we had seen earlier came out in his thick coat with his cap in his hand, picked up on Clifton Chenier calling out "Eh, Petite Fille," from Leonard's tape deck, smiled, sang a verse with Clifton, jiggled a little and flop-kneed on out to the car. His long body, pasty face, and gyrations made him look like an albino grasshopper on speed.

He reached the car dancing and grinning, stopped and laughed. "Damn," he said, "give an accordion to a redneck and all he can do is play 'Home on the Range' or some goddamn polka, give it to a coonass and he'll make the music crawl up your butt and play with your kidneys."

"That's right," Leonard said. He was standing outside the driver's door, leaning on the rooftop, listening. When the song finished, Leonard cut off the motor, and I started pumping gas.

"How're y'all," said the pale-faced man. He had a grin as infectious as syphilis.

"Good," I said. "Cold and a little damp, but good."

"Well, accordin' to the weather report, we're all gonna get colder and damper. Air is blowing ass over tea kettle down from Canada, churning like pig feet a boilin', only the air ain't warm. There's penguins would faint they knew something like this was comin'."

"Damn," I said. "That bad?"

"Let's just say them suitcases you got in back of your car there better not be filled with Hawaiian shirts and sun hats . . . hey, speakin' of pig's feet boilin'—"

"Were we?" I said.

"Well, I was," said the man. "I got some pickled ones inside that're peppered just right. Fifty cents a pig stump. You might like to try 'em. Just got 'em in. Can't keep 'em, they go so fast. Fellow I know out in the country makes 'em. Them buddies are so spicy, you eat one, you'll be able to do a push-up with your dick."

"Maybe I could use some of that," I said. "I was younger, I woke up and did a push-up with my dick without pickled pig's feet. Now, got to get enough sleep to do it, and then when I try to do it, I need sleep."

"Ain't that the shits?" he said. "Just when you get older and figure out what it's all about, what it's all about you ain't able to do."

"Say, listen," I said. "We're gonna get a couple of cans of oil too, but we're looking for someone. Main reason we stopped in here."

Leonard said, "Lady named Florida Grange."

"Oh, yeah. Nice lady. A looker too. She was around here a few days." He looked at Leonard. "You kin?"

"Nope," Leonard said.

"Boyfriend? Either of you?" He gave me a good hard look. "Though in this town, you better not say you are if you are."

"Nope," I said. "We're not boyfriends."

"She owe you money?"

"Nope."

"Y'all some kinda law?"

"Nope."

"Well then, let me say I tried serious hard and major purposeful to put the make on that little gal, but she wasn't havin' any. I think she has a thing about white guys. And not a good thing."

"Trust me," I said. "She does."

"Ah, so you tried her too?" he said.

"It didn't work out," I said. "You might say I'm an ex-boyfriend. But what we're lookin' for is to help out her current boyfriend who's worried about her. And we want to do it because we're friends of hers too. Sort of. Used to be."

"I see," the man said. "I think."

It grew very dark suddenly, then there was a crack of thunder and a sizzling race of lightning, and right after that it seemed as if a great tidal wave washed over us. The rain came down so hard it nearly knocked us flat.

"Goddamn," said the pale-faced man, putting his cap on. "There it is. Y'all come on in and we'll talk."

Leonard followed the man inside. I topped off the tank, hung up the gas nozzle, and damn near swam to the door. Inside, the store was warm and the lights were on, and the cold rain and midday darkness outside made the place seem tight and cozy.

The joint was stocked with pretty basic goods. Breads, crackers, a lunch meat cooler housing pressed ham, bologna, olive and liver loaf. There were soft drinks, peanuts, chips, that kind of stuff. Cans of oil, transmission and brake fluids. A rack of John Deere caps. A few straw cowboy hats. A cardboard display of colored plastic combs, and on the wall a dusty calendar over ten years out of date with a gorgeous, big-breasted woman in shorts and a halter top holding a wrench and smiling; the logo above her read January, and above that Snap Tight Tools.

Next to the cash register were two large jars containing yellowish brine water, and by my standards, some rather nasty looking pig's tootsies. Didn't appear to me that before they pickled them little delights they had washed the pig shit out from between the hooves, but maybe that was just a concentration of black pepper and meat gelatin.

There was a homemade oil barrel stove in the middle of the room, and there were lawn chairs and wicker-bottomed chairs pulled all around it. Near a couple chairs were two tobacco-splattered cuspidors, and the floor around them, which was covered with newspaper, was also splattered. Beneath the stove there was a large square of scarred, fire-spotted linoleum, and on it were tufts of dust bunnies, a chewing tobacco wrapper, and something that looked like blue glass or plastic that caught the electric light and pulled it in and winked it back.

There was a small stack of firewood next to the stove and there was a hatchet stuck deep in one of the logs and a gray lizard lay by the hatchet, attempting to trick us into thinking he was nothing more than a wood knot.

At the back of the store was an aluminum Christmas tree covered in lights and colored ornaments. The lights weren't on, and the angel at the top of the tree was too heavy for the little tip, so it leaned to one side, as if it were about to be cast from heaven.

Leonard paid for the gas and bought some oil, and when he got his change back, the pale-faced man said, "Y'all want some coffee?"

"You bet," Leonard said.

"I got a pot goin' in back. Sit down."

We took us a spot by the stove and sat. Leonard eyed the cuspidors and the tobacco wads, said, "Looks of this place, this ole boy talks to everybody, and for some time. He might know something nobody else does."

"And maybe just the weather report and where to get pig's feet," I said.

A moment later the man came back with two cups of coffee. He gave us a cup apiece, disappeared into the back of the store again, came back with a cup for himself and some ragged white towels. He tossed the towels at us. We used them to dry off. The station man sat his cup on the stove and took off his heavy coat and draped it over a chair near the stove, sat in another chair, put his feet up close to the heat.

"Now, you're lookin' for this gal?" he asked.

"That's right," I said.

"By the way, my name's Tim Garner."

"Glad to meet you," I said, and Leonard and I leaned forward and took turns shaking Tim's hand and giving our names. When we finished, Tim kicked back again and sipped his coffee.

"What do you mean she's missing?"

"Last time anyone's seen her we know about was here," Leonard said.

"No shit?"

"No shit," Leonard said. Outside the lightning gave the sky a workout and the flashes went all through the store. The lights faded, and the pickled pig's feet, for a fleeting instant, looked like strange body parts floating in jars in Dr. Frankenstein's lab.

"Goddamn," Tim said when the lights came back. "That was rich . . . let me see. She was here a few days, but she was having trouble finding a place to stay . . . you hang out here long enough, you're gonna discover this ain't a real opened-minded place."

"Naw," I said. "Say it ain't true. A homey burg like this."

Tim smiled at me. "Yeah, well, I guess you been talkin' to the Chief, so you know he's a bastard."

"How do you know that?" Leonard asked.

"That he's a bastard, or you been talkin' to him?" Tim said.

"Either," Leonard said.

"I come into town lookin' for someone, first place I'd go is the law. Am I right?"

Leonard nodded.

"And I'll bet old Cantuck sure was glad to see you two running around together. What he thinks, he sees a black and white guy together, is one of them ought to be riding in the back of a pickup with a rake."

"You're right," I said. "He wasn't glad to see us. I got the feeling just us being alive made him nervous. We met the fire department too. Now there's a bunch of regular guys. If you're white, potbellied, and stupid. Seems like they'd bore each other to death. What in the hell can guys like that talk about when they get together?"

"Pussy," Tim said.

"Well, all right," I said. "I can see that."

Tim took hold of the hatchet, lifted the log, and with a flick of his wrist, popped it loose of the hatchet and through the open stove door.

I was going to protest, since the lizard didn't have time to bail out, but Tim's move was so unexpected and so swift there wasn't a chance. The lizard gave a little pop when it went into the blaze, went black and turned to ash on his log; the last animated bit of him was his tail, which curled up and fell off. I decided not to mention it. No use putting an accidental lizard death on someone's head.

"Cantuck's a funny guy," Tim said. "Don't underestimate him. He ain't as stupid as he looks. And for a man with a left nut that looks like a softball in his pocket, he can move pretty fast too. No. He ain't stupid. And he ain't incompetent. Not really. He kinda uses that hick image to get his edge."

"I found that out," I said, watching the last of the lizard dissolve in the stove. The critter looked like a melted chunk of gummy bears.

"He's ignorant, but he's actually fair, and pretty law-abiding," Tim said. "In an Old Testament sort of way."

"Wonder how much he abided the law when that black guy hung himself in jail?" I asked.

"That weird sonofabitch had it comin'," Tim said. "He was a murdering bastard. I prefer he hung himself to the Chief doing it—and I don't think Cantuck would do it. Couldn't have. He wasn't even in town. That Soothe sumbitch was choked and stretched and put in the hole before Cantuck got back."

"Chief wasn't here," Leonard said, "but he could have made arrangements. Being out of town would be a good cover."

"I reckon," said Tim, "but I got to tell you true, if that sorry Bobby Joe fuck got a little help from the Chief, anybody, doesn't bother me a bit. That ole boy was into all kinds of shit. And I mean all kinds. Pretty smooth talker. Could stick his dick up your ass and tell you it was a turd, and you'd believe him.

"He's lucky he lived long as he did, considering how black folks are thought of here in Grovetown. I suppose he lasted 'cause he was a scary, dangerous bastard. And he could sing a pretty good tune. And there was some legacy to him, being kin to L.C. and all.

"Not that that's worth a big goddamn around here, but I reckon there's more than a few whites would hate to admit they enjoyed it when Bobby Joe come to town Saturdays, played over there in front of the courthouse with that ole slide guitar. Fact is, Saturday is normally the day all the blacks come in. Do their shopping, what they got to do. Hang out a little. Very little. Then go home. They got their own ways on the other side of town, and Bobby Joe was smart enough to keep most of his badness over there. Lot of folks here figured if it was just—and you'll pardon the expression—nigger business, then it wasn't no business of theirs. Figured too, niggers killing each other, giving each other a hard time, that wasn't nothing to be concerned with. One less nigger was like one less cockroach."

"'Course," Leonard said, "cockroaches can't play basketball."

"Yeah, the jump shots throw 'em. I'll tell you about Bobby Joe, kinda guy he was. He raped his own nephew's wife, then when she told on him and the nephew tried to do something about it, he cut the nephew up to where he near died, went after the woman. Rumor is he made her fuck his German shepherd."

"Oh, get out of here," I said.

"I'm tellin' you the story," Tim said. "I can't prove it. Haven't got photos or nothing, but I believe it. There wasn't nothing Bobby Joe wouldn't do short of a law degree."

"Man has to have some ethics," Leonard said.

"Our concern here is Florida," I said. "Only reason we're interested in Bobby Joe Soothe at all is Florida came down here to investigate things for some kind of article she wants to write about his death."

"I know about that," said Tim. "I got that much out of her. We talked a little when we saw each other. She was convinced Bobby Joe was innocent just because he was black and in a white jail."

"Innocent really hasn't got anything to do with it," I said. "Guilty or innocent, you're supposed to let the State of Texas do the killing, and with a needleful of poison."

"Yeah, well, we're back to where we started," Tim said. "Like I was sayin', I don't give a shit what happened to Soothe."

"Frankly," Leonard said, "I don't give a shit, if he had it comin'. I'm not as sweet as Hap. He still has all his Roy Rogers cap guns and stuff. But what we're concerned with is that Florida was in Grovetown, now she isn't, and she isn't home, and we're nervous."

"You're thinking bad business descended?" Tim said.

"We're thinking it might have, or can yet," Leonard said. "We hope we're just old worried grandmas."

"I don't know I can help you beyond saying I hope you're wrong," Tim said.

"Anything different about her last time you saw her?" Leonard asked.

"Maybe she was a little tired, or nervous, but you're black and hang out here, you're gonna get a little nervous. Don't believe in time travel, just hang around here a week. Better yet, don't."

"So," Leonard said, "you're saying' all the white guys in town, except you, were just perched like buzzards waiting to take her down?"

"I suppose you could say that."

"I don't doubt this town is backwards as hell," Leonard said, "but I don't buy every white guy here is a murderous prick. Is that what you're trying to tell me? You are, I got to ask, what makes you so special? You ain't threatening me. You wanted to fuck Florida. You don't seem like you're worried that the White Knights of the Asshole will come down on you with a barrel of tar and a basket of chicken feathers for wanting to bury your toad in some black hole, you got the chance."

"You're kinda dropping down on me pretty quick, aren't you, pal?" Tim said.

"Leonard's motto is 'Make a New Friend Every Day,'" I said.

Tim grinned that infectious grin. "Hey, it's all right. And you got some points, fella. But let me sorta tick 'em off. First off, my dick ain't no toad. It's just as pretty as a little old skinned banana, but a hell of a lot harder. 'Specially after I've had some pickled pig's feet. Pussy ain't a black hole. If it's black pussy, white pussy, yellow pussy, or red pussy, any other color, on the inside it's all pink and it all feels like a hot mink glove on your weener. So now we got that straight.

"Next thing. This town ain't filled with Klan types. It only needs a diligent few to be members. A few more who won't participate in their shit, but are behind them, and some others that might be against them, but are afraid to say anything, and for good reason. You don't believe me, let me tell you, not that long ago they sewed a little ole black gal's thang together and got away with it."

"So we heard," I said.

"They've been known to nail black men to trees and work them over with a blowtorch. Burn off their balls. You don't hear about all that goin' on, but it does. Maybe not right here in town, but round-abouts. And maybe not recently, but recent enough, and it could get real recent anytime.

"And I can hustle a little black tail if I want. You see, it's okay a white man wants to get him a dark piece, long as he has a sense of humor about it and thinks of the piece as just nigger pussy. 'Course, this white and black thing, here in Grovetown, it don't work in reverse. Black man wants to get him a white piece, well, that's considered unnatural and punishable by death.

"All that aside, main reason I'm left alone is my daddy. The old sonofabitch is Jackson Truman Brown. I've kept my mother's name. Anyway, Daddy's Grovetown's old-time swingin' dick. He's smooth, dresses in nice suits, can talk that shit, but he's at heart a plantation owner that misses the old days when you could work a black man to death and hang him for fartin'. His daddy's daddy, my great-grandfather, was famous for hanging a black man that looked at great-grandpa's wife a little longer than great-grand thought he should have. But hanging wasn't good enough. When the fella was dead, he propped him on a post out in his fields to use as a scarecrow.

Left him there for his black field hands to see till the body rotted away. In other words, he wasn't just scarin' crows. He was scarin' his slaves."

"What is it your daddy does?" I asked.

"He owns Jackson's Christmas Tree Farm and the lumber mill here. Both thriving concerns. Folks from all over Texas and the United States got to have their Christmas trees, I can tell you that. He's got these goddamn fir trees that all grow to look exactly alike. Not native trees, Yankee trees. They've been rebred, or whatever trees do to make more trees, and they can stand the Texas heat and the clay soil better than a native pine. He ships those dudes from here to Kansas City in air-conditioned trucks. And you want to work here in Grovetown, you want him to be happy with you. Because not only does he own the lumber mill and run the Christmas tree farm, he owns a lot of other things, as well as a lot of people. Black and white. Only things in this town he don't own are the cafe and the Chief, and maybe with the Chief it don't matter much. Like I said, he's honest and fair, but he and my old man share a lot of the same views."

"I notice you have an aluminum Christmas tree," Leonard said.

"Sort of speaks volumes, don't it?" Tim said.

"What about your station here?" I asked. "He own that?"

"Goddamn him, he owns that too. Loaned me the money for it—key word here is loaned, not gave, and he expects the payments, or I'll be back at the Christmas tree farm. I hate the bastard, and he knows it, and likes it. What I want most in the world is to get the money to pay him off, be a free man. Fact is, what I want most in the world is money. I admit it. Here I was, son of the richest man in town, and I was always wearing worn-out clothes with patches and carried my lunch in a fucking paper bag. Wouldn't even let me buy a lunch box like the rest of the kids. Thought it built character. What it did was it embarrassed me. I said I got older and got a chance to get money, I'd get it. The whole idea of going around poor, even owning this shitty filling station when I ought to have a good life, all the money he's got, I get itchy. Mad even.

"But I got my edge on him. See, I'm kind of an embarrassment. I actually had a couple years college in something besides business.

Anthropology. Though it didn't take. I can tell you a little about North American Indians, you want, but when it comes down to it, what I know is about as useless as tits on a boar hog. Still, I'm his son, and he's insurance for me. I wanted to, I could go over there and set fire to the cafe, and he'd make it so it was understood I was merely tryin' to warm up the place. But he wouldn't drop what I owe him on this station, and I don't pay it, he'll own the station. More coffee, fellas?"

Leonard and I declined. Tim offered us the pig's feet again, at a slightly reduced price, but we declined those as well.

"Let me ask you something," I said. "There anyplace we could rent a room for a few nights in this town?"

"I doubt it," Tim said. "I mean, I don't know."

"You don't know?" Leonard said. "Then let me ask you this. Where did Florida stay?"

Tim smiled, but the smile looked silly this time, not infectious. "Why, out at my mother's place."

IO

About noon, we bought some sandwich makings, and Tim called his mother, tried to get us a place to stay. Turned out his mother owned a few trailers she rented out, and one was available.

"I like you fellas and all," Tim said after the phone call, "but way it works, needing money like I do, you pay Mom, and you pay me a little finder's fee."

"What's a little?" Leonard asked.

"Fifty dollars."

"That's a little!" I said.

"It's how much it's gonna be you stay at Mom's trailer park."

Leonard grumbled, paid the fifty in two twenties and a ten.

"Florida pay you a finder's fee?" Leonard asked.

"You betcha," Tim said, folding his money into his wallet. "I never claimed I was a philanthropist."

Tim decided to close up and guide us out to his mom's place. He told us he had planned to stay open Christmas Day, partly out of boredom, and out of the fact he could snag a few extra dollars by being the only place available in town to pick up gas and goods, but the weather being the way it was, that turned out to be a pipe dream.

Still, bad as it was, it had slacked some, and we took the moment to get started. Tim drove an old four-wheel-drive, green, broad wheel-base pickup with gaudy tail flaps. One flap had the silhouette of a naked silver lady on it. The other would have had the same but it was ripped in half, leaving only the lady's head.

We followed in Leonard's heap, and as we drove, Leonard said, "He could have told us up front Florida had been staying with his mother."

"I think he was just being cautious," I said. "Watching out for Florida. Remember, he was mum until he asked if we were kin, boyfriends, or bill collectors? I think he didn't want to bring shit down on Florida, if he could keep from it. Or maybe he was watching out for his mother. Either way, I think he was being considerate. And remember, he didn't have to tell us dick."

"I don't like the dude."

"Really? He seems all right. Maybe a little too self-consciously folksy, but okay."

"A fifty-dollar finder's fee? I don't give a shit about his childhood money problems. I give a shit about my fifty dollars he's got."

"You are the most suspicious sonofabitch I have ever known, Leonard. He's a little overly money-conscious, and he strikes me as a would-be cock dog, but neither of those things are exactly criminal."

"Yeah, well doesn't he make you feel kind of creepy, him talking all that good ole boy bullshit?"

"Only thing creepy is how easy it is for me to do it too."

"There's some truth."

"Yeah. Well, what about that cockroaches can't play basketball thing?"

"I like that one," Leonard said. "But that aside, if Florida stayed out here, you got to bet this guy was sniffing her ass regular like."

"He may have wanted her, but trust me, my friend, if this gal doesn't want to put up with bullshit, she has a way of dealing with you that'll make you feel knee high to a cricket pretty quick. And maybe it takes a heterosexual to understand what I'm getting at, but this lady, young as she is, pretty as she is, she isn't any babe in the woods. Not about men, anyway. Maybe about other things, but trust me, she's got an A in Dealing With Men."

"All right. There's some more truth. I saw Florida drag you around by your ying-yang some, that's for sure."

"I ain't proud of it."

"Nor should you be."

One minute it was gray and damp, the heater humming, keeping us warm, the wipers thumping almost happily, and suddenly the sky went black as night and the rain fell down in silver sheets thick as corrugated tin. The air in the car turned cool and the heater moaned as if dying of pneumonia, the wipers swiped at the rain like a drowning victim trying to tread water.

Got so bad, Tim pulled over to the side of the road and sat in his truck. We pulled up behind him and sat too, waited. It was a full forty-five minutes before the rain subsided enough for us to continue, and as we drove on, slowly, I looked out my side, watched as we crawled past an old gray clapboard building. It was long and low-built and the walls were leaning, and you could tell the floor had long since lost its battle against gravity and was lying flat on the ground, the old support blocks having shifted and sunk. Through one of the windows I could see an unlit Christmas tree tilting to port, and an unlit neon sign over the front door that was impossible to read through the slash and thrash of the rain.

"A black juke joint," Leonard said.

"Yep," I said.

We continued at a drag, the water splitting before us and slamming against the bottom of the car, floating us left and right. I began to understand how it must feel to be in a submarine.

Tim's mother's place proved to be well outside of Grovetown, down some incredibly muddy roads, deep in some bottom land that made me nervous, weather being the way it was. I didn't know much about Grovetown, but I knew the dam for Lake Nanonitche was nearby, and not too many years ago it had burst and drowned three people and waterlogged enough property to cause Grovetown and surrounding burgs to become designated as a National Disaster Area.

When we got to the trailer park, I was even more nervous. I'd never seen anything like it. The park consisted of six nasty-ass mobile homes—one a double-wide—standing on stilts damn near twelve feet off the ground with crude wooden stairways leading to their doors.

We parked and sat in Leonard's car while Tim went up to the double-wide, climbed the stairs and knocked on the door. He went inside and stayed awhile.

When he came out he was under an umbrella with an older woman who was wearing an orange raincoat and matching galoshes. Tim beckoned us to him. We got out in the driving rain and met them at the bottom of the stairs. The woman was sixtyish, attractive in an "I've been hit by a truck" kind of way.

Tim said, "This is my mother."

"Y'all got money?" she said.

Like son, like mother.

"We can buy lunch and have dessert if the waiters don't wear suits," Leonard said.

Mom studied on that, said, "Come on."

We moved through ankle-deep muddy water behind them, soaked to the bone. The woman walked with her left leg stiff, her left hand in her raincoat pocket. She leaned against Tim as if she was trying to find her sea legs.

We climbed some stairs, the woman managing it with considerable effort, and stood on a platform in front of a trailer door that was all bent up with an aluminum strip peeling off to one side. There was a huge splotch of blackness at the edge of the door where fire had slipped from the inside and kissed the exterior.

Ms. Garner put a key in the door, and when it was unlocked, Tim got hold of the edge with his fingers and tugged at it. It screeched as if alive, then we were in.

It smelled doggy dank and burnt in there. There was a carpet that looked as if it had once lined a pigpen, and the dog odor came from it. The burnt smell came from a portion of the wall next to the door. That part of the wall was absent of paneling and consisted of charred insulation. The "living room" was furnished with one old rickety couch mounted on cinder blocks and a chair with a cushion that dipped almost to the floor. There was one little gas heater and it was missing most of its grates, and the ones it had were busted.

The kitchen was just another part of the same room, and you could see where there had been a grease fire over the stove. The dank carpet and burnt insulation odor that tracked us from the living room blended with the stench of rancid grease coating the stove top. The fridge hummed desperately, like a dying man trying to remember a sentimental tune.

"Well," Leonard said, "this is nice."

"Don't like it, go to hell," said Ms. Garner. She said that without so much as a change of features.

"So much for the big sell," Leonard said. "How much is it? Considering we'll be camping out."

"Ten dollars a day, pay by the day. Use too much gas or electricity, there'll be a charge for that. I watch the meters."

"This place looks like you found it when it floated downriver after a fire and tornado," Leonard said.

"It wasn't so bad six months ago," Ms. Garner said. "Morons moved in here were a bunch of them goddamn holier-than-thou Christians. Ones where the men wear their pants pulled up under the armpits and like green suits with white shoes. Women like to pile their hair on their head and wear ugly dresses."

"Pentecostal," I said.

"Morons," Ms. Garner said.

"Did they live in here with a herd of cows?" Leonard asked.

"You're a smart one, ain't you?" Ms. Garner said.

"My dearest friends call me the Smartest Nigger in the World."

"Yeah. Well, I believe it. What these Christian high-hairs had was a goddamn Chihuahua. One of them little ugly Mexican dogs looks like a shaved rat with a disease. Goddamned lab experiment material is what they are.

"Three men and three women, two kids. I charged 'em twenty dollars a day, there being so many. And they had a whole slew of Bibles and tracts and religious crap. Stupid morons."

"Calm down, Mom," Tim said. "You're gonna strain yourself."

"Don't talk to me like I'm constipated," she said.

"Whatever," Tim said, and shrugged his shoulders at us.

"Kids gave the dog a bath," she said, "and get this, they put the goddamn rat in the oven to dry. Turned on the oven and put the rat in there. He got dried up all right. Little turd caught on fire, starting barking—screaming, really. A dog gets hurt enough, it can scream. Heard him all the way over in my trailer. They let him out of the oven just before he was a casserole. He run all over the place. Caught them Bibles and tracts on fire, then that crap caught the wall on fire. I threw them Christians out on their holy butts. They had to tote what was left of that mutt off in a smokin' pail. Looked kind of pathetic, even if it was a Chihuahua. Nothing but that old blackened tail stickin' out of the top of that bucket, like a burned-down lantern wick."

"Yeeech," Leonard said. "I'm just glad it wasn't a real dog."

"Anyway, those irresponsibles burned up their dog and trashed my trailer. What a bunch of dipshits. I hope y'all aren't dipshits."

"No, ma'am," Leonard said. "Least I'm not. But I'll watch Hap for you."

"Yeah, well don't put him in the oven," she said. "And if you've got any more snide remarks about the accommodations here, you can hit the road before we get started. Let me tell you something. I didn't ask to rent to either of you. My son wanted me to help out, way I did that colored gal. I'd rather do without money than put up with shit. You boys got that?"

We said we had it.

She pointed to a dark and exceptionally narrow doorway. "Crapper's right over there. It's slow flush, so don't wipe so severe you cram the bowl with paper. You won't never get it down. Guess that's about it. Want the place or not?"

"We'll stay," I said. "But might I ask, as if I didn't know, why all these trailers are on stilts?"

"About five years ago we had a hell of a rain and a flood. Down here in the bottoms, it comes a good rain, you can catch catfish in the commode. Flood washed the entire park away. Fortunately I was in town. Couple old geezers renting the far end trailer drowned like ants in a ditch."

"That's what I was afraid of," I said.

"That's why I had these trailers put on stilts. These are good solid posts under us."

To prove her point she hopped heavily on her one good leg three or four times. "See there. Doesn't even move."

She pointed at the stove. "Top burners work. Oven don't. Damn dog fire messed it up. You won't want to cook much nohow. Even if you cook on the top burners, stove heats up, it smells like burning Chihuahua. I don't know about you, but that would set me off my feed."

"Yeah," Leonard said. "I think that would bother me too."

"Come on and I'll show you the bedroom. And by the way, I don't want y'all having anybody over. 'Specially gals. This ain't no brothel."

"We don't know anybody to have over," Leonard said.

"Good. Come on."

Tim looked at us, tried to grin, but couldn't quite make it. We followed Momsy into the bedroom. There was a single bed with a mattress that looked pretty dadgum bleak.

"Looks as if someone's been pissin' on it nightly," Leonard said.

"That Chihuahua," she said. "Sonofabitches would rather bark and piss than fornicate and eat. That's the thing about 'em. They got no priorities. My sister had one of them little poots, and she used to jack him off once a week 'cause he was tense. Never could figure what was wrong with the sonofabitch lickin' his noodle like any other respectable dog. Fact is, more men could lick their noodle, the world would be better off. Less mess'n around. Y'all just turn the mattress."

"I'll take the couch," I said.

"We'll flip for it," Leonard said.

"Hell, dog pissed on the couch too," she said.

"Dibs on the bed then," I said. "I'll turn the mattress."

11

Tim helped his mother home, and Leonard and I went into the living room and surveyed our surroundings. "Well, it's cheap enough," I said.

"Well, Smartest Peckerwood in the World, what do you expect? She should be getting top dollar for this? Damn, I'm cold."

We lit the suspicious-looking gas heater in the living room, found one of an equally suspicious nature in the bedroom and lit it. We lit the top cook stove burners as well, and the old lady was right. That rancid grease heated up, that dog in the oven warmed, the place began to smell like a rendering plant.

"I don't know which is worse," Leonard said. "Being frozen or stunk to death. Flip for the bed?"

"I already called dibs. Besides, you heard her. Dog pissed on both of them, so what's the difference?"

"Difference is the couch looks like some kind of torture instrument."

"I got dibs, man. Bed is mine."

The door scraped and squeaked, and Tim, dripping water, came inside and shoved the door shut.

"Shit," he said. "I ain't seen a rain like this since them old codgers drowned."

"That's good to know," Leonard said. "Give me a little something to think about tonight while I'm trying to sleep."

"Trailers weren't on stilts then," Tim said. He went over and got up close to the little heater. "Brrrrrrrr."

"Tim," Leonard asked. "Why didn't you tell us early on Florida stayed out here at your mother's park?"

"I don't know. She seemed like a nice girl. Woman. I didn't know what you guys were up to. I had to feel you out a little. She couldn't find a place, and she mentioned it to me, and I told her about here."

"Didn't have anything to do with you hoping to drop your anchor in her ocean, did it?" Leonard asked. "You having her out here, I mean? Handy. Kind of indebted to you?"

"I guess it did," Tim said. "Some. But I was trying to help her too."

"And pick up fifty dollars," Leonard said.

"That's right," Tim said. "Besides, how indebted is someone gonna feel staying here? This was where she stayed, you know? This trailer . . . besides, I don't need any grief, don't need the law on my back, and I didn't want to drag Mom into this. She don't need those Klan creeps on her for helping out blacks. It isn't like she was trying to be a Good Samaritan, anyway. She'd rent to anybody to make a few bucks."

"Gee, thanks," I said.

"You know what I mean," Tim said. "She wasn't making any kind of statement renting to Florida. It's not like she keeps this park up or nothing."

"No joke?" Leonard said.

"I try to help," Tim said, "but with the station and all, my own life. Hell, it's all I can do."

"You live out here too?" I asked.

"I got a place in back of the store. Once in a while I'll stay out here. It's rare Mom's got any boarders. Place like this mostly caters to a pretty desperate crowd. People come and go quick like. Lot of them are just one-nighters. Some guy renting so he can do the rodeo with some local poke. Right now, 'cept for y'all, and Mom, of course, the park is empty."

"Not to meddle," I said.

"Don't count on it," Leonard said. "Hap's got a black belt in meddlin'."

"Maybe your mom could stay at the store," I said. "This is pretty, well, bleak, isn't it?"

"She won't have it that way," Tim said. "She wants her own thing. When her and Daddy divorced, she had to go to work in the lumber mill, like one of the other wage slaves. She got caught in some machinery. She lost a leg. Has an artificial one. Her hand . . . well, it was mashed flat. Looks like a goddamn Mickey Mouse hand. No shit. Mashed flat like a cartoon hand. Only it ain't a cartoon. It's ruined. She's got where she ain't exactly right. Gets worse every year. But she remembers being independent, and she doesn't want to lose that. Sometimes, I think that's all that holds her together, being independent."

"She sounded all right to me," I said. "Ornery. But all right."

"This is one of her good days," Tim said.

"She's damn sure got them Chihuahuas scoped out," Leonard said.

"You can't put much stock in what she says," Tim said. "She'd probably have been less upset if one of the Pentecostals had gotten cooked by the dog."

"I can understand that," Leonard said. "Or maybe that's the Jehovah's Witnesses that bother me with the tracts and stuff, not the Pentecostals. I can't get 'em straight."

"Listen here, guys," Tim said. "I know you two and me ain't buddies or nothing. Just met you. But I got to give a little advice, tell you that messin' around in this town, a black guy and a white guy. It ain't good. If something did happen to Florida, whoever done it might be willing to do it again. This thing with Florida, maybe you ought to forget it. Let the Chief handle it. He's basically fair. Let him do your lookin' for you."

"I'm not sure he'll look that hard," I said.

"All right," Tim said. "But you wake up one morning beside the road with your throat slit and Leonard hanging from a crab apple tree, and his dick cut off and in your mouth, don't say I didn't warn you."

"I don't want my dick in his mouth, cut off or attached," Leonard said.

"You should be so lucky," I said.

"All right, guys," Tim said. "Have it your way."

We gave Tim some rent money for his mother, and he went away. When he was gone, I said, "Guess we shouldn't have jacked with him. He was just concerned about us."

"Hell with him," Leonard said. "Seems to me he's awfully anxious for us to leave matters in the hands of that ruptured cop. I think he's just worried he might get asked some questions. And hey, Bubba, let me give you some advice. Stay the hell out of everybody's business."

"What?"

"Stuff about his mama living at the store with him. That ain't your problem."

"You're the one thinks he's a money-grubbing untrustworthy sonofabitch. So if he's a sonofabitch, maybe he hasn't thought about it."

"Just keep your mind on askin' the insulting questions that pertain to Florida, and quit trying to take the world in to raise. I think that ole woman is just the way she wants to be, and that Tim's just embarrassed by her, and he's a selfish sonofabitch who'd take coins off her dead eyes to buy rubbers."

"Could be . . . man, she's something, isn't she. That story she told, about the Chihuahua. The Pentecostals. That's horrible, don't you think? Poor dog getting burned up like that."

"Terrible," Leonard said, then pursed his lips and smiled a little. "But it's kinda funny, you don't know the dog personal like."

12

We got our suitcases and sandwich makings out of the car, got soaked to the bone again. It had grown so dark outside, it seemed as if it ought to be bedtime.

Inside, we changed into dry clothes and sat on the floor by one of the stoves and made sandwiches of meat and bread and no fixings. We balanced the food on our knees and ate slowly and drank soda pops. Outside, the storm grew stronger and squealed like a pig having its throat cut.

When we finished eating we put the goods in the refrigerator, which was a filthy sucker and had a smell that refused to blend with the burnt dog, burnt wall, and pissed-on carpet. Its aroma was well sorted from the others, and equally overpowering.

The rest of the afternoon we sat by the fire with used paperbacks we had brought, and read. We were sharing some old books written by Michael Moorcock under the name Edward P. Bradbury. They were pastiches of Edgar Rice Burroughs, and they were fast and fun and pretty mindless.

Except for the odor, and the fact that over-forty-year-old bods have a little trouble sitting on the floor for an extended period of time without back aches and the legs going to sleep, it really wasn't, all things considered, too unpleasant. It had been some time since I had just settled in with a book and read, especially books like these, and my mind and emotions were just right to believe them, eager to get away from crack houses, a Chief of Police with swollen balls, and a missing woman I had once loved, and maybe still did a little.

When I was a kid, I read a book like this, I became the main character, and the characters I liked were big and strong and fearless and always got the babe. I thought my life would go that way when I grew up.

It hadn't.

But for a few hours I was away from what my life hadn't been. Away from worry and reality. I was on another planet, fighting monsters with my fine, sharp sword. And I was winning.

The pleasant feeling didn't last. I finally fell out of the book and hit reality. I thought of Florida. I wondered how she was, and feared I already knew. The rain quit being pleasant. It had gone back to making me feel cold and wet and sad.

When I looked up from my book, Leonard was looking at me. He said, "Hungry?"

"Didn't we just eat?"

"About three hours ago."

We ate again, more out of boredom than anything else, then tried to read some more, but I had lost it. So had Leonard. He found a couple of blankets in the bedroom, put one over the couch itself and took the other for cover. He took the old worn cushion off the chair and tried to make a pillow out of it. He stripped down to his shorts and covered up and lay there and blew out his breath, which frosted and made a fast dissolving cloud. He said, "You know, it's kind of funny, Raul not being around. I'd grown accustomed."

"I'm sorry, man."

"Me too. I reckon, thinking on it, I was kind of a jackass."

"That's hard to imagine."

"Ain't it? How do you put up with me?"

"Guess 'cause you put up with me."

"Thing throws me is how we can be so close, and yet I can't put together a relationship. You and me, we been through thick and thin. Been mad at each other. Gotten each other into shit—Naw, now that I think about it, it's you gets me into shit."

"You're probably right," I said.

"But here we are, two guys, friends, one straight and one gay, and we get along better with each other than we do with our chosen sex partners."

"Maybe it's the sex throws a wrench in things. Soon as you start doing the two-bear mambo, like those bears on that special, it falls apart."

"I don't know, those bears looked pretty happy."

"Yeah, but way it works in nature is the male bear loads the female bear with sperm, then he heads out, leaving the female bear to raise cubs by herself."

"That's not nice."

"No, it isn't."

"A little secret, Hap. When two guys fuck, neither of them gets pregnant."

"What I mean is, sex, one way or another, complicates things. I don't know how, but it's always in one way or another the turd in the stew."

"So you want to give it up?"

"I may not have a choice, way things are going, but no, I don't want to give it up. It's been so long for me now, the bear on the *National Geographic* special got the right look in her eye, I'd mount up."

"So, except for determining that you'd fuck a bear, we're no closer to solving the mystery of human and animal relations than we were five minutes ago."

"Maybe our friendship works out okay 'cause when I get tired of your shit, I go to the house till I get over it. I don't feel obligated to be with you, and I don't feel I'm deserting you if I go home. I have no sexual interest in you."

"That's hard to believe, being the fine specimen of gay manhood that I am."

"I know, but it's true. I also know we get sideways with one another, tomorrow, next day, everything's gonna be okay. You'll be there if I need you."

"You know, Hap, you've never sent me a valentine."

"Fuck you."

There was really very little to do with the rest of the day, and I was tired from the night before, so I went to the bedroom and got the remaining two blankets and lay down on the bed, but the odor of dog piss was too overwhelming. I flipped the mattress and there was the smell of Chanel No. 5.

Florida.

My head filled with her. Soft and dark and smart and sexy. I almost coveted the dog pee side. I lay there with the blankets over me, a thin pillow beneath my head, looked at the ceiling, picked out water spots, and listened to Leonard hum Country's Greatest Hits. He did that sometimes when he couldn't sleep, hummed tunes. Maybe that's why Raul left him. That and no respect for *Gilligan's Island*.

Eventually the water spots darkened into one large shadow as the gloomy afternoon became early evening. Leonard's humming became spaced, starting to drift off.

My eyes began to fill with tears then, and I can't honestly say if the tears were for Florida or for me. I had lost her and I wanted her back, and I knew that wasn't going to happen, no matter what. I knew I should think of her and what might have happened to her, harness some new game plan for finding her, but I lay there instead and felt sorry for myself, and was angry, because some part of me was enjoying the sorrow, and maybe, just maybe, there was a bad part of me that barked and howled and said, "See what happens you leave me, baby? You die."

Oh, God, Florida.

Don't be dead.

And then somewhere between all that and the sweet and over-whelming smell of Chanel No. 5, and Leonard slow-humming "Walkin' the Floor Over You," I dropped off.

The rain and wind beat and lashed the trailer and I could feel Florida beside me, and she was sweet with the scent of Chanel No. 5, and I reached to hold her, but couldn't. She was as insubstantial as the shadows, and then I opened my eyes from the dream, and there she stood at the end of the bed, looking down at me. It was dark in there, but somehow I could see. I could see she was naked. She stood like some kind of harpy, her legs bent, her body leaning forward, her fine breasts swaying down, the nipples taut with the cold. Her hair glistened red with East Texas clay, and her lithe body was slick with it. Chunks of clay clung to her pubic thatch like dirt dauber nests.

Then I realized not all the red was clay. Her head had a split in it, and some of the red that ran from her mound and down the inside of her thigh wasn't slick clay at all.

I tried to get up but couldn't. She leaned farther forward and reached for me. I didn't like the way her eyes looked. They looked cold and lifeless, like those of a fish in an ice chest.

She opened her mouth, and clay fell out. She said, "Hap, you got to help me."

"I will, Florida. I will. God, we thought you were dead."

She laughed and clay sprayed from her mouth as if from a nozzle.

Then I came awake, sat bolt upright, and there was Leonard sitting on the edge of the sagging bed. He reached out and touched my shoulder.

"It's okay, man," he said. "It's all right. Get your shit together."

I sat up in bed and pushed my back to the wall. "Damn," I said. "I thought I saw Florida."

"I know. You called her name about a half-dozen times. Woke me up. You all right, buddy?"

"Yeah. What time is it?"

"I don't know. Not too late."

"God almighty, I swear, that was as real a dream as I've ever had . . . Leonard, she's dead, man. She was all covered in clay, like she'd been buried."

"She's dead because you saw her dead in a dream? That don't mean nothing."

"She's dead because she is. Way dreams work is they put together what you know. She's somewhere dead and buried, and you know it."

"You don't know nothing."

"Yeah. Well tell me, what do you think?"

"All right. I think she's dead. I don't think she drove up here and just dropped off the face of the earth. No one has seen her in a while. Last stop was here. Not like there's lots of places to stay in Grovetown, so I don't think she's around. It don't look good, Hap."

"Yeah."

"Thing is, this is all just how I feel. It isn't worth anything."

"So what now?"

"We came up here to find her, and we will. Dead or alive. First thing to do though, is tomorrow morning, call Hanson or Charlie.

See they've heard anything from her. She may be back in LaBorde, and if so, Hanson probably hasn't even told her we're looking for her. He's too busy making up with her, layin' pipe."

"No, Leonard. He wouldn't do that. She's like a daughter to him. Remember."

"Yeah, right. I forgot."

"Damn, isn't this one hell of a special Christmas?"

"Yeah. Merry Christmas. Listen here, Hap. I ain't been sleeping all that good. Cold in there and the sweet aroma of dog whiz is about to make me puke, then you yelling and all, but it's also because I been thinking."

"Careful now. Don't hurt yourself."

"Much as I hate it, we call and Hanson hasn't heard anything, I think we got to go back to the Chief. Officially report Florida missing, set him on the case."

"What would he care?"

"Guy like that, he may already know what happened to her. It's not that I think he'll find her, but he may do something gives us a lead to where she is. Or gives us an idea what happened to her. We want to push him a little. Make him nervous."

"You think he's behind all this? Maybe head of the Knights of the Swollen Left Nut, or whatever they are?"

"I don't know. I'm clutching at farts, but we got to clutch at something. And speaking of that, I'm gonna go clutch at my blankets, and I'm coming back in here, and you and me are gonna share this bed."

"Oh God, Leonard, has my manly physique finally caused your hormones to bust the blood vessels to your brain?"

"No, but I'm cold, and I figure we can share our blankets and some body heat."

"You make me so hot when you talk like that."

"Hap, you tell any of my friends I shared a bed with a heterosexual, even if it was just to keep warm, I'll kill you. Thing like that got around, it could ruin my reputation. By the way, you wearing perfume?"

"Florida," I said. "It's in the mattress."

"Oh."

He came back with his blankets and we shared the mattress. Just before he closed his eyes, he said, "Wake me when Santa comes."

It was warmer that way, Leonard and I sharing. I slept better, deeper. But near morning I awoke from yet another dream.

This time Florida and I had been naked, sitting in lawn chairs, and we were on a little raft made of crude-cut logs, sailing down a dark river on a moonlit night. The moon was high in the sky and bright. When Florida turned to look at me her eyes were full of the moon. Two white orbs slick as wet bone inside dark tunnels. She said, "Come on and love me, Huck, honey."

Then we were beneath the water, cold and wet and alone. She had her arms around my neck, and she was heavy, and she was dragging me down, down, down to the bottom of the great black river, and no matter how hard I fought, she wouldn't let go.

I got up, dressed, had a soda pop and a couple slices of lunch meat, and waited for daybreak.

13

By morning the rain had slowed, and when Leonard woke we drove into town for coffee and a real breakfast. We had plans to call Hanson.

Grovetown was starting to stir. Christmas holidays were gone, and stores were open. The cafe was hopping. Tim's filling station had two cars in the drive. One driver, a fat lady wearing a bright field of flowers on a dress constructed of enough material to parachute a Land Rover from a speeding jet, was putting gas in her car, the rain beating down on her blue-haired head with a vengeance.

At the full-service pump, behind the wheel of a gray pickup, an elderly man with a face tight as a sphincter muscle rolled his window down and coughed blue-gray cigar smoke into the rain.

Tim was filling the pickup's tank, had his head bent so that water was running off his cap. Both the fat woman and the elderly man took note of us, just in case we were planning on hijacking their vehicles. Tim looked up, saw us, gave us a wink.

We went inside the store, hung around until Tim was finished. He came in and grinned at us. "Y'all decide you want some of them pickled pig's feet after all?"

"No," I said, "but we'd like to make a call to LaBorde, if you'll let us. I can give you enough money to cover it."

"Long as you pay, you can call goddamn Australia."

Tim showed me the phone behind the counter, and allowed me some privacy. I called Hanson at home first, didn't get him. Tried the cop shop, still didn't find him. I asked for Charlie, and they put him on the line.

"It's me," I said. "Checkin' in. Seein' if Florida showed up."

"Nope," Charlie said, "and that means you haven't found her either."

"It don't look good. She's been here, but she isn't here now. We're gonna look around today, but I don't get the idea the Chief here is much worried what happened to Florida. I think you need to get some real law down here. The Rangers maybe."

"Her not being there doesn't mean anything's happened to her."

"So I keep hearing, but I got some bad vibes."

"Thing occurred to me, was what if she used this trip to go on and leave Hanson for good? You know, an easy way to keep on going. It's possible."

"Yeah. But not likely."

"I wouldn't say that. Little something I found out was she took a lot of money with her."

"What do you mean?"

"I am a paid sleuth for the public, Hap. I called a friend of mine over where Florida banks. She withdrew her savings. Thirty thousand dollars. What you think about that?"

"I don't know. I guess she could have plans to leave, but that's not like Florida. She gets tired of a situation, she just hangs it up. She doesn't sneak. Besides, she has a law practice."

"She let her apartment go too."

"That could mean she got over her rift with Hanson, was planning on moving in with him full-time. As in marriage. But something, whatever happened to her, got in the way."

"I suppose. But I still hold for her just hauling ass on out of Dodge, and right on across the Badlands."

"I hope you're right, Charlie. Anything else shaking?"

"Hanson's gone off. On a drunk, I think. I can't get him at home, hasn't been in the office this morning. It's early, but I don't think he's coming in. Was supposed to. Me and him had some stuff to do."

"What makes you think he's on a drunk?"

"'Cause up until he asked you and Leonard for help, he was on a pretty constant drunk. I don't think he'll clean up his act just 'cause y'all are looking around."

"Not exactly a big vote of confidence from the Lieutenant. But I'll tell you something, Charlie. I don't blame him. Not about the drinking. About the lack of confidence. We're about as useful here as a spare pecker on a dead hog. We haven't seen hide nor hair of her, and investigators we are not."

"I'm covering for Hanson long as I can. But I don't know. You're around him enough these days, you kind of get the feeling his brain is coming apart."

"Alcohol is not noted for making someone smarter."

"True. I'm gonna give it up myself, soon as it kills me. Thing is, Chief gets wind Hanson's out, or on a drunk, that's another load of ammunition he's got against him. He'll be lucky to get a night job shaking doors at the Kroger."

"All this drinking has to do with Florida? Or is the drinking part of the problem with them? That shit he told us the other night sounded a little pat."

"I think he told you the truth. Stuff he said is how it is. He just left out that the drinking wasn't making matters better. He drinks 'cause he has problems, and the drink makes him have more problems. He's got a grown daughter he feels he's lost too much contact with. An ex-wife he still loves. Kind of an odd relationship with Florida. Bad work conditions. Hemorrhoids and the sauce. Tight as he is these days, you say something don't quite set with him, he'll burp a turd and fart his teeth."

"Yeah," I said. "I was remembering the lamp he threw at Leonard."

"I tell him what you've told me, I figure he'll show up down there where you are, ready to throw the town in the street, and to hell with all this checking around shit. Hell, he may not need to be told anything. He sucked enough Rebel Yell this morning, minus the Co-Cola, he could be on his way now."

"I don't think Chief Cantuck would take kindly to a black law enforcement officer with an attitude and whiskey on his breath. 'Course, could be interesting. Anything else?"

"Got a minute so I can whine and feel sorry for myself?"

"You bet."

"I'm not doing all that good either. Wife fussin' at me all the time. Can't do nothing right. She's pissed I can't fix the garage opener. She's got girlfriends whose husbands can fix anything. Hear her tell it, all them sonofabitches do is go around with a screwdriver and a pair of pliers, turning lawn mowers and garage doors into nuclear weapons. Let's see . . . I've quit smoking again, so I'm irritable. Wife said no more poontang if I don't quit, and I got to be quit a month before I get a taste."

"That's a goddamn death sentence."

"Yeah, well you haven't been gettin' any for a serious stretch, and you're still kicking, so I reckon I'll survive."

"You through whining?"

"Not yet. Guess what? I lost my shadow picture book. I think my wife hid it. I was just getting a whooping crane down. And you know what else?"

"Hit me."

"They're closing down the goddamn Kmart."

"Naw."

"Yeah, it'll be gone in less than three weeks. Can you figure that?"

I told him I couldn't, we talked a few more seconds, and rang off. Leonard took his turn at the phone, called home, hoping Raul had shown up.

I paid Tim some money for the calls, and Leonard bought a straw cowboy hat to protect his head from the rain.

Out in the car, Leonard said, "Charlie have any news?"

"They haven't heard from Florida. Hanson is a nervous wreck, possibly gone off somewhere on a drunk. Charlie's wife won't give him any and she may have stolen his shadow book, and he's got his panties in a major twist 'cause they're closing down the Kmart. And I told him he ought to get some real law down here."

"They're closing up the Kmart?"

"Tighter than a Republican's wallet."

"You white Democrats, you get on my nerves."

"Yeah, well what I can't stand is a black man doesn't have enough sense to know not to vote Republican. Shit, man. You look like a fuckin' fool in that hat."

"Let's not talk politics, Hap. It upsets your tummy. And I look fine in hats . . . Did Charlie ask about me?"

"Nope."

"Well, shit."

"Raul back?"

"No. But Leon said the *Gilligan* videos are a scream."

14

We drove across the street to the Chief's office and went inside. The lady with the wasp nest hairdo was behind her desk. The little Christmas tree was still in place, surrounded by its city of cards. She eyed Leonard as carefully and frightfully as the day before. He smiled at her, slow and suggestful, like he might be thinking about how nice it would be to fondle her hair.

There was a thirtyish officer in a straw cowboy hat and a tan uniform looking in a file cabinet drawer nearby. He pretended not to notice our coming in. Leonard asked the secretary if the Chief was in, and the officer pulled a file from the drawer, slowly turned, pretended he had just noticed us, and smiled.

"Something I can do for you fellas?" he said. "I'm Officer Reynolds."

He was a big man with a big belly and little pocks on his face. He'd pinched too much acne as a youth. His straw hat was expensive, with a rattlesnake band and a little red feather stuck in it. He had a Western-style revolver almost big as a howitzer in his holster. Three Tootsie Roll Pops stuck out of his shirt pocket next to a pen that, from the stain at the bottom of his pocket, appeared to have exploded. Belly or no belly, he looked like someone you wouldn't want to mess with, especially if he didn't like you. He had a face said he didn't like much of anything, except maybe a Tootsie Roll Pop.

Leonard took off his straw hat, said, "There. I feel smarter already."

Reynolds grinned. "Hell, I heard about you fellas."

"Yeah?" Leonard said. "I hope it was good."

"Oh no," said Reynolds. "I heard y'all was meddlers."

"Meddlers?" I said.

"Yeah," he said. "I heard you two limp dicks—sorry, ma'am."

The lady at the desk turned bright red and began to shuffle

papers. Reynolds smiled at her, said, "Why don't you get some coffee, Charlene?"

Charlene opened her desk drawer, took out a cup that had some kind of cartoon on it, scuttled in one place for a moment, her shoes making a lot of noise, like a poodle with overlong toenails turning in a circle. Finally, she disappeared without a word from the room.

Reynolds turned back to us. He still had that nice smile. "She goes to a lot of church. Words like dick cause her consternation."

"Ah," I said.

"Consternation," Leonard said. "That's a big word for a police officer, ain't it?"

"Maybe," said Officer Reynolds, placing the file on top of the cabinet. "I also have a few nice phrases. Like 'The nigra died slowly and painfully after a methodical beating'."

"Nigra is one of those words that always bothers me," Leonard said. "It's not quite respectful. Like 'Negro,' but the talker can't seem to go all the way and say what he or she really wants to say, which is 'nigger'."

"I work for law enforcement," said Reynolds. "I am one third of the Grovetown Police Force. Me, the Chief, and Charlene, we're not allowed to call you a goddamn shit-eating nigger. That wouldn't be right. Sir."

"It's certainly nice to talk to a public servant," Leonard said, "but your boss, he does say nigger. We've heard him."

Reynolds didn't respond. He spent some time checking Leonard out, and Leonard checked him in return.

Reynolds was larger by a head than Leonard with wider shoulders. Big in the belly but hard-looking, with massive arms and tree trunk legs. Leonard isn't all that big, but he's got the look. One that tells anyone with half a brain that he can be dangerous. But there was a part of me that knew this Reynolds character was no lightweight either. He had the look too, like a man who had seen the elephant and seen it well, and maybe even put his arm up its ass and pulled its intestines out.

He and Leonard went toe-to-toe, I'd put my money on Leonard. But maybe because he was a sentimental favorite and I knew I'd help him.

Reynolds put his thick fingers together and pressed and popped them. He leaned against the file cabinet, still smiling, one hand resting on the butt of his revolver. His fingers looked like thick roots, his knuckles like lug bolts. He said: "I hear you two gentlemen are acting like you're some kind of law or something."

"We heard the same thing about y'all," Leonard said.

Reynolds's smile changed just enough to allow his top lip to snarl. "You think I can't arrest you for messing with a sworn-in law officer? You think I won't get tired of this and chunk your ass behind bars?"

"What's the crime?" Leonard said. "Greater wit than your own?"

Reynolds's face showed he had lost his sense of humor, but he never got to let us know how much. A door at the back of the office opened and Chief Cantuck came out. He was hatless and sweaty-looking. His nose was red and highly porous today, like maybe he'd had a little too much Christmas cheer the night before. Way he was sweating, you'd have thought it was a hundred degrees. His belly hadn't gotten any smaller, and neither had his ruptured testicle. He looked as if he might blow a major hose at any moment.

"Chief," Leonard said. "My man. How's it hanging? . . . Oh, I see."

"They think they're funny," Reynolds said.

"Hey, I've been real quiet," I said. "Leonard's the one talking."

"I've already caught their act," Cantuck said. "It wasn't any better the last time."

"You want me to lock 'em up for a while?" Reynolds said. "Just so they can hone their material?"

"No crime in being an ass," Cantuck said. "Reckon you two are here for some reason other than trying to outwit my officer or make fun of my balls?"

"Both are easy," Leonard said, "but we're here on official business."

"All right," Cantuck said. "I'll play. Come in the office."

As we followed Cantuck, Reynolds said, "By the way, nigger. I'll remember you."

Leonard paused, said without the slightest hint of anger, "In case you might forget, I'll leave my business card with the secretary."

★

Cantuck's office was relatively neat. His wall was covered in photographs of a boy, who from his wasted appearance and resemblance to Cantuck, without a swollen nut, had to be the son he'd told me about.

There was a middle-aged woman in some of the photos with the boy, and she looked plain and worn-out, like her daily job was the Augean Stables.

On Cantuck's desk were pictures of himself, the boy, and the wife, as well as a plastic container backed by a cardboard frame for donations to MS. It had some change in it, and a couple of bills had been rolled and stuffed inside. On the left-hand side of his desk was a can with a label that suggested you should "Give to the Handicapped," and on the other side of the desk was a can that pleaded for money for cancer research.

It was very odd, the cans and the cardboard donation container being there. I wondered who had put the money in the cardboard container. The Chief? Reynolds? Charlene? Assorted prisoners? Had Florida dropped in some coins?

Cantuck sat down behind his desk. We took chairs on the other side. Leonard placed his hat on the edge of the desk and used a finger to turn it from time to time.

Cantuck picked a picture of the boy off his desk and held it in his lap and looked at it. He put it back. From the way he moved, I could tell it was an unconscious ritual.

"Your son?" I said.

"Yeah," he said. "What do y'all want?"

"We want to make an official report," I said. "Concerning Florida Grange. We fear foul play."

"And, of course, we here in Grovetown are the culprits, just because a lot of us are segregationist?"

"She was here," I said. "She's not here now."

"So, she's shacked up with some buck somewhere. Check out the Southside of town. Ten miles out. That's the colored section."

"We were sort of hoping you'd do that," I said. "It is your job."

Cantuck studied us. He unsnapped his shirt pocket and took out a tightly rolled package of chewing tobacco. He unrolled it, opened it, pinched out a wad, put it in his mouth, started chewing. He chewed slowly, as if activating brain cells.

"You gonna fill out the papers for a missing person?" he said around the tobacco.

"Yeah," I said.

"I doubt you need to," he said.

"You saying we fill it out you won't look?" Leonard asked.

"No. I'm saying I doubt you need to. She'll turn up. My guess is she's oiling some coon's pole out niggertown."

"Careful now," Leonard said. "Words like that, you might hurt my feelings."

"Shit," Cantuck said. "I wouldn't want that. Let me put it to you straight, numb nuts. You fill out a report, that gives me work to do. Well, I don't want work to do. Not when I think it's bullshit work. But no matter what you may think, you fill out that report, I'll look for her. I'll find her if she needs finding. I'm just a small-town cop, and as you both know, not very smart and I got a ruptured turnip. But I got a job here. The law says it includes whites and colored. I don't have nothing against colored. You being an exception, Smartest Nigger in the World . . . that is how you introduced yourself, isn't it?"

"That's right," Leonard said. "But when it comes out of your mouth, it stinks. My name's Leonard. Leonard Pine."

"What you want . . . Leonard . . . is me to respect you because you're black," Cantuck said. "Not because you're worth a shit. You want me to be polite and sweet when all you've done, the both of you, from the first moment I've seen you, is come on with an attitude. An attitude that says: We're better than you. We're smarter than you. We're a couple of hip-hop guys . . . I believe that's a term they use, isn't it?"

"Close enough," Leonard said. "But not around my house."

"Not once," Cantuck said, "have you treated me with the respect deserving of any human being, or someone of authority. Yet, you expect me to be all sugar and syrup and suck your dick."

"You did sort of threaten us," I said. "You even pulled your gun on me. That seems to have faded from your memory."

"I don't deny it. But you fucked with me, treated me stupid, then wanted me to give you a hand job and smile. I don't think your mamas would be proud of the way you two have conducted yourselves."

To tell the truth, neither did I.

"There was that talk about the fire department and being burned up with white trash and a nigger," I said. "Remember that?"

"I wanted you scared, out of here, before somethin' happened we'd both be sorry for. You two being sorry while it was happening, and me after I heard about it—for about five or ten minutes, anyway. You see, it's not bad enough I got you two pencil dicks, I got the Texas Rangers now."

"Texas Rangers?" I said, and thought I looked pretty innocent. Charlie damn sure wasn't fucking around. He'd gotten on the horn the minute I hung up.

"This nig hung himself here," Cantuck said. "Word's got around it ain't no suicide. Maybe that was your gal Florida did that, got 'em stirred. Maybe it was you. But about five minutes ago I got the call. They're sending in some Ranger dick to look things over. Show our not-so-smart three-person police force how the horse ate the apple. I don't like it. I don't like you. I wish you were both home. I wish your daddies had pulled out right before comin'. That way, the two of you wouldn't be nothing to me or nobody else."

We sat for a moment. I said, "Can we fill out the missing person report now?"

"When you do, why don't you head back to where you come from. Find someone else to insult and make fun of. I can't help my balls, boys, and I can't help that I believe the Bible insists that blacks and whites not intermingle, outside of work and a few laughs together."

"Shit," Leonard said, "you and me ain't been laughing none at all."

"Bottom line is," Cantuck said, "when I'm not worked up, I'm not so bad. And I can do my job. You leave, I won't be worked up. She's around here, I'll find her. She's gone somewhere, I might find that out. Black and white ain't gonna have anything to do with that."

We sat in silence for a moment. Cantuck reached down behind his desk, came up with a stained coffee can. He spat a stream of tobacco into it, put the can back. Some of the juice ran over his bottom lip and down his chin. He wiped it away with his sleeve. He looked at his sleeve. "Bad habit," he said. "Wife hates it. My boy used to call it slime. Let's get a report for you to fill out. And Smartest Nigger?"

"Yassuh, Massa, Chief," Leonard said.

"Stay away from Officer Reynolds. He's not a nice man like me. And don't forget your hat."

Cantuck stood up and we stood up with him. Cantuck said, "Before you boys go, would you mind dropping a coin or so in these charities? I try to support them, get others to do likewise."

We were blank for a moment, then slowly Leonard opened his wallet, took out a dollar bill and rolled it tight and pushed it through the slot of the MD container.

I did the same.

We went into the office where the secretary once again sat behind her desk. The Chief followed us out. Reynolds wasn't there. Cantuck had Charlene give us a missing person's report. I filled it out and gave it back.

Cantuck picked it up the moment I laid it down. "All right . . . Mr. Hap Collins," he said, reading my name off the report. "Me and this investigation are open for business."

He went back to his office and closed the door.

Charlene looked at the closed door, looked at Leonard.

"Like the hair," Leonard told her.

15

When we left Cantuck's office, we saw Officer Reynolds standing in the hallway near the exit, adjusting a plastic rain cover on his straw hat. He turned and looked at us. He carefully withdrew a Tootsie Roll Pop from his shirt pocket, unwrapped it, and tossed the wrapper on the floor. He stuck the pop in his mouth, winked at us, went out into the rain.

I said, "Think you could take him, you had to?"

"I don't know," Leonard said. "I don't know the both of us with clubs could take him. But the trick is, we don't let him know we think that."

"Frankly, I don't think it matters what we think."

"Know what? I sorta think he's cute."

"Oh, shit."

"I'm not kidding, Hap. I like the way he sucks that Tootsie Roll."

"He's a thug."

"I didn't say I liked him. I just wouldn't kick him out of bed for eating crackers. Tootsie Roll Pops either."

"Jesus, Leonard. He wouldn't get in bed with you unless it was to tie you to it and set it on fire."

"Wow. Really think so?"

Leonard chuckled. I picked up the Tootsie Roll wrapper and put it in the trash container by the door. Leonard put on his hat and we went outside.

We got drenched going out to the car. Leonard cranked the engine, turned on the heater.

"I feel kinda bad about Cantuck," I said. "I wanted us to push him, see if he knew more than he was letting on, but I feel kinda mean-spirited."

"Hell," Leonard said. "I did all the pushing."

"Making fun of a man's balls is pretty low, you know?"

"I admit I feel a little bit like a horse's ass myself. All those pictures of his kid, weird shit with the charities. I feel sorry for him. What did you tell me the boy died of?"

"Muscular dystrophy."

"Yeah, well, just because he loved his son and likes charities, doesn't mean he isn't a worthless dick."

I could feel my wet jacket sticking to Leonard's upholstery. The heater was slow to work. My stomach grumbled from hunger and need of coffee.

I said, "I hate to sound like you, but just because he's a dick doesn't mean he's a real villain."

"Jesus," Leonard said, "you're right. I'm starting to sound like a knee-jerk liberal asshole. I been around you too long."

"When I was growing up, Leonard—"

"Oh, Christ, another parable."

"Listen. My dad had the worst rhetoric you ever heard. He could get so worked up over 'the niggers,' he would vibrate."

"I've known people in my family to be the same way about whites."

"Yeah, but you know, one time I went down to my dad's garage, and there were a bunch of little black kids there, laughing, and my dad was giving them five-dollar bills. Apiece. It wasn't like we had lots of money, and when the kids were gone, I said, 'Dad, what are you doing?,' and he said, 'I was afraid they might be hungry.'

"Dad hated the black race, but liked them as individuals. He hated some as individuals too, but you get my point."

"I do."

"I'm not defending his racism. I detest it. I think that's one reason I hate it so much, my old man being that way, and otherwise being just the kind of man I wanted to be."

"Just because your old man was a good man, does that mean Cantuck is? It's hard to believe he'd go out of his way to worry about some black girl that might have gotten killed."

"You knew my daddy, it would be hard to believe he would give five dollars apiece to a handful of black kids too."

"We're not dealing with your daddy, though. This Cantuck, we know nothing about him. Say he wouldn't do anything to hurt Florida, he's still convinced she's out shacking up. Blacks are all a bunch of animals to him. He figures all we want to do is eat and fuck."

"That's all I want to do."

"Maybe that's all anyone wants to do. As for the Chief, he might not swerve to hit an animal, but he still knows he's dodging one. And when it comes to blacks, well, he might not go out of his way to do one harm, but he wouldn't expect anything of them but the most basic of animal behavior. Like being shacked up somewhere."

"So, we don't know any more than we knew when we went in."

"We know he's got an officer that isn't a nice person. Even Cantuck says so. And I know this. I'm one hungry sonofabitch. I say we go over to the cafe and get breakfast."

"You know how that'll go."

"We came here to be maggots in the shit. Squirm around, see if we can find what we want. What better way to stir the shit than to jump right in."

"I like the more casual approach. One where I don't have to get doo-doo on me."

"You sit here and be casual. I'm hungry, I'm wet, and I'm cold. The cafe is bound to be warm, and they've got coffee. I'll bring you some."

"We really ought to go over to the black section of town. Ask around there."

"We will."

"What's wrong with now?"

"You're stalling, Hap."

"Just as long as I can."

Leonard cut the engine, put his hand on the door handle, turned and looked at me.

"Oh, all right," I said. "What's a few stitches among friends?"

16

Leonard was right. The cafe was warm. It was also crowded. The brothers who I had warned about the ants were there, and their mother, of course. There were also a lot of burly types, and old men. The blue-haired woman I had seen at Tim's filling station was also there. She was sitting with an elderly man who, from the look on his face, appeared to be dealing with some sort of digestion problem.

I could see a gray-haired black cook through the order window at the back. He had on a white cook's hat, a stained white shirt, and lots of sweat. He hadn't been working Christmas Day when I was here. He didn't wave as we came in. Neither did anyone else. The mother of the sweet boys who I had spoken with on Christmas smiled at me, the sort you give someone you know probably has a short time to live. Or maybe she just loved me and my little friend.

The cook looked at Leonard, shook his head, went to furiously scraping at something out of our sight.

We went over to a couple of stools at the end of the counter, sat down in front of a rack holding salt and pepper shakers, a bottle of ketchup and a bottle of Tabasco sauce.

There was a plump middle-aged man sitting next to Leonard. He was smoking a cigar. He blew out smoke, rolled up the newspaper he was reading, put it under his arm, picked up his coffee cup, found a seat beside another man in a booth at the back.

"Did I fart?" Leonard said.

The smiling woman came over. She looked nervous. "Would you gentlemen like something to go?"

This, of course, was the better idea, and I'll be honest, I was scared, all those fuckers looking at us, licking their chops, but I'd seen too many cowboy movies, and a cowboy doesn't run.

Of course, a movie cowboy usually has a stand-in.

"No," I said. "We'd like something to stay. I want flapjacks and eggs and biscuits and coffee. My buddy here will have the same."

"I will?" Leonard asked.

"You will," I said.

Leonard tipped his hat at the lady. "I will," he said.

The woman looked at us sadly and went away.

The brothers came over and stood by me, one on either side. The one with the bad mustache smiled, said, "There ain't no Christmas ants, are there?"

"No, son, guess there aren't," I said.

"You lied to us?"

"Yes, I did."

"That was a good one," Bad Mustache said. He grinned at me, then he and his brother moved to the rear of the cafe and took a booth together.

The door opened, let in the cold wind. We turned toward a voice saying: "You boys passing through?"

The voice belonged to a man in a gray waterproof topcoat and an expensive gray cowboy hat over which was attached a clear plastic rain cover. He eased off the topcoat, shook the rain from it onto the floor, hung it on a peg by the door, put his hat on another peg.

He looked to be in his sixties. He was the only man in the place wearing a suit. It was a nice, dark gray suit, expensive in a J.C. Penney's best sort of way. He had gray hair, perfectly combed, not mussed by his hat. It was held in place with enough hair spray to make an evangelist proud. He wore a bright red tie. It was tacked with a gold horseshoe to a crisp white shirt. He had on gray lizard-skin cowboy boots. He had a muscular build, with a slight paunch. His skin was very pale. He looked very proud of himself.

On one side of Gray Suit was a rather sizable gentleman who looked as if he could snap a baseball bat over his knee. I affectionately thought of him as Bear.

On the other side of Gray Suit was an even larger gentleman with enormous shoulders, a big belly, and a very wide ass. He looked as if he'd enjoy jerking a knot in a gorilla's dick on his worst day. I affectionately dubbed him Elephant.

"What'd you say?" Leonard asked Gray Suit.

Gray Suit grinned. He had a very precious deep dimple in his right cheek. I think he liked that dimple. I think he thought it got him lots of pussy. I wished I had a dimple. I wished I had all my hair. I wished the gray in my hair looked as cool as the gray in his hair. I wished I'd stayed home. I wouldn't have minded some pussy either.

Gray Suit kept right on smiling. "I said, are you two passing through?"

Before we could answer, he went over to a booth, and the men sitting there got up casually, with their plates and coffee, and found another seat. Gray Suit slid in against the wall. Bear sat in the seat beside him. Elephant took a seat across the table from Bear. The rain outside came down hard and consistent. Good sleeping weather.

Leonard said, "Naw, we ain't passing through. Actually, we was sorta thinking of moving here."

"And for what reason?" Gray Suit said.

"We were thinking of opening up a little Afro-American Cultural Center. That's a black thing, see. Hap here would be working for me."

"I does right," I said, "sometimes, Mr. Leonard, he lets me takes off a little early on Friday afternoon and he give me a fifty-cent tip."

Gray Suit smiled, said to the lady behind the counter, "Maude. I'd like some coffee. The boys here would like some too. Keep it coming."

Maude gave Gray Suit a look that could have raised tumors.

Gray Suit acted as if he hadn't noticed. He turned his attention back to Leonard, said: "You know, when I was a little boy, right here in Grovetown, we used to have traveling minstrel shows." He paused and looked at Leonard. "You know what those are, boy?"

"I ain't wearing no knee pants," Leonard said. "Don't call me boy. Don't call my friend here boy neither."

"All right," Gray Suit said. "Man. Isn't that what you people prefer? Man?"

"Man's nice," Leonard said. "Man sound good to you, Hap?"

"I like it," I said. "Even if I'm not a 'you people.'"

"When I was a little boy," Gray Suit started, then paused to poke a cigarette into his mouth. Bear whisked out a little box of kitchen matches, struck one on the bottom of his shoe, offered it to Gray Suit. Gray Suit held Bear's hand, touched the match to his cigarette, puffed. Bear dropped the match on the floor.

Maude said, "Pick that up."

No one picked up the match. No one seemed to notice she'd spoken.

"What I remember fondly," Gray Suit continued, "was white folks doing colored minstrel shows. They wore blackface. Shoe polish. Big white lips. They did some jokes. And they were real funny. You know," he pointed the cigarette at Leonard, "you remind me of them minstrel folks, but you're not in blackface. Least I don't think so. And you know what? I think you're real funny. That makes me nostalgic. I like that. I like having you here. I didn't realize how much I'd missed being around funny niggers. And what I got here is not just some white man in blackface playing nigger, I got the real thing. I got me a genuine, born-of-black-hole nigger."

"Don't talk like that," Maude said, coming out from behind the counter with a pot of coffee. She put the pot on their table. "You're in my place, don't talk like that."

"It's all right, Maude," Gray Suit said. "It's just men talkin'. Ain't that right, nigger?"

Leonard didn't answer. He just tipped back his straw hat, sat there, patient.

Gray Suit turned his coffee cup upright and poured coffee. Maude rubbed her hands together, clasped her fingers, pulled, let go and went back behind the counter. I could hear her breathing behind us. Nervous, short breaths; kind I'd have been breathing had I not been holding my breath.

"I tell you, buck," Gray Suit said, "you look to me like someone who was bred of good stock. You know, that's why there's so many of your people can play basketball and football well. We white folks bred you. Got the biggest dumbest nigger bucks we could find, put them with some big ole black mammy could take about a ten-inch dick big around as a man's wrist, and that ole buck, well, he was the kind would mount a cow if our grandaddies told him to—and most likely if they didn't—and he'd bang that black bitch till she couldn't take no more. Then maybe our granddaddies would have a pony or a jackass do her, just to get a little spice in the stock. And through all that planning, down through generations of nigger kennelin', we ended up with solid, strong-lookin' niggers like yourself. And just as an added note, I got to tell you, I've always been partial to a nigger in a straw hat."

Most everyone in the place laughed. Even the blue-haired lady laughed. When the laughter died—

"Mama said don't talk that way in here!"

I turned and looked. It was Bad Mustache. His bubba was beside him. They were out of their booth, standing. The other brother said, "That's enough! Mama said that's enough."

"Billy, you and Caliber just relax," Bear said. "No one wants you hurt. Y'all sit down and have some coffee."

Billy and Caliber didn't move.

Leonard said, "Well, that certainly explains some things about us black folk, don't it?"

"Oh yeah," said Gray Suit, and he laughed a little, and the others laughed.

When the laughter slowed, Leonard said, "You know, every one of us, when you think about it, just missed about this much," Leonard held up his hand and made a C with his thumb and forefinger, "being a turd. Every one of us. I mean, there's only about this much space between one hole and the other. And we all missed the shithole by this much." Leonard lowered his hand, looked at Gray Suit and smiled, "Except you, mister. You made it. Your mama shit a turd, put a suit on it, and named it you."

Gray Suit turned red as a sun-ripe tomato. Bear started out of the booth then, but before he could shoot the distance, a blast of cold air blew through the cafe, and Officer Reynolds came in with it. He was sucking another Tootsie Roll Pop.

Everything stopped. Reynolds looked around. He eyed Bear, halfway out of the booth. Bear slid back into his place. Gray Suit raised up so Reynolds could see him, said, "Willie, it's me."

Reynolds pulled the Tootsie Roll Pop from his mouth, held it, said, "Yes sir." He turned to the woman behind the counter, said, "Maude, you got that breakfast?" He looked right at us. "To go?"

Maude glanced around, as if on the lookout for a miracle, sighed, went to the kitchen, came back with a greasy brown sack. She gave it to Reynolds.

Reynolds said, "Certainly glad I didn't see no unpleasantness here. Wouldn't want that. Chief wouldn't want that. I seen something like that, didn't do anything about it, he'd fire me. I don't like the idea of being fired. I like my little check. But, say I leave, how the hell am I gonna stop something gets going?" He looked at Leonard. "Any idea how I could do that?"

"There was," Leonard said, "you'd find a way around it."

Officer Reynolds smiled, put his Tootsie Roll Pop back in his mouth, went out with another blast of cold December air.

Bear stood up, arms crossed on his chest. Elephant stood up, opened and closed his hands—very large hands, and leathery. Probably got that way from strangling children. He was maybe six-six, and his shoulders were even wider than I first thought. So was his ass; even front on, you could tell that hunk of meat was enormous.

"You boys don't get in no fights now," Maude said. "This here is my cafe, and I don't want no fights. They were just leaving." She leaned over the counter, touched me on the shoulder. "You were just leaving, right?"

I was agreeable to this, but before I could say anything, Gray Suit said, "That's right, they were just leaving, but not under their own power."

"This ain't no cowboy movie saloon," said Maude. "This is my place."

"Mama said that's enough." It was Caliber. He and Billy were easing slowly to the front of the cafe. No one was paying them much attention, however. They were watching to see if Leonard and I were going to shit our pants. I don't know about Leonard, but I felt a rumble in my tummy.

I began to grope for a graceful way out. Even a not so graceful one, but Leonard, as is often the case, closed the door.

"Before we get on with the butt-whippin'," he said, sliding slowly off his stool, turning his body slightly to the side. "I got one question for the big guy." Leonard gestured to Elephant. "Man, tell me true. Is that your ass following you around, or are you pullin' a trailer?"

17

Elephant was a step closer than Bear, and no sooner had Leonard finished his remark than he stepped with his right foot and threw a hot haymaker at Leonard's head. It was such a wide and uncalculated blow, Leonard could have eaten a plate of eggs and biscuits and half a cup of coffee before it got there.

Leonard stepped in and blocked with his left hand and hit Elephant on his left temple with the edge of his right hand; hit him hard enough Elephant's greasy black hair flew up like a frightened monkey springing for cover.

Before the hair settled, Leonard captured Elephant's punching arm, swung under it, pushed against the big bastard's elbow and drove his head forward into the lunch counter, smacking Elephant's noggin into it with a noise akin to the crack of doom.

Leonard grabbed Elephant's hair, jerked his head up, brought it down into the counter again, let him go. What was left of Elephant's face smashed into a bar stool. Some of his cheek turned red and greasy and slid to the right of the stool while the rest of him fell left. I tell you, it was enough to make me lose my breakfast, had I eaten any.

All of this took no time at all.

Bear was on me then. I had already reached back and got hold of the ketchup bottle, and I swung it. It was still in the rack with the salt and pepper and Tabasco, and the bottle and the rack caught Bear alongside the head solid enough the ketchup exploded. Wads of red went all over Bear and across the cafe and onto Gray Suit's coat.

Gray Suit said, "Goddamn!"

The world froze. We were like prehistoric flies in amber, but one look at the fine citizens of Grovetown, and I could sense a sort of fire building inside them. Nothing like a nigger smacking a white man to stir a bunch of crackers, and a white man taking a black man's side didn't cheer them much either. The first was like being made to eat shit. The second was like making them eat it and smile.

I dropped what was left of the ketchup bottle and the rack. It hit the floor with a sound so sharp we all jumped. Then things went still again. I couldn't take it anymore. I said, "Well, you assholes gonna do it, or what?"

"Don't y'all do it," Caliber said. "You leave 'em be. You do it, you're gonna pay damages. You're gonna pay lawsuits."

Gray Suit said, "Git 'em! Kill the sonsabitches!"

And the mass of them came unstuck in time and space, rushed fast and hard, and I swung an elbow and saw someone's teeth fly, then I got hit on the right side of the jaw and a floating rib ceased to float, and I got my fingers in one guy's face and raked his eyes, side-kicked his knee out from under him, then someone was on my back and I was swinging my elbows, trying to throw him, but someone had me around the waist, and I couldn't get the torque, and out of the corner of my eye I saw Leonard dot a fat fucker's eyes with a rapid left, right, then kick another fatty between the legs solid enough to lift him. He back-elbowed an old guy, who spat his tobacco onto the back of Leonard's head, then Leonard was swarmed. He went down beneath a pile of writhing, punching bodies, his teeth clamped on some dude's ear, his hat beneath another's feet.

I saw Caliber launch a punch at someone, but he caught a solid one to the side of the head and went down. I saw Billy grabbing men and jerking them away from me and Leonard, but it was like trying to bail out the ocean. Gray Suit was standing up in the booth looking down on the action like Xerxes watching the last defenders of Thermopylae go down. He had a fresh unlit cigarette in his mouth.

Bodies were pressing me so tight I was using nothing but elbows, leg stomps, head-butts, and knees, but it was useless. I started falling. I was being hit so hard and often my face felt as if it were exploding. I came down hard on my back, and above me were thrashing legs and bleeding, hateful faces; the fat guys, the old men, the blue-haired lady.

Their fists and shoes tumbled down on me like an avalanche. My balls took a few shots. I wondered if Chief Cantuck and I might be able to get matching trusses. Maybe he could wear his nut to the right, I could wear mine to the left. We could walk side by side. Kind of a balance thing.

The lights of the cafe went dark, then bright again, but I was seeing them through a sheen of blood, and it was my blood.

Too much pain.

My last vision before darkness was the blue-haired hag's shoe coming at me, accurately aimed at my head.

When I awoke, I was in great pain and I was wet and getting wetter and I was shaking from the cold. I realized too I had pissed myself and there was vomit on the front of my shirt and jacket. I was up against an alley wall, out back of the cafe most likely, and it was raining hard, and my mouth tasted of copper and one of my eyes was nearly swollen shut. One of my teeth felt loose. My kidneys hurt. My ribs hurt. It hurt to breathe. It hurt to think. I feared if I moved too rapidly an arm or a leg might fall off.

I could hear grunting and I turned my head, carefully, just to make sure it didn't bowl a strike. The alley was full of people from the cafe, and the alley was full of rain.

Two fat guys, one with a couple of black eyes, the other with a wide split in his lip, had a mostly unconscious Leonard held up between them. His knees were bent and his legs were flared out behind him, the tops of his boots dragged the ground. His head was about the size of a medicine ball, and his lips and nose and eyes blended together in a knobby topography of swollen flesh. His breath steamed from his mouth and turned into little white clouds that faded to nothing.

The blue-haired lady was in front of him. She said, "Hold him up better."

She tried to kick Leonard in the balls, but the alley was wet, and she slipped and fell on her ass. The crowd moved toward the woman, and two men pulled her to her feet. When the crowd moved, I saw that Billy and Caliber were lying in the alley too. They looked to have taken a pretty good beating. Their mother was between them. Her hair was plastered to her head like seaweed to a rock. She was screaming her boys were hurt and wouldn't somebody do something, but nobody did. She squatted next to Billy and held his head in her lap, screamed, "Stop it! Stop it! Now! Stop it!"

Billy's hand came up and touched her hair. He said something, not very loud, then his hand went down again. He got the hand under him and pushed to a sitting position and scooted his back against the alley wall. He didn't look as if he cared much about what was happening now, long as it wasn't happening to him.

Maude rose suddenly, pushed through the crowd and went inside the cafe.

The blue-haired lady had a solid stance now. She kicked Leonard firm in the nuts with a football style kick. Leonard let out a burst of air, it puffed white and went wide and far, like a blast from a dragon. He sagged between the two men even more. The old lady said: "Niggers is what's wrong with this country."

I tried to get up, but couldn't. I fell over on my side and watched the alley wall lean at me. I turned my head toward Leonard, saw that Blue Hair had been replaced by Gray Suit. The rain had pushed his evangelist do apart and it had fallen into his face. I noticed, pushed down like that, he had been covering a half-dollar-sized bald spot at the back of his head. Good. I was glad he had a bald spot. I really didn't like this guy.

He had ketchup on his suit and the rain had spread it into rusty patches all over his jacket. His white shirt looked as if it were spotted with blood. He said, "Hold him," and the two guys picked Leonard up higher and held him firm, and Gray Suit began to work on him. Pounding him in the stomach, once in the jaw, but that hurt Gray Suit's hand. He jerked it back, said "Damn," and kicked Leonard in the shin. Then the leg. Leonard's bad leg.

Gray Suit reached in his pants pocket and got out a large pocket-knife, pinched a blade open.

I tried to crawl toward Leonard, but I wasn't making any time at all. I felt like a slug nailed to the ground. I felt like I was in a car and it had skidded off the road, and everything had gone slow motion, and I could see a telephone pole coming through the wind-shield and there wasn't a thing I could do about it.

Gray Suit said, "Way you tame a nigger . . . way you make 'em good, is just like you do a rambunctious stallion. You got to severely lower their testosterone level. All that ball juice just leads a nigger to trouble."

The men in the crowd laughed. One came forward, got hold of Leonard's zipper and pulled it down, reached in his pants and pulled out Leonard's equipment.

"No," I said. "Don't," but my words sounded like coughs.

Gray Suit turned, looked at me. He showed me that pretty dimple. It looked so deep now you'd have thought it ought to have a winch and bucket perched over it. He said, "Well, the nigger lover's come around. I cut this nigger's boo-doodles off, I'm gonna put 'em in your pocket, boy."

Gray Suit came forward and grabbed Leonard's testicles and lifted them and reached with the knife, and a gunshot split the air.

It was Maude. She had a pistol in one hand, a Winchester in the other, tucked under her armpit.

"You ain't gonna do this. Not in my place. Not out back of my place." Maude fired a shot with the revolver and made a trash can jump. She pointed the revolver and the rifle at Gray Suit, who still held Leonard's balls and the knife. She said, "Jackson Brown, you cut that nigger, you touch one of my boys, you come for me or that fella on the ground over there, any of you make a move to do that kinda business, I'm gonna blow what little brains you got out of the back of your head. And I'll do it too. Don't think I won't. Now all you cretins get on your horses and ride."

Gray Suit said, "You're gonna bring yourself some serious grief, Maude."

"You don't own my place yet, Jackson. You don't threaten me. You hear? Let go of that nigger's rocks."

So this was Tim's father. Jackson Truman Brown, the Lord of Grovetown. Standing in a wet alley with a pocketknife in one hand, Leonard's balls in the other.

Gently, the Lord unhanded Leonard's gonads, folded up his knife and put it away. Way he did it, you'd have thought he just used it to clean his fingernails. The two fatties dropped Leonard on his face. He hit so hard he cut a fart, then lay still.

A siren whooped once, went quiet. I turned to see the Chief's car at the mouth of the alley. Officer Reynolds was driving. He got out of the car and strolled up the alley, sucking his last Tootsie Roll Pop. "That's enough," he said. "All y'all go home."

"Draighten and Ray are on the floor in the restaurant," one of the fatties said. "These fellas hurt 'em bad."

"Yeah," Reynolds said. "Well, haul 'em off. Get 'em a doctor, they need it. I want all y'all out of here. Now."

"Officer," Jackson Brown said, "you don't want to get too carried away."

Officer Reynolds studied Brown for a few seconds. His face took on a pleasant look. "You know how it is, Mr. Brown. Think about it a minute. The position I'm in."

Brown took the minute offered and considered. "There'll be another time," he said.

"That may be," Officer Reynolds said. "Maude, put them guns up before you shoot yourself or wound that nigger. We wouldn't want something to happen to that nigger. Niggers are special, you ought to know that. Government protects 'em, like some kind of goddamn endangered species." He looked at me. "And nigger lovers are special too. Damn precious, in fact."

Maude lowered the guns. Caliber limped over and took the Winchester from her, then the revolver. Billy turned so he could use the wall to get up, clawed his way to his feet. He and Caliber looked rough. But not as rough as Leonard. I figured I didn't look too pretty myself.

The crowd began to break up. Brown looked at me, creased his dimple, said, "You boys weren't tough as you thought, were you?"

It took me a couple of deep breaths to say it: "Could be. But all I can say for you is, you certainly handled Leonard's nuts like a natural."

Brown glared, turned, paused long enough to look Maude over good, nodded at her, then went through the back door of the cafe and out of sight. The others had already gone, and now there was only Maude, her sons, me, Leonard, and good ole Officer Reynolds.

"That nigger don't look so smart now," Reynolds said. "Neither do you. You want to say something smart?" I was on my knees, using my hands for support. Officer Reynolds came and stood over me. "I said, you want to say something smart?"

"No," I said.

"Good. Now, get your nigger. Put his dick back in his drawers, zip him up, then you and him get out of Grovetown, and when you get home, find you some pretty stationery, purple or pink would be nice, and write me a thank-you card for not letting them folks kill you. Write Maude one too. And you keep your nigger and your nigger-lovin' ass out of Grovetown, Texas. Only thing I regret in all this is not gettin' to try your nigger. I think he might have thought he could take me. I'd like to have shown him he couldn't."

Officer Reynolds went down the alley, opened his car door and turned. "Billy. Caliber. Y'all see them guns get put up."

"Yes sir," Caliber said.

I lay down, slowly, the side of my face resting against the freezing, wet alley floor. My face was so hot from injury, it actually felt good. The rain felt good. My eyes, heavy as stones, began to close.

I heard Officer Reynolds drive away.

18

The oaks and pines and hickory trees that grew close to the road were dark with rain. Visible through the boughs, when there was any visibility at all, was a grim, gray sky. The sound of windshield wipers beating back and forth, the vibration of tires on cement, seemed at first to be the rhythm of striking fists and feet on flesh.

For an instant, I thought I was in the midst of another beating. I hurt so bad, I figured I couldn't distinguish the pain of the old beating from the new.

It took me a moment to realize I was in a car, an old blue Ford Fairlane, and that it was not night but late morning, and that the beating was over, and not long over. My face was turned toward the door and my forehead was resting on the rain-beaded passenger glass of the front seat. I could feel cold air leaking in around the window and hitting my feverish face, and it felt good. I smelled like dried urine.

I had no idea who was driving and for an instant I didn't care. I sort of thought I was on my way to the river bottoms where a rusty transmission would be tied around my feet, and I would be sent down to inspect the river mud for about three minutes, then it would all be over. A year from now, maybe two, some fisherman would snag his line on what was left of me, pull up my rotting head, call in the law, and dental records would reveal I had six cavities, was dead, and that I was Hap Collins.

When I felt strong enough to flip a whole loaf of bread over by myself without verbal encouragement, I turned my head and saw the driver.

It was the cook from the cafe. He wasn't wearing his white hat, but he still had on his stained white shirt. He said, "You might as well go on and sleep. You took a hell of a beating."

"Yeah," I said. "You should have seen the other guy."

"I seen them other guys, and compared to you two, they look pretty good."

"That's what I was afraid of."

"Then again, Draighten and Ray don't look so good. You gave them two a righteous ass-whuppin'. Bopped some eyes and mouths and noses on them others too. Hadn't been so many of 'em, so crowded, I think you and your friend might have done some serious whup-ass. 'Course, I only sort of saw it in passin'. I went out the back when things got goin' good, went over to the antique shop, told 'em to call the Chief, say there was a ruckus. That's how come ole Officer showed up."

"Thanks."

"'Course, Officer might not be who you want to show up. He got connections with the Klan."

"As does Jackson Brown?"

"Yep. They tied at the hip. Mr. Jackson, he's the Grand Cyclops or some such shit for that bunch. They don't call themselves Klan exactly, but that's what they are. Ole Officer, he kinda in a spot. Even for Grovetown, he got to play by some rules. You best be glad all this didn't happen out in the woods somewhere."

"I hear that."

"Did, ants be eatin' your ass right now. In town, Officer got to keep the Chief happy some. Chief not someone gonna invite me over to his house to supper, but I reckon he's good enough, it come down to business. He ain't gonna stand by let something like that happen on purpose."

"That's good to hear. Thanks again."

"Don't give too big a thanks. Tore the cafe up too bad, I'd have lost my job. There by the skin of my teeth anyway. Cafe ain't like a McDonald's chain, you know? It loses money couple, three weeks in a row, it's gone. Damages could make it gone quicker."

"What about Leonard? Man that was with me?"

"Back seat. Now, you talk about a beatin', he took it. You boys lucky you in pretty good shape."

"Rose field work. Cheap food. No sex. Makes you strong."

"My name's Bacon, by the way."

"Bacon?"

"Yeah, like in slices of."

"Your mama named you Bacon?"

"My daddy. He always liked bacon, so he named me Bacon. I don't think he liked me near good as bacon, though. Least not the way I remember it."

I managed to turn and look in the back seat. Leonard was stretched out there, lying on his back, and he looked awful. His face appeared to be the end result of a radiation experiment. Had I not expected him, I don't know I would have recognized him. His smashed straw hat lay over his crotch.

"He needs a doctor," I said.

"Gonna get one. Wouldn't no white town doctor gonna look at him. Not after they find out Mr. Jackson Brown was the one wanted y'all beat. Reason he got that hat with him like that, wasn't no one wanted to put his dick in his pants."

"That'll slay him. He thinks his dick is his best feature."

"Caliber, he got him two sticks and tried to do it, but he couldn't do nothing but pick it up and move it left and right. Couldn't get it to go inside the pants, and he wasn't gonna touch it. Me neither. So we put that hat over him."

"Very innovative. He's lucky he's still got a dick. That Brown fella didn't mind touching it. Or cutting it."

"I don't think he really gonna cut it off. He knows how far he can push, and he can't push that far. Not in town. Not all them witnesses, even if most of them deny they saw anything happen. They know someone got to pay. And if it's somethin' that bad, a ball-cuttin' downtown, they only gonna lie so far."

"In other words, they won't go to the pen for Jackson Brown?"

"That's right. But way it stands now, Chief ain't gonna do nothin' to that Mr. Jackson, even he wants to. Mrs. Rainforth—"

"Is that Maude?"

"Uh huh. She gonna say what happened, and her boys gonna say, but all them other people, they ain't gonna say, 'cause they was in on it. Them two y'all whupped up bad. They'll take the fall for all that ruckus. 'Cause that's what they're paid for."

"Where are we going, and how come?"

"You goin' to my place, least for a bit. And the reason how come is Mrs. Rainforth done paid me to do it. Said I should take you home and take care of you awhile. She's paying me some extra."

"So this isn't out of the kindness of your heart?"

"I ain't got nothing against you. I think what happened was a shame, but I wasn't gettin' paid, and wasn't gettin' Mrs. Rainforth's blessing on this, you'd still be out there in that alley. 'Sides, my place only a little better than the alley."

"And how come Mrs. Rainforth is doin' this?"

"White ladies are hard to figure. She don't like Mr. Jackson, for one. He owns most everything in town, wants to own the cafe, and she won't sell, and on top of that, him and her husband, Bud, they hated each other. He's dead now, but Mr. Jackson, he ain't one to forget, and Mrs. Rainforth, she ain't neither. It's not she's suddenly grown to like niggers, but then she don't exactly hate nobody neither. She don't like that kinda business come down on you two."

"What about you? She like you?"

"Shit, boy. I'm the cook. I been there so long she don't think about me one way or the other. I'm like furniture and . . . Wheeee! I tell you, mister . . . Who are you anyway?"

"Hap. Hap Collins."

"I tell you, Mister Hap. We got to get you out of them piss-pants. You makin' my eyes burn."

19

There's no other way to describe Bacon's home other than to say it was a real shithole. It was down in a wash and the yard was full of water. Decorating the place like yard art was a worn-out washing machine, the lid up, the drum overflowing with beer cans. Near that, like a dead companion, a refrigerator lay on its side with the door off; its interior was nasty black with moss and grime and an abandoned bird's nest.

Out to the side of the house I could see some kind of heavy machinery and a truck under a weathered tarp. There was just enough visible that I could tell that, but not enough to identify the machinery or the make of the truck.

Bacon coasted slowly through the water, drove right up to the front porch, which sagged a little and dripped water. Worse yet, it looked like the porch was holding the house up. The house looked to have been made mostly of plywood and suspicious two-by-fours pried off a burned-out building. The roof was primarily tin and the rest was tar paper and the water ran off it in great gushes.

Bacon got out, waded to the front porch, which drooped beneath his steps, and opened the front door. He went inside for a moment, came back, opened my door, said, "You gonna have to help me with watermelon head here, Mr. Hap."

"I'm an injured man," I said. "Couldn't you carry me in and leave him here?"

Bacon grinned. "You sore. You banged, but you're all right enough. They spent their steam on your buddy."

"Thank God," I said. "They could have hurt me."

I eased out of the car into ankle-deep water. I felt as if someone had wrapped me in razor wire and set me on fire with a blowtorch. I found I couldn't completely straighten up. Bacon opened the back door, got Leonard under the arms and pulled him forward, out of the car. "Get his feet," Bacon said.

"I just hope that damn hat don't fall off his dick," I said.

It was painful, but we got Leonard inside, carried him into one of the three small rooms—a bedroom. It was actually pretty cozy in there, considering there was no heat, and it looked a hell of a lot better than the exterior. One corner of the room sported a commode and a bathtub right out in the open. Half the room had carpet in it that might have once been beige, but was now greasy brown with a flecking of black spots that wasn't design.

"The decor," Bacon said, "is late slave or early nigger."

I saw what Bacon had done when he went inside. He'd gotten a paint-splattered drop cloth and put it over the bed, and we put Leonard on top of that. There was a little heater in the corner of the room, and Bacon lit that while I took off Leonard's shoes. Bacon got a couple of army blankets out from under the bed and laid them over Leonard without removing the hat from Leonard's crotch.

We went back to the living room. It was small with a shelf of dust-covered knickknacks, a well-worn couch, a large space heater, and a coffee table bearing an ancient television set festooned with foil-covered rabbit ears. Bacon saw me looking at it. He said, "I didn't have to eat regular, I'd get me a satellite dish."

"Quit running yourself down," I said. "I hurt too much to feel sorry for you."

"You think I'm running myself down, then you full of shit. Don't sit on the couch there till you get out of them piss-clothes."

"What am I gonna do, sit around in the nude?"

Bacon disappeared into the bedroom, came out with a pair of khaki pants, some dry black socks, and a plaid shirt.

"You gonna have to let it all hang. I ain't got no clean underwear."

I went to the bedroom, moving slow, bent over like Quasimodo, and took off my clothes. There was a full-length mirror leaning against the wall, and I looked at myself in that. My face was swollen, there was dried blood on my upper lip and over my eyes, knots the size of Ping-Pong balls swelled out of my forehead, and there were great black-and-blue bumps and bruises all over my body. Even my balls were swollen and blue. I had to hold them with the palm of my hand to keep them from hurting as I stepped into the tub and cleaned myself. It was a painful ordeal. The hot water was slow to come and cooled quickly.

I put my pants and shirt in the tub with me, ran water over them, twisted the water out best I could, draped them over the faucets. The water that ran out of the tub didn't go down a drain, it went straight to the ground. I could feel the cool air whistling up under the house, blowing through the tub's drain. It was a simple approach to plumbing. Easy. Efficient. And a bad idea.

I got out and dried on a suspicious-looking towel and put on the clothes Bacon had given me. The pants were too long, so I cuffed them. The shirt was big and loose and felt good on my damaged body.

I went over to the commode to take a leak. The pot's interior was dark with urine stains. It looked as if the last time it was clean was when it came out of the box. I pissed, and the piss was full of blood.

I'd had it happen before. It does that, you take good shots to the kidneys, but it was always scary to see.

I flushed, wondered if the contents of the toilet went straight to the dirt below the house along with that of the tub, then picked up my socks and shoes, stopped by the bed and looked at Leonard.

It was all I could do not to cry, he looked so bad. I touched him gently on the shoulder, went to the living room. I sat on the couch, put the socks and shoes beside it. I said, "What about this doctor?"

"He gonna be here," Bacon said. "Mrs. Rainforth called him. Told him we was comin'. He live on the far side of here. Probably be a few minutes. If the rain's worse on his side, he's flooded out, who knows?"

The third room was a kitchen, but it was a room only by definition of containing a butane stove, a refrigerator, a sink, a table with chairs, and a large lard bucket that collected water dripping from a hole in the ceiling. There was a window over the sink, but a big square of warped plyboard had been nailed over that. Bacon lit the greasy cook stove and the space heater, and the house, small as it was, began to warm.

Bacon said, "You gonna be here just a little bit, then I'm gonna run you off. I don't want no trouble with them Ku Kluxers. You want some coffee?"

"Might as well. Jesus, I don't know when I been hurt this bad and was still able to stand. I mean, I been hurt worse, but not in this way."

I was thinking about being shot. That had been damn serious, and scary too. Leonard had been hit worse, and he almost lost a leg. But those times were not times I liked to think about often. I had a feeling this little escapade wasn't going to be one of my top ten on memory lane either.

"You think you hurt now, give it a couple hours, tomorrow morning," Bacon said. "You be stiff as a young bull's dick, only not as happy. You know that was all a setup don't you?"

"Back at the cafe?"

"Uh huh. They layin' for you and the other'n. Mr. Hat Over His Dick."

"Leonard," I said.

"They just waiting for you to be where they want you, and I guess the cafe got as good as they could get. I think Mr. Jackson, him not liking Mrs. Rainforth had somethin' to do with it too. He don't go to the cafe. Never. Not even for coffee. Reckon he figured he was gonna shit off the papers, he oughta do it someone else's place. Someplace where there was plenty of folks behind him. They don't show a little support, they could lose jobs. 'Sides, I think they really liked beatin' on y'all."

"They did seem jovial. I would have thought he'd have picked a more private spot."

"He might have. But I figure, right now, he just want to run you off 'cause you askin' too many questions. He like to sport a little for the town too, keep showin' 'em who's boss. Show the law don't worry him none."

I lay down on the couch very carefully. It was damned uncomfortable and smelled musty. I turned my head and saw the shelf of dust-covered knickknacks. I said, "You don't look like a man likes knickknacks."

"Can't live without them. I had my way, I'd have a room with them and nothing else. Especially they was ceramics of little kitties or ducks. . . . Them's my wife's."

"Where is she?"

"Dead."

"Hell, I'm sorry."

"I ain't. I been meaning to sack up that shit of hers for years, throw it out, but I just ain't had the time. Ain't got no milk, want some sugar in yours?"

"Just black," I said.

"Way I like my women," he said. He brought the coffee in, said, "Sit up, man, I got to have some room. 'Sides, I got a program to watch. I like the noon news. I like to know who's killin' who."

"I'm injured here."

"Sit up anyway."

I managed myself to a sitting position, slid down to the far end of the couch and took the coffee he was offering me. "Thanks," I said.

"Don't make nothing of it. I was gonna fix me some anyway."

Bacon turned on the television, adjusted the rabbit ears for a while, did everything with them except tie them in a knot, but he didn't get a picture. Just snow.

"Shit," he said, and turned off the set. "Guess we got to talk."

"Do you think Jackson Brown did it? Hung the fella in the jail?"

"Bobby Joe? If ever anybody needed hangin', it was that sonofabitch."

"He's certainly popular around here. I haven't talked to anyone liked him."

"Nothing to like. I enjoyed puttin' him down."

"Come again."

"I buried that fool. Dug the hole for him, anyway. I do backhoe work, I'm asked. Make a little on the side, digging ditches, sewer lines, and graves. Gotta stay on top of stuff, you gonna make ends meet."

Now I knew what kind of machinery was under the tarp.

"Well, do you think Brown did it?"

"He may not have done it himself, but he probably behind it, 'cause I don't think Bobby Joe hung himself. I think he con that white sonofabitch down here with that music business, thinking he gonna get big money out of him, then Bobby Joe got drunk, and didn't think it through, decided to go for the short change. Just killed him for what he had in his wallet. Bobby Joe like that. Mean as ass rash. He might just thought it would be funny to see that peckerwood squirm. You know how they found that white man?"

"No."

"Hung by his heels from a tree with his throat cut."

"Damn. Taking another angle on the subject, thing we came here for, Bacon, reason we ended up takin' this beatin', is we're trying to find a woman."

"What man ain't?"

"A certain woman. Named Florida. Good-lookin' young black woman, came here not long back? You saw her, you'd remember her."

"That black fox? Shoot, she here fifteen minutes, everyone knew it. Every hard dick in niggertown was after her, and the peckerwoods was watchin' too. I was still able to trot, I'd have been after her."

"She was interested in the Soothe case. She was here to look into it. Do you know what happened to her?"

"She a fool. Come down this side of town talking about how she wanted to maintain Bobby Joe Soothe's legacy, like he had one. It was ole L.C. had the legacy. Bobby Joe could pick a guitar some, but he was a scum hole, and a scum hole don't deserve no legacy, 'sides that hole I dug for 'm. If'n he'd a takin' up preachin', he'd have been the perfect villain. As was, he once cut up his nephew."

"I heard that story."

"Hear about the German shepherd?"

"Yeah."

"Well, that ain't true. That ole dog was part collie."

"I don't suppose you caught the dog's name?"

"Ralph. Tell you another one. Bobby Joe, he goin' to one of the joints, and he stepped in some cat shit by the door. Fella owns the joint, he got all kinds of cats. Don't really take good care of 'em none. Just lets 'em run wild. Throws a little food out the back, and well, them cats ain't spayed, and next to a rat and rabbit, ain't nothing likes to fuck better'n a cat. So they always makin' baby cats. Cat shit all over that place. Bobby Joe, he did his drinkin' there 'cause everyone was scared of him, and he liked that. He liked to go a place where people was afraid of him. Made him feel like a big dick. Anyways, he steps in this cat shit, and you know what he does?"

"I can't even begin to guess."

"He goes in and gets him a beer mug, and he scoops up some cat crap with it, then he comes in and makes the owner buy himself a beer. You know, take money out of his own pocket and put it in the register."

"Least he gets the money back," I said.

"That's right. Who says life ain't fair. Well, Bobby Joe makes this owner, Tiny Joe Timpson, called that 'cause he's big as a bear standing on a block of wood, makes this guy pour that beer on top of the cat shit, and drink it. And Bobby Joe, he ain't no big guy. Ain't no midget, but ain't no big guy either. That Tiny, he done killed six folks this year. Caught two of 'em breakin' in the place, killed two others 'cause he was fuckin' around with their wives and they caught on, and done killed two women. One of 'em 'cause she got mad Tiny was keepin' her husband down at the bar all hours of the night. She complained and words got tossed, then Tiny shot her. Called it self-defense. Cantuck, he looked into it, but wasn't no one contradicted Tiny. Said she tried to kill him with a beer mug."

"What about the other woman?"

"She was asleep in the driveway, and he backed over her."

"She pass out there?"

"Yeah, right after Tiny hit her in the head with a Coke bottle."

"Cantuck didn't do nothing?"

"He tried, but black folks, they keep things to themselves, and the white folks, they let 'em. But you can see the kind of guy Tiny is, and this Bobby Joe, he makes Tiny drink this beer with the cat shit in it."

"Man, I don't think that'll catch on."

"Tiny made sure it didn't. Next day, he got his shotgun, and he shot all them cats, and when he run out of shells he beat the rest of 'em to death. He wouldn't even hang a picture of a cat in his place now. That cat shit, it's always right there in the back of his throat."

"I wasn't under the impression Florida was here to find out about his legacy. She was planning to write some kind of article on him."

"Heard some of the guys say somethin' about that, but I don't know about it. She liked to hang over at the roadhouse, talk to people about Bobby Joe like he was some kind of star. She wanted to buy his guitar, music tapes, stuff like that. She had the money for it and she told anyone would listen to her she did. Them boys over there, they was tellin' her all that shit about how L.C. and Bobby Joe sold their souls to the devil at the crossroads and drank the devil's piss and such to play guitar, and she was eatin' it up."

"I don't understand why she'd talk to just anyone about buying Soothe's stuff."

"'Cause she couldn't find none of L.C.'s or Bobby Joe's stuff on her own, and his relatives didn't have nothin' of his, didn't want nothing to do with him. They were scared of him. Hell, he used to rape his own sister. They say a female dog run across the yard, he'd chase it down, fuck it and kill it. They wasn't no sorrier sonofabitch than Bobby Joe. He born bad, man. All that legacy stuff started 'cause Bobby Joe did a little playin' around Tyler, and someone on some magazine or paper or somethin' interviewed him, and he told all these stories about how he had L.C.'s stuff, and he talked that voodoo jive, said he had some unpublished songs L.C. had written out, and he had a couple songs on tape was recorded way back but never put on record."

"Did he?"

"Not that I know of. Not that anyone I know knew of."

"You're sayin' Florida was fishing?"

"And she was offering money for information. Lots of money. Them roadhouse lizards, about half of 'em ain't worth a shit. They'd tell her anything she want to hear they think they might make'm a dollar or get 'em some pussy. And it piss me off when anyone try to make somethin' special out of that nigger. He was sorry, just plain sorry. He meet that white boy at a roadhouse here. I seen 'em there. I was drinking a beer and watching 'em, and ole Bobby Joe had that white boy eating out his hand. Talkin' that music shit, playing like he some kind of jive nigger, and that ole white boy, he just shakin' his head like he was talkin' to some kind of god. He was talkin' to the devil, that's who he was talkin' to. They left together in that white boy's car, and wasn't more'n a couple hours after that, they found that peckerwood with his throat cut, hanging from a tree just off the highway, right by the goddamn road led up to Bobby Joe's house. Bobby Joe smart in one way, but in another he just a drunk field hand with a bad temper. He didn't think no farther than the length of his dick or the deep of his thirst. That's the way he was, and that's all there was to it.

"All that voodoo shit didn't do him no good when that Officer Reynolds show up. After ole Officer find out about that dead white boy, he went over to the roadhouse, asked around, and me and some others told him we'd seen Bobby Joe and the white boy together, seen 'em leave together, and when ole shitass Officer kick Bobby Joe's door off the hinges, there's that drunk fuck sittin' at the table with that peckerwood's watch and wallet, countin' the money. Bobby Joe tried to fight that big cop with his guitar, and Officer just tore that all to hell, then ole Officer stomped the stuffin' out Bobby Joe, opened that boy's mouth, made him bite the edge of the table, then slammed him in the back of the head with his forearm, knocked out all of his front teeth."

"I believe that's police brutality."

"Way the law works here. You don't fuck with the white law. 'Course, Bobby Joe had it comin'. Law or anyone couldn't have done nothin' to that jackass would have bothered me."

"How do you know it happened like that?"

"Filipine told me."

"Filipine?"

"That's what we call fella lives down the road here. His mama black, but his father was one of them Filipinos. He went with Officer to show him where Bobby Joe lived. He probably didn't have no choice but to go. Didn't want to go, ole Officer would have kicked his ass up around his ears."

I thought about all that, realized suddenly why Florida had withdrawn her money from the bank. She was a woman with a plan. A bigger one than I had first thought. She saw herself not only as some sort of crusader, but as someone who was going to preserve a heritage, and maybe get some notoriety in the process. She had envisioned Bobby Joe as some kind of Robert Johnson. Magazine articles. A book. TV movies. That would be her approach. Florida was one ambitious rascal. She'd most likely given up her apartment with plans to live here, near her subject matter.

I heard a car splashing through the water outside and became, to put it mildly, tense.

Bacon got up, went to the window, pulled back the curtain and looked out. "Doctor," he said.

The doctor came in wet and old, bald-headed and grumpy. The black skin on his forehead was deeply wrinkled, the wrinkles sagged like worn-out venetian blinds. The water beaded on his gray slicker like blisters on a rhino's hide. He had a bag in his hand, not a little black bag, but a big red plastic bag, as if he'd just come from shopping at a toy store. He sat the bag down, took off the slicker and dropped it on the floor and the water pooled beneath it.

"What the fuck you doin' to my floor?" Bacon asked.

The doctor looked the place over, then looked at Bacon. "Say what?"

"Yeah, well, all right," Bacon said.

The doctor picked up his bag, and Bacon led him back to where Leonard lay. A moment later Bacon came from the bedroom and shut the door, said, "He always was a dickhead. But he's a good doctor. Only lost a few dogs he's worked on, and they'd been hit real bad by cars. He do all right with horses too. He's had a lot of cats die on him, but I never did give a shit about the outcome of cats."

"He's a veterinarian?"

"He do a little side work, it comes up. Only real black doctor lives fifty miles away, and I'll tell you now, in this rain, this being Grovetown, he wouldn't have come."

"Great. A vet."

Twenty minutes went by and the doctor came out of the bedroom with his big red plastic bag and sighed.

"How bad is he?" I asked.

"Looks hell of a lot worse than he is. Took a good beatin', but folks doin' it didn't do too special a job, all things considered. He's a tough sonofabitch, and he'll be all right. I worked on a hog like that once. Some kids climbed in a pen with a bunch of hogs, took baseball bats to 'em, but this old boar took a good beatin', got one of the kids down and ate part of his face 'fore the kid could get out of the pen."

"So he'll be all right?"

"Not tomorrow, but he'll heal. Don't seem to have no real internal injuries, which surprises me."

"He knows something about covering up, going with the flow," I said. "Experience."

"I put his dick in his pants, by the way."

"That's good," Bacon said. "Me and him wouldn't do it."

"I wore gloves," the doctor said. "Well, let me look you over, whitey. Take off them duds."

I could hardly rise off the couch. In fact, I couldn't. Bacon got hold of me and lifted me up. He smelled of fried foods and sweat. My muscles ached deeply and I felt ill to my stomach. Standing was the most painful thing I'd ever done next to paying taxes. I gingerly unbuttoned my shirt and the doctor helped me take it off. My skin had turned purple and black and green where I had taken shots from fists and feet. The lump on the side of my head hurt the worst.

The doctor poked and prodded, felt and looked. He said, "That one there, that's a shoe caught you."

"Reckon so," I said. "Can't say as I was takin' notes."

"Take off your pants."

I did. My balls were the color of plums going to rot and were doubled in size.

"You better get you some underwear," the doctor said. "These dudes swinging will make you see elephants."

"I hear that," I said. "They aren't ruined are they?"

"No. They'll heal. Ought to get you some Epsom salts, put it in the tub with hot water and soak for an hour or so every day." He looked at my head. "This is really the worse shot you got. You have any memory loss?"

"I don't remember."

"Ha. Ha," the doc said. Nobody had a sense of humor anymore.

"Bacon, you watch him. He shows trouble remembering, repeating of phrases, then . . . well, I don't know. Give him a couple of aspirins, keep him awake."

"Shit, man, he ain't my problem. I don't even know this guy. He go to sleep and die, it ain't my fault. He die, it won't be on my head. I'll sleep like a lawyer. It wasn't me got him into this. Him and ole Swole Head in there is the one's crapped in their nest, not me."

"Well, that's between you and him," said the doc. "He ain't none of my problem neither."

"Sure I am," I said. "You're a man of medicine."

"Just counts on animals. Someone found I was checkin' on you, they'd take my license. 'Sides, you seem all right to me." He poked me in the ribs with his finger. "That hurt?"

"Hell yeah."

"Good. I'm through. You gonna live. Just stay out of trouble for a while. I tell you, both you boys, you the luckiest fellas I've seen. Ain't neither one of you look like much, but you're both tough as a roadhouse steak. The one in there, his head wasn't like that before the beatin' was it?"

"No."

"Then he's tough, not just ugly. Y'all be all right. That's sixty dollars apiece."

"Apiece?" I said. "What do you charge dogs?"

"I don't charge them nothin', but their owners pay me sixty dollars apiece for a lookover like this."

"We get anything for pain?"

"My sympathies and Bacon's aspirin. I can't be dolin' out medicine. I'm a vet."

"Hell," I said, and gave him some of the money Charlie had given me.

About ten P.M. the rain slacked. I hadn't moved much from my position on the couch, and that had been a mistake. I was very stiff now. Bacon fixed some fried egg sandwiches and finally got the TV to work. He found an old black-and-white movie about gangsters, interspersed with long stupid commercials, and we watched it. When we finished the sandwiches, Bacon said, "You want some whiskey? I likes a little jolt or two before bedtime."

"I gave up drinking anything but nonalcoholic beer."

"You a drunk?"

"Nope. Just felt it wasn't healthy."

"I'm gonna take me a little jolt. All that pain and such, you might want you a little."

"Oh, all right, what the hell, just a shot."

He poured us both some in plastic glasses and gave me a handful of aspirin. I took the aspirin and we sipped and watched the movie. I finished off my whiskey and began to nod. The gangsters were taking another gangster for a ride when I lost track of the plot. Next thing I knew it was morning.

20

I tried to get up and go pee, but it wasn't as easy as I would have hoped. It was a job just to get my legs over the side of the couch.

I saw Bacon in the kitchen, sleeping on a cot with a blanket pulled over him. I finally got up and old-man-stepped to the bedroom/bathroom, pissed and checked on Leonard. He opened his eyes and looked at me.

"I got to go," he said.

I pulled back the covers, discovered he had been dressed by the doctor in some of Bacon's old clothes. Helping him took about twenty minutes from bed to toilet. I wasn't all that brisk myself. Leonard took a leak and looked in the mirror. "Oh, my God," he said. "I look like the Elephant Man." I led him back to bed. We were doing better, it only took ten minutes to get back.

"I feel awful," he said. "Where are we?"

I filled him in.

"Bacon? His name is Bacon?"

"Yeah, and he's grumpy. The doctor, you remember him?"

"Not really."

"He was grumpy too. And he's a vet, not a real doctor."

"That figures."

"Everybody is grumpy in Grovetown. I want to go home."

"Me too. Hap?"

"Yeah."

"This Bacon, he can't hear me, can he?"

"No."

"Then I got to tell you, just between you and me, I was really scared. I mean really. I don't know I could face any of them guys again. I'd wet myself."

"You already have."

"Oh yeah."

"And I forgot to tell you, you cut a big fart when you fell down in the alley. I was really embarrassed for you. And they messed up your hat too."

"I looked good in that hat."

"No, you didn't."

"I been whipped before, but not like that," Leonard said. "I've never been humiliated that way. I've strapped three and four fuckers at a time. So have you. Like the assholes next door. The crack house. I whipped them like they were nothing."

"In this case, we were vastly outnumbered, the space was small, we did not have the element of surprise, we're older today than we were yesterday, and to be just goddamn honest, Leonard, those bastards, young and old and female, were about as tough and determined as any I've fought, and they came on like a tidal wave. Under the circumstances we did pretty good, and the fact that we're mostly bushed and stove up and not broken and killed is due to the fact that we have some manly skills in the art of self-defense."

"I figure we just lucked out."

"Actually, me too."

"I really want to go home. For the first time, I really want to give up. Why'd you have to tell me about the fart and the dick part? The pissin' on myself was bad enough."

"I didn't think you'd want it coming from someone else. And besides, misery loves company."

"We were certainly cocky before all this, weren't we?"

"You were. I wasn't."

"Now I don't know if I want to shit or wind my watch."

We sat for a while, not saying anything. I said, "You hear the joke about the lonesome cowpokes."

"Ah, Hap, not now."

"Just to cheer you up."

"You can't tell a joke for shit, Hap."

"You see, there was this cowboy town, and this guy rides in—"

"Hap, please."

"—and he goes to the bar, and he has a few drinks—"

"You're going to do this anyway, aren't you?"

"—and after he gets pretty lubricated, he says to the bartender, 'Where are all the gals? Hell, I ain't had a woman in six months.'"

"Is this going to be sexist?"

"Probably."

"Well, all right, go ahead, even if it's the wrong sex for me."

"We can change it to a gay cowboy. The line is now, 'I ain't had a man's ass in six months.' We have to take for granted that this is sort of a progressive cowboy bar, okay?"

"Just get it over with."

"So, the bartender says, 'Hell, there ain't no gals . . . guys.' You know, Leonard, for this one to work it has to be gals."

"Okay. Whatever."

"The bartender says, 'There ain't no gals, but we got something we do for that little problem.' Cowboy says, 'Yeah, what's that?' And the bartender says, 'Show 'em, boys.' So the boys take the cowboy out back of the saloon, and there's this watermelon patch."

"I see this coming."

"No you don't. They take him over to the fence and he looks at the watermelons growing there, says, 'I don't get it,' and one of the cowboys says, 'We just cut us a plug out of one of these melons, and on a hot night like this, we fuck it, and it feels damn good.'"

"This is disgusting, Hap. Go on."

"So the cowboy, he's, to put it mildly, shocked, but as we have established he hasn't had any in six months, so he climbs over the fence, looks around, sees him a fine-lookin' melon, one of those striped rattlesnake melons, and damn if he don't actually feel a little something for it. A stirrin'. He picks it up, takes out his pocketknife, starts to cut him out a plug, when suddenly all the cowboys gasp and fall back. He turns, looks at them. Says, 'Hey, what's wrong?'

"'Why stranger,' one of 'em says, 'you're playin' with fire. That's Johnny Ringo's girl.'"

A long moment of silence, then Leonard sighed. "Oh God. It's worse than I thought. That's tasteless. Which is okay. But it's not funny."

"Is too."

"No, it isn't. Hap?"

"Yeah."

"You know what?"

"Yeah. One way or the other, we got to finish what we started."

Leonard wasn't much fun. He hadn't liked my joke and fell asleep while I was talking to him. I went back to the living room. Bacon was up. He had put the cot away. He was wearing boxer shorts with flowers on them, a stained T-shirt, and old brown slippers. He was standing by the stove. He said, "Want a scrambled egg, somethin'?"

"Egg is fine."

"How about two and some biscuits?"

"All right."

I went into the kitchen and sat at the table. It was warm in the kitchen. Bacon had slept with the oven lit and the oven door open. He took a can of biscuits out of the fridge and whacked it on the edge of the counter, plucked the biscuits out and snapped them into a greased pan. He paused to scratch his ass, went back to his business. I tried to keep an eye on which biscuits he handled after the ass scratching, so I could locate them in the pan.

He put the pan in the oven, closed the door, went to cracking eggs. "You feel any better?"

"A mite. More than I ever expected."

"You're lucky the couple guys knew how to really throw punches were the ones y'all took out right at first. They can do some damage, them two. See 'em again, won't be so easy. They weren't expecting all that Jap stuff."

"Korean, actually. Hapkido."

"All the same to me. See 'em again, they gonna come on hard, if they don't shoot you."

"I don't want to see them again. I want to go home."

"There's an idea. You damn sure ain't stayin' here. You look well enough to me to stay somewheres else, and I wish you would. I don't want no more troubles than I got."

Bacon cracked eggs in a bowl, poured some milk from a carton into the bowl and started whipping them up. He poured the results in a lightly oiled frying pan, stirred them as they cooked.

A moment later the food was on plates. He pulled the biscuits out of the oven, sat the pan on the counter. "Your buddy want to eat?"

"I'd appreciate it if you'd make the trip to go ask him."

"You don't move them muscles, much as they hurt, you're just gonna get stiffer'n shit."

I sighed, made my way to the bedroom. Leonard was asleep. By the time I got back Bacon was through eating. Half the biscuits were gone. There wasn't any margarine left for the biscuits, just a greasy wrapper, and the eggs on my plate were cool.

I eyed the biscuit pan. Two of the biscuits were the ones Bacon had handled after scratching his ass. I ate the others, and the eggs.

"What happened on the movie last night?" I asked. "I fell asleep."

"These two guys, they got roughed up, so they decide to go back and do the guys in did it to 'em. They got killed."

"Did not," I said.

"You're right. They went home and lived happily ever after, and the guy they was stayin' with 'fore they did got him some peace and goddamn quiet and died with a hard-on."

"Did not."

"I got to go to work. There's Epsom salts by the tub, you want to soak."

"Bacon?"

"Yeah."

"Thanks for letting me sleep on the couch, taking the cot and all."

"Don't keep expectin' it. I didn't get paid that much. I don't reckon no one knows where you are right now, but give it a few days, it'll get out. Word always gets out."

I got out my wallet and gave Bacon a twenty. I said, "For food."

"Thanks," he said.

"I'd appreciate it if you'd get some vanilla cookies. Leonard likes vanilla cookies a lot."

"Vanilla cookies," Bacon said, and left for work.

21

Around five o'clock that afternoon the rain stopped. I was at the window looking at the sky, the dark line of trees below it and the highway beyond the water-covered yard. The sky looked strange. All red and swollen, as if it were bleeding behind transparent skin. The highway was red with sunlight and glistened like a fresh-licked strawberry freeze pop. As I watched, a car splashed into view, turned off the highway onto where the drive would have been had it not been covered by water.

It was Bacon's old wreck. Two cars pulled in behind him. I felt my innards churn, then saw one of the cars was Leonard's and Tim was driving. The windshield had been knocked out on the passenger's side and black plastic had been stretched across it and held there with gray tape. The driver's side still had glass, but it was fractured and webbed.

The other car was the Chief's car, and Cantuck was by himself. Bacon got out with a grocery sack in his arms, stood by his car in the ankle-deep water with his head hung, as if he had just been forced to give all the dogs at the pound a blow job; then write a favorable report on it.

I let the curtain drop, went to check on Leonard. He was awake. I propped him up, told him who was out there, then we heard the front door open. I went into the living room, leaving the bedroom door wide so Leonard could look out and hear.

Tim managed to come inside first. He looked tired and vacant-eyed. He needed a shave. He didn't quite look at me. He sort of smiled out of the corner of his mouth. I figured I wasn't much to look at.

Bacon eased inside carrying his dripping shoes and socks in one hand, the grocery sack in the other. He sat the sack on the television, reached inside, got out a bag of vanilla cookies, tossed them at me. "Little goin'-away present."

I caught the cookies, let them dangle by my side.

Cantuck was standing in the open doorway, carefully scraping mud off his boots with the bottom of the door frame. He finished and closed the door. His right cheek was stuffed with chewing tobacco and his ruptured nut looked extra lumpy today, as if it might burst open at any moment giving birth to deformed twins. When he spoke, flecks of dark tobacco juice jumped from his mouth and onto his lips.

"Where's the Smartest Nigger in the World?"

"In the bedroom. Right now, he's the Most Swole Up Nigger in the World."

Cantuck didn't look in the direction of the open bedroom door. He said to me, "You boys know a fella named Charlie? Cop in LaBorde?"

"Charlie Blank?" I said.

"That's the boy," Cantuck said. "He called up the office. Said to tell you boys to come on home. Said to say a fella you know, a colored cop named Marvin Hanson, was in a coma."

"A coma?"

"Got drunk, wrecked his car on the way here last night. Got caught in the rainstorm, run off the road and didn't have on a seat belt. Hit a tree. Jolt shot him through the windshield, bounced his coconut off a limb after he went through a barbed wire fence."

"Oh shit," Leonard said.

"This Charlie, he said you'd want to know, and to tell you to come home. I told him I'd pack your bags for you. And I have."

"We went by the trailer and got your stuff," Tim said. He stood with his hands in his pockets, as if he might reach down far enough to find a crawl space into which to pull himself. "Leonard's car, the window's busted out of it."

"I saw," I said.

"Goddammit," Leonard said.

"Don't know who did it," Tim said. "They cut up the upholstery too, broke the tape player and all the tapes."

"Hank Williams too?" Leonard asked.

"I don't know," Tim said, looking toward the bedroom. "I reckon. They put all the pieces in the glove box. They slashed all your tires. I replaced them. Bill's in the glove box with the tapes. I know it's a bad time, but I got to remind you, I need my money."

"You'll get it," I said. "How bad is Hanson?"

"A coma's bad," Cantuck said. "You know all I know."

"How'd you know we were here?" I asked.

"I told them," Tim said.

"And how did you know?" I said.

"Maude told me. I went over to apologize for the way my father acted. Or rather to distance myself from the old bastard. Got a little carpenter work too, fixing what y'all wrecked. I can use the money. I said I was a friend, she told me how bad you two were hurt, where you were. I told the Chief, offered to bring out your car."

"Great," I said. "And I guess Officer Reynolds knows where we are too?"

"No," Cantuck said. "I didn't tell him. There's places where me and him don't see eye-to-eye."

"Only because he's taller," I said.

Cantuck grinned at me. "You really don't know me, son. Not even a bit. Hey, Bacon, where can I spit this shit?"

Bacon disappeared into the kitchen. I heard him scrounging around in the garbage. I sat down on the couch. I was past standing up. Bacon came back with an empty corn can. Cantuck took it, spat a cancerous wad of chewing tobacco into it, sat the can on top of the television next to Bacon's grocery sack.

Bacon said, "You was gonna have to leave anyway, Mister Hap."

"Before you head out," Chief Cantuck said, "let me give you a little report. . . . Bacon, got any coffee?"

"Yes sir."

"Make us some."

"Yes sir."

I watched sadly as the old black man shuffled into the kitchen. He had gained ten years and lost twenty points off his IQ the moment Cantuck arrived.

The Chief took hold of a rickety chair, straddled it carefully, adjusted his nut, said: "On this gal."

"Florida," I said.

"Yeah, well, you boys may be right. I think maybe she might be in trouble. Or beyond it."

"No shit," Leonard called out.

"There's stuff don't add up," Cantuck said. "Tim, give me that spit can."

Tim, with a scrunched face, picked the can off the television set and handed it to Cantuck by holding it with thumb and forefinger. Cantuck put the can in front of him on the chair, peeled back his coat, pulled a pack of Beech-Nut from his shirt pocket. He carefully unfolded the pack and opened it. The smell of the tobacco was fresh and sweet, like syrup on pancakes. Too bad it didn't taste that way.

Cantuck poked tobacco into his mouth as if packing a cannon. He worked his mouth a little, wiped spittle on his sleeve and said, "There's some kind of tie-in in all this. Bobby Joe's death, this Florida gal missing."

"So we're not quite the assholes you thought," I said.

"No, you're assholes all right," Cantuck said, "you're just a little smarter than I expected."

I could hear Leonard moving in bed, trying to find a better listening position.

"This mornin' a Texas Ranger came down with the County Sheriff, Tad Griffin. They had a fella with 'em. Some kind of coroner, or dead body expert, whatever them sonofabitches are."

"Forensics," Tim said.

"That's it," Cantuck said. "They come to dig up that dead nigra. Bobby Joe. Wanted to see if he'd hung himself or someone hung him. They got ways of tellin'. Did you know that?"

"All I know I get from the movies," I said.

"They look at the marks on his neck, the strangle marks, and they can somehow tell if he did it himself or had help. Or so they claim. I'm not sure they really know shit."

Cantuck paused, poked two fingers into his mouth to line his chewing tobacco up right, then wiped the fingers on his pants.

"I'll bite," I said. "Was he hung, or did he commit suicide?"

"Don't know," Cantuck said.

"When will you know?" I said.

"No idea, because they didn't find the body," Cantuck said.

"What?"

"I put him down," Bacon said. "You was there."

"I know," Cantuck said. "Went out there, dug where he was supposed to be, and he wasn't there. Wasn't nothing there, unless you want to count earthworms. Big old bastards. Make good fishing bait."

"You're sure he was in the coffin to begin with?" I asked.

"He was there," Cantuck said. "I went out and supervised the burial. Bobby Joe's family wouldn't have nothing to do with him. Thought he had the taint of the devil on him. Was a voodoo person, they said. I was at the undertaker's when they closed him up in his box, and I was there with a Baptist reverend when they put him down in the colored paupers' field. Bacon dug the original hole. I watched him dig it."

"Colored?" Leonard called out. "You can't be consistent, can you, Chief? Are we niggers, colored, or nigras?"

"Take your pick," Cantuck said.

"Just as long as you don't use a term like People of Color," Leonard said.

"Don't worry," Cantuck said. "I won't."

"You mean someone stole the body?" I said.

"Unless it turned into a worm and crawled off. Coffin, body. Gone. Bobby Joe wasn't embalmed 'cause wasn't nobody paying for it, so whoever took the body had'm a pretty ripe job."

"Any ideas who might have stolen it?" I asked.

"Few," Cantuck said, changing his tobacco to the opposite cheek. "Could be kids fuckin' around, some of that Satanist shit."

"Oh, come on, Chief," I said.

"Didn't say it was," Cantuck said. "Said it could be. It could be other things. Folks might not want him buried out there near a loved one."

"I know one family was real upset about it," Bacon said. "They was upset enough, they could have moved him."

"Who would that be?" I asked.

"Mrs. Bella Burk's folks," Bacon said.

Cantuck nodded, picked up from there. "They come to me about it. Wasn't nothing I could do. Burks didn't want Bobby Joe laid down near their mama on account of him into black magic, not being baptized and all. Her people covered her grave with crucifixes, charms. They may have decided that wasn't enough, dug him up and disposed of the body. They did, I wouldn't hold it against them."

"And if they didn't," I said, "what's that leave?"

"What you might suspect," Cantuck said. "What you been thinking all along. Someone got rid of the body so there's no evidence Bobby Joe didn't commit suicide. If he didn't."

"That's the case," I said, "him not committing suicide, someone might think your office could be involved. He didn't hang himself, that points a finger at you, doesn't it?"

"It do," Cantuck said. "In fact, they're thinkin' along that line right now. Sheriff and Ranger told me that right out. Frankly, I'm startin' to think that boy was hung."

"While you were away, of course," I said.

"Yeah, while I was away. I was there, he wouldn't have been hung. He might have lived to have gotten the needle, but I wouldn't allowed nothing like that. I keep tellin' you that."

"That's right," I said. "I thought I'd heard it before."

"Man does a crime like that, sets it up way Bobby Joe did, had that stupid Yankee come down here with money to buy stuff didn't exist . . . Well, the Yankee was stupid, but his only crime was being stupid, and legally, that ain't no crime. Bobby Joe could have had that Yankee's money without killin' anyone. Could have conned that city fuck and come out good, but Bobby Joe thought it was too much fun to kill him. Maybe 'cause he was white. Maybe 'cause Bobby Joe was drunk. Maybe 'cause he just wanted to."

"Sounds more like it," Tim said.

"But there wasn't no excuse to gut him like a hog, do him the way he did," Cantuck said. "Even if he was a Yankee. I got nothin' but contempt for Bobby Joe."

"You and everybody else," Tim said.

"But," Cantuck continued, "he was in my jail, and I put a prisoner in my jail, he's supposed to be safe. People work for me are supposed to make sure he's safe. They don't, and I find out they didn't, then I'm gonna want to see they get a trip to the death house, get that needleful of shit in the dead man's place. I don't allow that kind of shit."

"Does Reynolds know you don't allow that kind of shit?" I said.

"I reminded him this mornin' after that body come up missin', and I told him if he had his fingers in any of this, well, I was gonna see they got cut off."

"How'd he take that?" I asked.

Cantuck paused. "Nervous. I thought he looked a little nervous when we went out to the gravesite, for that matter. And damn relieved when the body wasn't there."

"So, you think Reynolds was surprised it wasn't there?" I said.

"I don't think nothing."

"Meaning, he didn't move the body," Leonard said.

"Meaning nothing," Cantuck said. "I'm sayin' he looked nervous, then relieved. That could mean somethin', and it could mean diggin' up corpses don't give him a hard-on. Then, knowing he wasn't going to have to see a dead body after all, it cheered him up. I'll tell you, seeing a body don't give me no hard-on neither, so I can understand that. Fact is, ain't nothin' gives me a hard-on anymore."

"Not even chickens?" I said.

"Not even chickens," Cantuck said. "But I don't know, I look at them little pin feathers around a chicken's butthole long enough, maybe I'd heat up."

"Still," I said, "you're suspicious, aren't you?"

"Maybe."

"You went far enough to talk to Reynolds about it," I said.

"I did it to see if the water rippled or splashed. It might have rippled a little, but it didn't splash. Then again, Reynolds ain't easy to read, and if I had my druthers I wouldn't work with him. 'Sides, he's fuckin' my secretary, and she's a married woman. I don't like a man workin' on a married, and I don't much care the woman don't mind givin' it up. She's got kids and a good husband. I had concrete evidence I'd fire 'em. And her a big churchgoer. You say shit, she acts like you just gave her a mouthful, and I know she's fuckin' that big sonofabitch every goddamn chance she gets. Can't prove it, but I know it."

"You sound jealous," Tim said.

"I am a little. I don't feel good about that, but I guess I am. I've thought about her some myself. I'd like to get my fingers in that hairdo. But I'm a married man, and a married man ain't supposed to do stuff like that, so I don't. Bible said it was okay to go around pokin' any hole you wanted, I might look at it different, but it don't say that."

"Nice of you to tell us all about your office problems," I said. "Come in here and shit all over your deputy."

"Yeah," Leonard yelled. "That's damn white of you."

"Can't help myself," Cantuck said. "I just plain don't like Reynolds. I don't like my secretary either."

"You don't like them, fire them," I said.

"Not that easy. Charlene needs the job. She's got them kids. And Reynolds, I didn't hire him in the first place. Town pushed him on me. Actually, Brown pushed him on me through the Mayor. That's the way politics are played, so I ended up taking him on. He's good enough at what he does, but he ain't all that fair about things. He's crafty, but he lets personal get in the way."

"You think Brown has Reynolds in his pocket?" I asked.

"Not his front pocket, right next to his dick, but his hip pocket maybe. Mainly Reynolds is just Reynolds. He does what he wants 'cause he wants to, and a lot of what he wants ain't all that good."

"Certainly nice of you to drop by and tell us all this, Chief," I said. "Why?"

Cantuck considered a moment. He laid his hands on the back of the chair and leaned back. As he did, a shaft of red sunlight poked through the curtain and landed on his left eye. He jerked his head from the light and leaned forward again, said, "Reckon I should have taken this colored gal's missin' more serious."

"And maybe you want us to feel so warm toward you we'll go home and forget all this mess. Just leave it to you. Trust you to do what's right."

"Could be," Cantuck said.

Bacon brought coffee in, two cups at a time. One for himself. He stood by the television and sipped his.

"What about all those guys jumped us?" I asked.

"Your word against theirs," Cantuck said. "Draighten and Ray say they got into it with you two on their own. Claim there wasn't no one else involved but them, and it was just y'all caused the ruckus."

"You believe that?" I said.

"Don't matter what I believe. We get through sortin' it all out, it'll come down to you two fought them two, and it'll be your word, and Maude's and her boys against all them other folks who saw it and say it didn't happen way you say it did."

"What if we press charges?"

"They'll press charges back."

"So what's next?"

"We put your asses in your car and send you home."

22

Leonard and I decided to wear our own clothes. Tim went out to Leonard's car and brought in our suitcases, then asked Bacon to drive him home. Bacon left with Tim, and I went into the bedroom and closed the door and changed clothes and helped Leonard dress. While I held him under the arm and he painfully slipped into his pants, he said, "You think the Chief is telling it the way it is?"

"I don't know," I said. I helped Leonard sit on the side of the bed, then folded up the clothes Bacon had given us and placed them on a chair.

I helped him into a shirt. He buttoned it slowly. He didn't look at me when he said, "I'm glad we're going home."

"Me too."

"There was a time when I thought I couldn't be broken, but I don't know now. I hear a sound, I get tense. I hear it twice, I damn near shit myself. I think it's that bunch coming down on me, all of them, and I figure right now, if I was solid and sound and they came, I might just ball up like a baby and let them have me."

"You wouldn't, Leonard. It's not in you."

"I wouldn't have thought that just a day or so ago, but I think now I've just been lucky."

"No one survives all you've been through and calls themselves lucky. Your problem is you've lost your boyfriend, taken a damn good beating, and everybody saw your dick. Not to mention you cut a fart and pissed on yourself."

"Thanks for reminding me."

"Trust me. You'll get over it."

"You comin' back here, Hap?"

"Come on, Leonard, let's go."

"Hap?"

"I don't know."

The Chief and I loaded Leonard into the back seat of the car with a blanket we borrowed from Bacon, and as a last thought, the Chief gave us his thermos. I took it inside and the Chief came in behind me. I poured what was left of Bacon's coffee into the thermos.

I said, "You wouldn't happen to have some sandwiches, would you, Chief?"

"You boys hit the road, and don't come back," he said. "You were fortunate this time. I see you again, and you get to stay at the jail a while. Like maybe till I retire."

"Been nice visiting your little town, Chief."

I took the thermos and went out to the car, the Chief walking behind me.

The sky was dark again. All the red had bled out. The Chief said, "You start now, you won't get home late, and you might beat the storm. It's coming, but it'll be at your back, you don't fuck around. You've got a full tank of gas, courtesy of me, and you got hot coffee and I don't want the thermos back. I don't want anything that'll have to do with me seeing you again. Comprende?"

"But we will get a Christmas card from you next year, won't we?"

"Sit out by the mailbox and wait on it. And, son, Happy New Year."

I opened the car door and tossed the thermos inside. A pillow had been laid across the ripped-up driver's seat, and I put my ass on that and started the car and turned on the lights.

As I backed out of the drive, the Chief lifted his fingers and waved bye-bye.

I drove until I reached the highway, then pulled over beside the road.

"What's up?" Leonard said.

"One minute," I said.

I got out and paused to look at the sky. It was dark all over, but behind us there was a greater wad of blackness, like soot-stained cotton, and it was balling and twisting and tumbling our way. The wind was cold and wet and smelled of lightning.

I opened the trunk of the car, got a handgun and the strapped Winchester and made sure they were loaded, brought them around, laid them in the front seat as I climbed behind the wheel.

"Thought you didn't like guns," Leonard said.

"Today, I'm trying to be more open and friendly toward them."

"Let me have one for back here," he said. "As a pacifier."

I gave him the revolver and he put it in his waistband. I patted the stock of the Winchester on the seat beside me, said, "Good boy. Stay. Good boy."

As I drove, the sky grew black as the bottom of an ancient outhouse. The trees alongside the highway became little more than an outline and appeared to be sketched from charcoal. The storm behind us was rolling faster than I was, and I could feel it as it descended on us like a heavy, alien cloud. Rain splashed the windshield and the tires began to sing in the water; a nasty little song that hinted of blown tires, skidding machinery, and twisting metal.

It had been hard enough to see with the cracked windshield, but now, with the rain coming down the way it was, it was damn near impossible. I slowed, leaned forward, tried to make out the yellow line so I could hold the car steady. I really should have pulled over, but I didn't want to. Not until I had us and Grovetown many miles apart.

Another few miles and I glanced in the rearview mirror and saw lights. Then behind those lights, others. The lights were moving toward us pretty fast, much too fast for common sense in weather like this.

I watched the lights in the rearview mirror when I wasn't struggling to hold Leonard's junker on the road, and they were closing with a determined pace. I felt my bowels weaken, then the car was filled with the light. A big dark pickup was riding right on our bumper, so close, at a glance you might have thought I was towing it. The truck fell back, charged forward, fell back, broke around us and passed.

I glanced at the truck as it went around me. It was big and black and souped-up and rode on oversized tires that splattered the water on the highway with power and grace. You got the feeling that goddamn truck could ride on the surface of a lake. The windows were tinted and it had grown quite dark, so I couldn't see anyone inside. The pickup glided around us quickly, then way ahead, and I watched as its taillights bounced out of sight.

I glanced in the rearview mirror, saw the other set of lights moving forward, and there were lights behind those lights. I looked at Leonard. He was lying on his side, looking at me. He said, "Trouble?"

"I don't know."

I dipped Leonard's junker down into a drop in the road and a fog thick as the wool on a sheep's back clouded over the windshield. I inched forward and out of the rise, and at the top of it the fog thinned, and directly in front of me, pulled crossways across the highway, was the big black pickup, the lights poking toward the woods and a marshy pond festooned with dried weeds and cattails. There wasn't even a half lane between the nose of the truck and the marsh.

Behind me one set of lights rushed forward like a falling pair of meteors, rode my bumper. The other set filled the passing lane.

I wasn't going backwards, and I couldn't go forward. I thought about ramming the truck, but figured I tried that I'd move the truck all right, but what was left of me and Leonard wouldn't have been enough to pack a gnat's ass.

I decided I had only one avenue, and that was to swing wide left in front of one set of lights, try and race around the pickup, glance a blow off of it, get back on some free and straight highway.

Temporary fix. I managed that, then I could gun Leonard's junker all the way up to sixty, if the radiator didn't blow out through the hood or the tires didn't pop. That would keep us ahead of that souped-up truck for almost ten seconds.

One cliff at a time.

"Hang on, buddy!" I yelled at Leonard, and tried to put my foot through the floor. The car didn't exactly leap, but it surged a little. I saw the driver's-side door open on the pickup and a man wearing a white sheetlike outfit and a hood stepped onto the highway. He had a shotgun in his hands and he lifted it at me.

I jerked the wheel to the left as the air exploded with a sound like thunder, but it was shotgun thunder. Pellets tore through the black plastic side of the windshield and carried it away. I heard

Leonard cuss and I cussed, then I was going around the front end of the truck, hitting gravel. There was a noise like a cherry bomb going off, and less than a second later I knew the left front tire had blown. The car made a weave, and I tried to turn in the direction of the skid, but couldn't figure out which way it was skidding, then—

—we were airborne. Went way up and out toward the marsh and the car hit the water and the water parted and came up high and washed through the windshield and cattails leaped out and away and the car rode up as if it might coast the water, then went down again, dipped its nose slightly forward. Water lapped through the windshield, over the dash and sloshed my legs.

Leonard said, "Go for it, Hap. Get out of here."

I climbed over the back seat and grabbed Leonard, tried to open a door. Couldn't. Water pressure.

"Let me go, Hap."

The car dipped forward again and more water came in, and Leonard said, "On second thought, drag my ass out of here."

"We're going through the windshield," I said.

Leonard helped all he could, and I got him tugged over the seat, into the front seat, which was half filled with water. I got hold of the rifle, which had fallen onto the floorboard, and used it to knock out what was left of the flimsy windshield, flung the strap over my head and shoulder as the car took a nosedive.

I got Leonard by the coat collar, pulled him straight through the windshield, and we went down, down into that cold, dark murk, and for a moment I couldn't figure if I was trying to break the surface or diving for the bottom, then realized the truth, pushed off from the car with my feet and changed direction, fought the tug of the sinking car.

I pulled at Leonard, but couldn't get much movement. He was too heavy and not able to do much. I actually considered letting him go, then tightened my grip and decided it was both or nothing. The darkness above me bloomed with light, and I broke the surface, yanked Leonard up behind me.

Leonard's head from the mouth up was all that came out of the water, and he bobbed like a cork. We gasped for air. The rain pounded on us. It was still dark, darker than before, in fact, jet as night and the air had a stench to it. Rotting vegetation, fish, mud. It was a strong, almost overwhelming reek activated by the blowing wind and the rain.

I readjusted my grip on Leonard, started to swim toward shore, then there was a crack and the water jumped like a frog leaping.

I glanced at the highway, the source of the lights, realized the lights were the headlamps of the pickup and the two cars that had been behind us. They had parked in such a way to use their head beams as spotlights. I realized too that someone had just tried to clip me with a thirty-ought-six.

There were several white-gowned and hooded shapes near the lights, and they had rifles pointed at us. Then that damn shotgun roared and the water popped all around us and a pellet went into my cheek, and almost simultaneously the sinking car created a delayed suction, and we were pulled back down into the depths.

23

Only I hadn't realized the depths weren't that deep.

We hadn't dropped far below the water when my feet hit the back of the car, which was nose down in the muddy bottom. I pushed off and swam laterally, got into a tangle of weeds and vines, panicked, nearly lost the rifle, floundered and split the surface.

As I bobbed above the water, gasping at the cold, throat-searing air, clinging to Leonard, I decided if I was gonna die I wanted a bullet in the head, not water in my lungs. Even though I was a decent enough swimmer, the idea of drowning terrified me, and it seemed nearly drowning was something that happened to me on a regular basis. Leonard once said if there was two feet of water within a hundred miles of me I'd find some way to fall nose forward into it. And probably take him with me.

We had come up in a thicket of dried weeds and cattails, and nobody had ventilated our skulls. It was starting to rain harder, and the rain came down in chilled pills and moved the water around us. I could see the car lights through the weeds, and they were hazy from the rain, and I could see the hooded assholes moving down close to the bank, looking around, chattering like squirrels. I realized they couldn't see us, at least for the moment.

They were fanning out to our left and right, around the marshy pond, and the pond wasn't all that big. I knew pretty soon they'd spot us, and when they did, it would be as easy for them as shooting decoy ducks.

My cheek stung where the pellet had gone in, and I was already a mess to begin with. My legs hurt from treading and I was so cold, my balls felt as if they had crawled up inside me for warmth.

But one good thing, I wasn't thinking nearly as much about all the pain the beating had given me. I was too concerned with freezing, drowning, not getting my head scattered like a rotten pumpkin. Just like they say, every cloud has a silver lining.

Leonard looked weak as a pup with distemper. He couldn't really tread. I was holding him up and it was about to do me in. I tightened my grip on his collar, pushed backwards with my legs, silently as possible, backstroked and dragged Leonard with me. It was a hard go, and I was swallowing that foul water and I almost decided to lose the rifle to make going easier, then thought better of it.

The weeds around me parted and rustled and I heard a voice out near the highway, then there were a couple of shots. They popped next to Leonard's head, and I looked at him. He was all right, just spitting water.

"Hang in there, buddy," I said. "They can't see us, just the weeds moving. They're taking pot shots."

He shook his head a little, cocked an eyebrow. "Ain't this somethin' for the scrapbook?"

I kicked on back, and pretty soon my feet were touching the bottom, I pushed up, rolled over and scuttled onto shore behind a blind of weeds and cane and cattails, dragging Leonard with me. When I had him on shore, I found I couldn't make my hand let go of his jacket; it was cold and cramped. I had to use my other hand to free it, work the fingers, press my thumb into the center of my palm and squeeze, try to bring my paw back to life.

I took a gander at Leonard. He lay on his back, shivering. He turned his head toward me. His teeth chattered. He said, "Hap, that goddamn Cantuck. He set this up. He sold us down the shit river. And I'm mad. Real mad."

I reached out, patted his shoulder. I thought that's right, Leonard. Get mad. Real goddamn mad, 'cause right now, that's all we got.

"Still got the revolver?" I asked.

He pushed his wet coat aside and lifted his shirt. The revolver was still in his waistband. He pulled it free and poured water out of the barrel.

"All right," I said. I looked behind us, trying to take in our position. The roots of great willows and oaks grew down from the bank behind us and wound their way into the water and knotted near our feet. Some of the roots were wrist-thick, and some of the thicker ones came down from where the bank was higher than where we lay. Above all this, falling down on the water like a blot of ink, was the great darkness of the woods. I was glad for that, but not ecstatic. Darkness cannot deflect bullets. A shotgun can clean out darkness as easy as light.

Out through the weeds I could see their car lights. Shadows, like goblins, moved in front of the lights. To our left I could hear someone tromping along the marshy water's edge, someone about as sneaky as a bull rhino on its way to mate.

Leonard very softly said, "Use the rifle. You know how you can shoot, Hap. I know you don't want to hurt nobody, but you know how you can shoot."

I squatted and hooked Leonard under the arms and got back in the water with him, pulled him toward where the roots were thickest. When I got him there, I whispered, "I can't pull you on shore far enough, get you hid in time for them not to see us. I go by myself, I can make it faster and I can get their attention and pull them away from here. Stay hid. No arguments."

"Hap. Use the rifle."

I shoved Leonard through a split in the roots, and the roots and the muddy overhang and the darkness from the trees and the blackness of his skin concealed him well.

We squeezed hands and I pushed away from him, scooped mud from the marshy bottom and rubbed it on my face and the backs of my hands as I went. I got hold of roots and pulled myself out of the water, crouched and tried to go along the edge of the bank quietly where there were some reeds and trees for camouflage.

But I wasn't as quiet as I hoped. I sloshed as I moved and my shoes made sucking sounds. I slung the rifle off my shoulder, backed into the woods about even of where Leonard hid in the roots just below the bank. I got positioned just as around a row of high reeds came a big bulky shape in a muddy white outfit and hood. The goblin was armed with a shotgun.

I thought, if you're trying to be sneaky, you dumb sonofabitch, you need to lose that Kluxer suit. It stands out like a white tent in a bombing raid.

He came along crouched. As he neared I felt sick and weak and scared. I could have shot him in the head effortless. He wasn't expecting me to have a gun, and he didn't know where I was. Maybe he thought I had drowned or was somewhere in the water. Maybe he thought he found me, killing me would be easy as stomping an ant on a piece of stale bread.

I waited on him, keeping an eye and ear out for others and not seeing or hearing them. When he was alongside me, I stepped out from the shadows of the trees quick-like and brought the Winchester stock around and hit him hard as I could in the side of the head. He had seen me move a second sooner than I hoped, so he reacted enough that the blow was a glancing blow and didn't knock him out, but it was still a good hit and he lost his peaked hood. It flew into the water, and in that instant, even in the dark, I could see it was the big bastard from the cafe that I had called Bear. Ray, his name was.

He stumbled toward the bank and the mud crumbled beneath his big feet, and one leg went off the edge of the bank so hard the other leg was forced to bend quickly to try to hold his weight. It couldn't. I heard his knee snap. The big bastard screamed, fell into the water, still clutching the shotgun. He floundered and splashed and started to yell, but suddenly the yell was cut, and I knew he had fallen near Leonard and Leonard had reached out and got him. Probably had that goddamn choke hold on him he did so well. Leonard could go either way with it. He wanted, he could end your life by strangling you, or he could use another version, shut off the blood supply to the brain. You'd be out quick that way and not wake up too soon, if ever, and you'd never know you'd been got, because it didn't take any strength to make either choke work, just skill and determination.

I slipped back into the woods and went along the trees, clinging to the shadows. The lights through the reeds and cattails seemed to die at the trees, and when I looked back at the marsh the lights made the water look dark blue, as if it had been dyed, and the rain moved the blue and it was oddly mesmerizing and beautiful.

I found an oak with a fork in it, slung the rifle over my shoulder, climbed up and eased onto a big limb that went way out to where I had a good clear look at the marsh and the highway beyond. The leaves were all gone off the oak, but the limb was thick and there were two big limbs jutting out from it like a Y and there were some little limbs too, and I figured they'd hide me pretty good if someone wasn't expecting me to be ten feet up.

I hooked my legs around the big branch and rested an elbow in the Y and sighted down the barrel. I knew even in the dark, if I wanted to, I could shoot clean across the marsh and give a frog a hemorrhoidectomy. No brag. Just fact.

There was one hooded figure over by the truck, waiting, using the rifle to lean on. He was probably there to make sure someone didn't come along and run the hell over the cars and the truck. I slung water out of the rifle barrel, hoped it would still shoot, then lined his head up in the sights. I figured I splattered his brains all over the place, the rest of them, wherever they were, might opt to head to the house, but I couldn't do it. It would have been an easy shot for me, but I couldn't do it.

Then I saw lights on the highway and the hooded man by the truck turned and looked in that direction, and I wondered, what you gonna do now, Bubba? How you gonna move the truck and two cars? How you going to explain this? Then, I thought, oh shit, he might not explain anything. He might just start shooting. He might decide not to leave witnesses.

The car came into view and slowed, and I could see now that it was Chief Cantuck's patrol car, and I thought, you double-talkin', big-balled sonofabitch. You set us up. You got us on the road, then you had us followed out, knowing our old wreck wasn't going to make much time. Had us followed because we were on to the fact that you hung that guy in jail or had it done, and you didn't want us to spread the word. That's why we hadn't been charged. That's why the snow job.

Cantuck stopped the car and got out. Across the marsh, floating on the night air, I heard him say: "You might as well go on and throw that rifle down, Leroy. I know who you are and know them other two cars, and I ain't gonna let you go on with things."

"It's a nigger," Leroy said, "an out-of-town nigger. And he's got that nigger lover with him."

"Put the gun down," Cantuck said, and I saw his hand go to where his holster hung.

I thought, now wait a minute, what's this? Then I saw to the left of the pond one of the Kluxers was sneaking around some reeds, and he squatted with his rifle across his knees, thinking he was hid. I saw to the right of the marsh that another Kluxer, or whatever those bastards called themselves, was easing up on that side. He slid into the woods behind a tree. I knew as soon as I saw him, even under that wet sheet, that it was Elephant. He was big and had an ass that poked out behind like . . . well, what Leonard had said. Like he was pulling a trailer.

"Throw down the gun," I heard Cantuck say.

The man at the truck said, "Can't do that, Chief. Can't go back with you. None of us can."

"I think you oughta," Cantuck said, and at that same moment the man by the truck used the toe of his shoe to kick the stock of the rifle up, tried to catch and pull it under his arm for action, like he'd seen in some cowboy movie, but Cantuck had seen the same movie. He drew his pistol and shot Leroy through the head and I thought I saw a shadow jump across the front of Leroy's hood but realized it was blood, then Leroy was down, on his back, his heels pushing at the highway, pushing so hard he went up under the truck about a foot and lay still, legs spread, knees up, as if accepting a lover.

Another shot cut through the night, and I realized too late it was the man at the left of the pond. He stood up and fired and the shot hit the outside driver's mirror on Cantuck's car and glass leaped from it and Cantuck let out a yell and jerked his head so hard his hat flew off. He stumbled back, grabbed his eye and fell down. The Kluxer fired again, hit the back of the car, near where Cantuck lay writhing, holding his eye.

I repositioned the rifle, sighted the shooter, and fired. My shot hit where I meant for it to hit. The peaked hood. It ripped it off his head, knocked it back and away.

The de-hooded shooter couldn't quite place where my shot had come from. He shuffled left and right, and across the pond I heard Elephant yell, "Goddamn, Kevin, you shot Cantuck."

Kevin, a middle-aged dark-haired man, was crouched, twisting left and right, trying to locate me. He said, "Shut up. That last shot was at me."

Elephant yelled, "What?"

"Shut up," Kevin yelled back, and I got a bead on the stock of his rifle, fired, knocked the gun back into him. He dove for the dirt and I put up a line of fire around him, snapping three shots near his head, making the dirt fly. He lay facedown, the rifle in one outstretched hand, the rain pounding down on him. He didn't look like he had any intention of moving.

While I was so engaged, Elephant came up from his side and located me. He fired a shot that shattered the limb I was resting my rifle on, and though the slug missed me, the sudden impact caused me to lose my balance and fall out of the tree. As I hit, the Winchester bounced away from me and fell into the wet leaves.

I was going to make for it when I heard the cocking of a rifle, looked around, saw Elephant standing just inside the line of trees. He had me in his sights. The hood was wetly plastered to his face, and I could see the outline of his nose and mouth beneath the material, clinging to him like wet baking dough.

He reached up and swept the hood off his head. He was grinning at me. "You nigger-lovin' piece of shit. I'm sending you to the devil."

I was still on one knee, waiting for the end, when suddenly there was a roar and a flash of red light. Elephant seemed to take a football kick at the sky with his right leg, only the leg was twisted funny and it went out longer than a leg ought to. The kick pulled his ass out from under him, and he came down with a scream that made my spine knot up.

Behind him, lying on the shore, looking as if he had just crawled through hell with the lights off, was Leonard. He was lying on the ground, holding Bear's shotgun.

I ran over to where Elephant was screaming and got hold of his rifle. I nodded at Leonard, said, "Stay low," moved back into the woods, out of the line of fire, scouted for Kevin. He wasn't where he had been. I glanced across the marsh, saw him making for one of the cars.

I got a little higher ground, and watched him run. He got in one of the cars and backed it around quickly. I jerked up Elephant's rifle, took out one of the headlights, but Kevin kept turning about. I fired and took out a tire, but he kept going, blubbering along the wet highway on the rim.

I collected my Winchester and went to examine Elephant. His right leg was all but gone, cut off at the knee except for a few strings of muscle and flesh. He was screaming and howling like a dog with ground glass in his belly.

I went past him, on down to Leonard. Leonard was starting to lose his grip, slide back into the water. I tugged him to higher ground, said, "Where's the other one?"

"If he didn't drown," Leonard said, "he's still down there stuck between roots. I choked him out. Bound him up with my belt."

I took Elephant's rifle and the shotgun and tossed them in the water near the bank. I slung the Winchester off my shoulder.

"I wanted to kill him, Hap, but I didn't because I knew it would disappoint you. Same with the other fuck."

"Killed either one of them, you'd have been justified," I said. "And to hell with me being disappointed. Cantuck's here. He's been hit."

"I heard," Leonard said. "Guess I was wrong about him."

I left Leonard on the bank with the Winchester, went back to Elephant. I got hold of the white sheet he was wearing, pulled it over his head while he screamed and cussed me. I said, "You can let me tie up this leg, what's left of it, or you can try and give me shit and bleed to death."

He didn't answer, just screamed and groaned, but he lay back and I used the sheet to tie off his leg above the wound. The sheet turned red immediately.

I went back to Leonard. Leonard said, "How is he?"

"You may have killed him anyway," I said. "He's bleeding like a leaky water hose. I got to get to Cantuck's radio, call in some help."

"I don't think he's got any help back where he's from," Leonard said.

"Then we've got to do different."

I went down in the water and found Bear, his arms bound behind his back with a belt that was looped around a root. He had slipped down into the marsh so far it was washing under his nose. He was still unconscious. I unfastened the belt, got hold of him and pulled him out of there. On shore, I ripped off his white tunic, tore it up, tied his arms behind his back, bent his legs up and tied them to his wrists.

Leonard grunted and groaned as I helped him to his feet. But his sounds were pretty well muffled by Elephant screaming and rolling about in the wet leaves. He hadn't stopped that for a moment.

Leonard nodded toward Elephant. "He Draighten or Ray?"

"Can't say as I care," I said.

Elephant stopped rolling. Just lay there, shivering, holding his hands above his chest like a dog lying on its back with its paws up.

We started for the highway.

24

When we finally made it to Cantuck, he was on his feet. He was leaning against the side of his car, his gun in one hand, his other hand over his eye. Blood was running from under his palm, through his fingers, and the rain was washing it away as fast as it came. Still, the blood had managed to stain his khaki jacket and had dripped onto his pants.

He said, "I got glass in my eye."

"We're going for a doctor," I said.

"Go to LaBorde," he said. "You don't want to go back way we come. There's no hospital fifty miles beyond Grovetown."

"There's an asshole in a bad way out there in the woods," I said. "He doesn't get a doctor soon, he'll die. He's one of the guys jumped us in the cafe. One with a big ass. There's another one out there tied."

"Draighten," Cantuck said, then sagged to his knees and began to pant.

"Hang in, Cantuck."

I opened the back door of the car, assisted Leonard inside, got Cantuck up and helped him. He was wobbly and heavy, and I was so weak from injuries, the swimming, the fighting, that now, with the adrenaline gone, I was feeling more sore than ever and sick to my stomach.

I put Cantuck in the front passenger seat, stumbled to the pickup, got hold of the dead man Cantuck called Leroy, boosted him on my shoulder, thumped him into the bed of his truck.

The keys were in the pickup. I started it, backed it off the highway, tossed the keys underneath it, staggered to the car they'd left. The keys weren't in it, but it was unlocked. I put it in neutral, went to the rear, gathered my resources, pushed it toward the marsh. It nose-dived into the edge of the water where it was shallow and stuck its tail in the air.

I climbed into Cantuck's car, felt so weak suddenly I had to put my head on the steering wheel, let it rest there for a moment. I said, "Chief, you got to call help for those bastards."

I removed the microphone from the rack and gave it to Cantuck. He mumbled through a call to a LaBorde emergency crew, gave them the location.

I couldn't wait for them to arrive. I was too sick and scared that the bastard who had driven away on the bad tire would come back, or reinforcements would arrive. Cantuck was bad off with that glass in his eye, and Leonard had gone deathly quiet. I looked back at him. His eyes were closed. He was breathing badly.

I cranked the car, flipped on the heater, pulled on the lights, took a deep breath, pulled onto the highway. The rain was still coming down and the sky was black as midnight, but Cantuck's motor was better than Leonard's had been, and so were the tires, and that was some kind of comfort.

I wondered about Draighten and Ray, but I didn't wonder too much. I couldn't. It wasn't my fault. I didn't want any of this to go the way it had, but there wasn't any undoing it. I told myself if it bothers you don't think about it. Think about the road, the yellow line in the headlights. Hold this thing in the lane and don't pass out. You pass out, it's all over. Hold on, and don't pass out.

Cantuck fumbled the microphone into place, leaned back with his hand still over his eye. In the green light from the dash his face was streaked with blood and some of the blood had dried and it looked like a big birthmark.

"The eye's gone black," Cantuck said.

"It's all right," I said, as if it really were.

The rain pummeled so hard the wipers were near useless. My breath was dry and hot and my body jerked with nervous tension.

And so it went, the seconds crawling along, me looking through that windshield at the rain and the stormy darkness, watching and listening to those pathetic wipers working so hard and doing so little.

*

Rain on the windshield. Rain on the glass.

When I awoke, I felt as if I were still behind the wheel of Cantuck's car, but I was in bed and three weeks had gone by. It was still raining and had pretty much rained the full three weeks. Lakes were swollen, rivers were overflowing, some areas were flooded out, and the news said the dam near Grovetown looked ready to go.

I was lying in bed looking at the window glass, watching rain bead onto it, beginning to realize that's what I was doing and that's why there were no windshield wipers; I was lying in bed, shaking off the last bad vibes of a dream.

It wasn't the first time I'd dreamed I was in Cantuck's car. Ever since that night, especially that first of two nights in the hospital, I'd had a series of dreams and none of them were very comforting. For a time, before all this Grovetown business, I was having a recurring dream about screwing this beautiful Mexican woman I had seen in a magazine. I guess I was dreaming about her then to get Florida out of my head. I had animated her in my mind and made her ravenous for my root. I was such a stud in my dreams she couldn't get enough. I liked the way she screamed and grunted and called me baby in that sweet high Spanish. Even if in the end she was nothing more than a paper memory in my head, a pillow in my arms.

But after the stuff in Grovetown that dream went away and I couldn't call it up any more than I could whistle down a 747 and cause it to light on a high line. If I tried to call it up the Mexican lovely would not stay static. She went to pieces like fog. In her place I had the other dreams.

One was of Florida wandering about. She was a cross between a zombie and a ghost. I was always walking along a highway, a road, or in the woods, and I'd see her up ahead, not looking at me, just crossing in front of me, wearing one of her short dresses with high heels, going into the cover of the trees, and I'd run after her. Only when I got to where she had gone into the woods she wasn't there, and I couldn't find her.

I dreamed too of the marsh that night, and of Draighten screaming and his leg all gone to pieces. I found out a short time later he had died before the emergency crew made it. Bled to death. He deserved what he got, but I couldn't get him out of my mind. Somewhere he had people who loved him and he'd loved them back and he'd had plans and thoughts just like everyone else. Meaner thoughts, but thoughts.

Had Leonard not shot him, I'd have been the one six feet down in the ground and Draighten would be lying in bed, maybe watching a little wrestling on television or pulling his pud. It was something strange to consider.

The part about him being alive and wanting to watch wrestling. Not the part about him pulling his pud. I tried not to think about that; it was too horrible to visualize.

I was thinking about pulling my pud, when the rain picked up and I began to feel cold, even under my blankets. I got out of bed, pulled a robe over my naked self, picked up the .38 revolver from the nightstand where I kept it all the time now, and made for the bathroom.

I brushed my teeth, looked at the wound the shotgun pellet had given my cheek. It wasn't much. It was healing nicely, but it looked as if it would leave a small puckered scar. The doctor had put medicine on it and a Band-Aid, and I'd been doctoring it at home, but I had begun to suspect a stitch had been needed.

Then again, wasn't like it was going to ruin my native good looks. If I'd had any, that crowd at the Grovetown Cafe had rearranged them. I did look better than a week ago, though. Both eyes seemed to be lined up—sort of—and the bruises had changed from the color of eggplant to a sort of raw spinach green.

I picked the gun off the sink, toted it with me around the house while I lit the butane heaters, then fixed myself a little breakfast of cereal and coffee and sat at the kitchen table with my friend the .38 snub-nose revolver and stared out the window at the rain coming down. My yard looked a lot like Bacon's yard, without the refrigerator and the washer. There was a dead squirrel out there, though, and I'd been thinking about moving it. Another week or two, however, I figured it'd be pretty much dissolved. I thought I could hold out.

My days had been like this for two weeks. A little coffee and cereal in the morning, the dead squirrel watch, worrying about how I was going to pay my hospital bills, then a morning movie if I could find one worth watching. All this hinged, of course, on how often I was asked to come in and see the cops. They insisted I drop by for talks.

They held meetings in LaBorde, since it was the county seat, and the law was a Texas Ranger and some detectives from somewhere, and then Charlie, who was kind of a moderator. I even saw Cantuck a few times, going out as I came in, a big swathe of gauze over his eye, always wearing a cheap black suit that offered plenty of room for his balls. He'd smile and say, "Hap," but keep right on walking. I even saw Jackson Brown once. He was dressed in a bright blue suit, a white cowboy hat with a beaded band, and shiny black cowboy boots. We passed right by each other. He was walking with a thin, attractive woman with tall blond hair and an empty look to her eyes. He smiled at me as he passed, said, "Tell the nigger Jackson says hey."

It was tempting to see if I could turn his head completely around on his neck, but I didn't. I just walked on.

The cops liked to talk. They liked for me to talk. They loved hearing my story. Separately, they talked to Leonard too. They liked his story. We told it so much, I thought maybe we ought to work out a dance routine, so if we ever told it together, maybe we could do a few steps in concert.

But for now the cops seemed through with me. I had gone a few days without seeing their smiling faces, and I wanted it to stay that way. Without them, I could maintain my mind-numbing routine.

After the movie every morning there was lunch, usually a sandwich, or more cereal and coffee, then I'd go out on the front porch bundled up in a coat with my revolver and sit in my glider and listen to the rain until the cold got too much. Then it was back inside where I'd strip off and get under the covers again, and with my revolver on the nightstand, I'd crack open the book I was currently reading.

As I sat that morning with breakfast, I kept thinking in time I wouldn't feel the need to carry the gun with me everywhere I went, to sleep with it nearby, feeling greater comfort in it than I might a woman. But that beating I had taken with Leonard, and that night at the marsh with the Kluxers, had changed me and I wasn't sure there was any going back. I wasn't sure I could be Hap Collins the way Hap Collins used to be. I was still him, but I wasn't him, and I didn't know who I was or who else to be.

I thought about giving Leonard a call, but feared Raul would answer the phone. I'd heard he'd come back, and for some reason I didn't like the little sonofabitch anymore, though I wasn't sure I'd liked him in the first place. Fact was, all told, I had spent little more than an hour with him, so my opinion was bullshit anyway.

I was jealous. I had been Leonard's friend longer than Raul had been his lover, and when they split up and Leonard and I got together again and went to Grovetown, even with all that had happened, at least we'd had each other, and it was like old times. There had been that special warmth between us, that understanding, that lack of explaining, and now Raul was back and I had a robe to wear, a gun to tote, and my dick to jerk. I wished with all the blackness of my heart right then that Raul was forcing Leonard to watch the *Gilligan's Island* reunion episode, which I understood he'd finally acquired. I wondered whose dick he'd sucked to get it.

Goddamn, Hap, don't think like that. That's homophobic. That's evil. Just not nice.

No, hell, it isn't any of those things but the last. It's not nice. You're just mad so you're thinking mean and you better not keep thinking that way or you will be mean.

Why in hell had Raul come back anyway? I asked myself, and self answered: Because he heard Leonard was hurt and needed him, and he came back and things were all right now in their relationship. They were close again, and that was good.

Sure. Sure it was. It was good. Liver was good, if you closed your eyes and rinsed your mouth and ate ice cream afterwards.

Shit, don't think like that, Hap. You're being an asshole. Leonard's got his right to happiness, even if his boyfriend is as shallow as a saucer and likes *Gilligan's Island*. Who are you to stand in the way of Leonard's love life? Friendship isn't about that. It's about being happy your friend is happy. That's the true nature of friendship.

I sat and wondered if I could think of any more folksy homilies, but nothing came to me.

Me and my gun got us a cup of coffee and went into the living room and turned on the television and surfed the channels until we found an Audie Murphy Western.

The movie was coming to the end when I heard a car, got hold of the gun and took a timid peek out the window.

It was Charlie driving up. He got out, wearing a beige belted raincoat and a porkpie hat with a plastic cover on it. He was holding a black umbrella over his head, tiptoeing toward my door through puddles of water like a schoolgirl trying not to get her stockings wet.

I cut the television, stuffed the gun beneath a couch cushion, hoped Charlie would have good news about Hanson. Hell, good news about anything.

25

I opened the door before he was on the porch. He smiled at me, closed the umbrella, leaned it against the porch wall and shook hands with me. "I see the squirrel's still hanging around."

"Yeah," I said. "He likes it here. I call him Bob. He calls me Mr. Collins."

Charlie took off his hat, removed the cover and draped it over the handle of the umbrella. He put his hat back on, took off the raincoat and stretched it over my glider. All of this was done very slow and precise.

When he came inside he tossed his hat on the couch, took off his cheap sports coat, hung it over the back of a chair, sat down beside his hat and smiled in that pleasant manner he has, loosened his threadbare tie, crossed his legs, wiggled a Kmart shoe.

"Are those shoes real plastic, Charlie?"

"You betcha. I don't stand for imitations."

"And that hat, isn't that like Mike Hammer wears?"

"I certainly hope so."

"Want some coffee?"

"You betcha."

I fixed us both a cup, sat back in my chair and stretched my feet out.

"Christ, Hap," Charlie said. "Put on some drawers, or cross your legs different. I don't want to look at your balls."

"That's not why you came out?"

"Come on, man."

I went and pulled on some faded jeans, but kept the robe on. I came back, recovered my coffee. Charlie was in the kitchen, pouring himself another cup. He went through the cabinets and found the bag of vanilla cookies I keep on hand for Leonard. He opened them, brought them into the living room, put the bag on the couch next to his hat and began eating the cookies.

"Want one?" he asked.

"Only if you're sure you don't mind."

"Not at all."

He held the bag out and I took one, dunked it in my coffee and ate it. Charlie said, "Nobody eats these with as much pleasure as Leonard."

"You're right."

"I like to watch him eat them," Charlie said. "He gets that look that cartoon dog used to get when he was given a dog biscuit. You know, the one hugged himself and floated up and then floated down, he was so happy. What was that fuckin' dog on? *Quickdraw McGraw?*"

"I think so," I said. "How's Hanson, Charlie?"

"Same."

"I think I'll go by and see him."

"Go by, or don't. He won't know one way or another. You come in there butt-naked with a feather up your ass, or dressed in your Sunday Go to Meetin's, it's all the same to him."

"What do the doctors say now?"

"Not much more than before, only they're less optimistic."

"I didn't know they were ever optimistic."

"You hear them now, you'll think before they were goddamn foolish with optimism."

"Shit."

"Yeah. Shit. Another week, they think he can go home. Might as well, he can hold down a bed there good as he can at the hospital. They'll send some tubes and pee-bags with him when he goes. Maybe, on good days, he can be used for a doorstop. Just roll him up to the door to hold it open."

"Who'll take care of him?"

"He's going home to Rachel."

"His ex-wife?"

"Yeah. Go figure. It was her idea. She and her daughter are gonna take care of him."

"I thought Rachel had a boyfriend or something."

Charlie made a patting motion at his shirt pocket, like he was looking for cigarettes, didn't find any, put his hand back in the vanilla cookie bag and pulled out a wafer. He waved it at me, said, "Did. And the boyfriend wasn't keen on the idea, but she sent him packing. Believe that? Hanson and Rachel. They haven't lived together since I don't know when, and now she's gonna take him home and empty his pee and make sure he's got gruel in his food tubes, washrag his balls and wipe his ass. I don't get it."

"Me neither. Must be the daughter's influence."

"Maybe so. Tell you something else, Kmart is all but gone. Another week, won't be nothing there but an empty building and the parking lot."

"So, that's why you came. You want to hold a little memorial service or something?"

"What I come to say is you and Leonard are in pretty good shape."

"We going to court?"

"Only to testify against folks. I don't think you'll get much backlash. It'd just make those fuckers look stupid. Ray Pierce, one you call Bear, he finally broke down and named Kevin Reiley as the other Klan man, which is of course who Cantuck said it was all the time. You know, I don't think that Cantuck is such a bad guy, you get to know him."

"Good. What about Brown? Pierce name him?"

"No. There was enough business there for us to bring him in for questioning, but we didn't nail him. And I wanted to, believe me. He's a smug sonofabitch. White trash with money and a business degree. They're like roaches, guys like that. They're hard to get rid of, hard to kill . . . oh, and Pierce didn't name that officer—"

"Reynolds."

"—yeah, him. He didn't name him either. He claims they did it on their own. One of them supposedly saw your car go by when you took the Grovetown turnoff toward LaBorde. He told the others, they got their sheets and came after you."

"So, there's nothing to prove anybody else had anything to do with what happened?"

"That's right."

"I don't believe it. I got a feeling that whole nest of Klan assholes knew where we'd be, and not by seeing us go in that direction. I think Brown was involved, and those boys aren't talking 'cause he's paying them not to talk, and maybe he's giving them a little something to worry about besides jail. Like what might happen to their families."

"There's nothing to prove you were set up, is what I'm saying. But the Klan not only found you and Leonard, they found that black fella helped y'all out. He got his the next night."

"Oh no, Bacon? I hadn't heard."

"I didn't think you needed to before. You were dealing with enough. Handful of Klan members went out to his house and jumped him. Tarred and feathered him, locked him in his car trunk, drove him down to the river bottoms, tossed the keys and left him there. He'd have died of exposure if the trunk had been any good, but it wasn't and he was able to kick it loose, hot-wire the car and get out of there. They say he was hurt pretty bad. He was in a hospital over in Longview couple days."

"Ah, hell. He was scared to death they were going to catch up with him on account of us, and they did. How'd the Klan find out?"

Charlie shrugged. "Maybe Cantuck can tell you, or the Ranger on the case. I don't know they know. Can't say. Damn, I wish I had a cigarette. I think about smoking now and then, you know, sneaking one, but my wife, she smells it on me. I don't care I do it outside in a high wind, little gets on my jacket, in my hair. She smells it."

"And no pussy."

"Yeah. I been thinking about striking up a relationship with the cat. Is that some kind of incest or something?"

"Bestiality."

"Well, I tell you, I'm tired of whackin' off. Funny thing is, you know you're not gonna get any, it's all you think about. Pussy. Pussy. Pussy. When I used to get it now and then, not knowing when, but figurin' I would, I didn't whack off near as much. You whack off a lot?"

"Just once or twice a day. Would you like to know about my bowel movements?"

"Naw, I was just interested if you whack off. Some of the guys at the station, they think it's odd if you whack off. They all say they quit that shit when they were fifteen, or when they started gettin' pussy."

"Everybody whacks off. I don't care what they say, they whack off. Maybe if they're poking someone every night they don't, but when they're not, they whack off. But on a less serious note, about me and Leonard not going to court. You sure? We're okay?"

"Looks like it. I can't guarantee anything. Not really. But Cantuck spoke for you again, said you and Leonard didn't have any choice but to do what you did, tells how you saved him, drove the car through a storm, all that shit. You know the story. Same one he's been telling. You'll talk some more to the law, but I figure you're all right."

"That's good. How's Cantuck?"

"Well, his eye didn't grow back. He's still blind, and he's got a patch. He looks like a pirate turned pig farmer turned small-town cop. He's taking it well enough, I guess. Oh, you or Leonard will have to pay a little fine for having those guns you used. Hidden weapons. I talked to the Highway boys. They agreed to let the rest of the guns in Leonard's trunk get lost so it wouldn't look like you were loaded up and spoiling for a fight. That damn near caused you trouble, all them guns, but Cantuck stood up for you again. He can talk a pretty good line of shit, he wants to. Even if he does refer to Leonard as 'a good nigra.'"

"That's high praise from Cantuck," I said. "Will Leonard get his guns back?"

"Don't try to skin your rabbit and keep it as a pet too, Hap. They agreed to lose 'em, not oil 'em and give 'em back to you with ammunition. Be glad you're not paying big fines and doing a little time. This is serious shit, killing a fella."

"Leonard didn't mean for Draighten to die. He had, he'd have shot his head off from the start. It's not that he gave a shit, frankly, but he didn't kill him outright 'cause he didn't want to hurt my feelings. In the long run, it was self-defense, plain and simple."

"That's why you're not doing time, you and him. This is Texas, after all. And you did save an officer of the law from being killed, and you got him to safety and a doctor. Shit, Hap, you and Leonard, you're goddamn heroes."

"I'm so glad."

"I finish up here, I'm going to drive over and tell Leonard how things are."

"You could call him from here."

"Yeah, but it's an excuse to see him. And I thought you might want to go."

"I don't know."

"You and his boyfriend don't get along, do you?"

"I think it's me that doesn't get along."

"It was that way with me and Florida. I liked her, but the moment she and Hanson got together, well, things weren't so good between me and Marve. She had a way of looking at him out of the corner of her eye, making him nervous. I tried real hard not to say shit or fuck or talk about my wife not giving me pussy when I was around her, but I don't think I could ever do right."

"Some women are just born spoilsports."

"Hell, I don't know. Marve might feel . . . might have felt that way about my wife and just didn't say nothin'. Hard to say. Relationships are funny stuff. I tell you though, I took a peek up Florida's dress a few times. Couldn't help myself. She was something else."

"I think maybe it was your cultured manners got on her nerves, Charlie. She just hadn't been around so much class before."

"There you go. You got any cigarettes? Cigars? Pipe? I might even chew, you got some Beech-Nut or somethin'."

"Nope. I gave my pipe up. Now I do a cigar couple times a year. This isn't one of those times, so I don't have any. Besides, you don't need it. You're doing good. You smoke, you won't get any from the wife."

"Yeah, okay."

"Do a few shadow figures, keep your mind occupied."

"I do shadows pretty good now, but I've had to quit for a while. I got strained fingers."

"Get out of here."

"No, really. Kind of a carpal tunnel thing from twistin' my hands and fingers around."

I finished off my coffee, asked what I had to ask. "Since we were speaking of Florida in the past tense . . ."

"I guess I shouldn't talk that way about her. About looking up her dress and all, not getting along with her. I know how you feel about her, Hap. And she was Hanson's lady and all. I shouldn't talk like that."

"She was here right now, I'd try to look up her dress too. She wore dresses designed for that, and I think she knew it. She'd never admit it, but she knew it."

Charlie nodded. "We don't know anything we didn't know before. Ranger went in there, checked around some, and knows what we know. She was there, then wasn't. Evidence is thin."

"What about the juke joints? No one had anything to say there?"

"Sure, they did. We think of some things, Hap. You see, we do this for a living."

"I didn't mean to offend you."

"I've kept up with this case, even though it isn't mine. Know what I'm sayin'?"

"Sure."

"Florida went in there, tried to see this Soothe as some kind of martyr, and what he was was an asshole. No one disagrees on that. His own folks didn't have nothing to do with him. Everybody was glad he got dead and wasn't nothing more to worry about. Those recordings, the songs written down. That was just his line of shit. No one believes there were any recordings, written songs. None of that stuff. So no one much cared what happened to the guy. Except Florida. And I figure her trying to find out about what happened to Soothe, she maybe put her nose where it didn't belong, and got it pinched. But good. Same stuff you and Leonard think. Nothing new."

"Well, someone cared about Soothe. Or was worried about him. His body was stolen."

"Ranger, Highway boys, think it was voodoo shit."

"Voodoo is primarily charm stuff, mixed with a little Christianity. East Texas cops love to think devil worshippers or movie-style voodoo business is going on in the backwoods. It makes them feel their job is a little more important, less boring if they're dealing with El Diablo."

"Yeah, I see that. I could use a little voodoo now and then. This old-fashioned crime, drugs, spouse abuse, good ole boy murders are wearing me out. As for Soothe, all I know is the body's gone and there's no evidence where it might be. Florida, she was sure this Cantuck had Soothe murdered. A racist thing. I don't think that stands up so good. I think Cantuck done that, he wouldn't have been trying to keep you from getting killed. This Officer Reynolds, I don't know nothin' about him."

"He's some piece of work is what he is, but I can't prove he did anything. He might not be any worse than Cantuck, who seems to be all right on some days. I sort of like it better like the old movies, where you could tell who the villain was because they wore black and twirled their mustache. What's never been explained to me, Charlie, is how Cantuck knew me and Leonard were in trouble."

"Instinct."

"Saying he had a hot flash sheet-heads were trying to kill us, so he saddled up Trigger and came after us?"

"Way he tells it, he packed you up, sent you on your way, got to feeling guilty 'cause the two of you weren't in that good a shape, decided he ought to make you park Leonard's junker and take you into LaBorde. So, he went to catch up with you. I believe him. I think he's a fart on the surface, but underneath he smells a little better, just sometimes he's got to settle down long enough for the sweetness to surface."

"So right in the middle of a rerun of *The Beverly Hillbillies* he decided he was an asshole and ought to come out and check on us?"

"He never got home. Drove to the office, got to thinking about it from there, came after you."

"And in the meantime, Big Butt Draighten and his buddies just happened to spot us and come after us?"

"Yeah."

"Kind of coincidental, isn't it?"

"Life's full of 'em, but I don't see this as coincidence. Those shitters saw you, followed you out, and Cantuck, not being a bad guy, got to feeling like a turd, came to check on you. Everything comes together. It's not that wild."

"What about Bacon?"

"Like I said, I don't know. But them finding out Bacon helped you might not be that hard. People see things, people talk."

Charlie went into the kitchen to fill his coffee cup. He stood at the counter and drank it. I went in there and sat at the kitchen table with my empty cup. He got the coffee pot and poured me what was left.

"Going with me to Leonard's?" he asked.

"Not this time," I said. "I'll call him later. Maybe I'll drive over there."

"Sure. You know, he's healing up fast. Moving around pretty good. 'Cept for his leg. You should go by and see him."

"I will."

Charlie sipped the last of his coffee, put the cup in the sink, said, "Sometimes, under stress, guys close as skin and bone can feel a kind of, I don't know, postpartum-style depression."

"Neither Leonard nor I have recently given birth, Charlie."

"Postpartum Scary Event Syndrome."

"What?"

"I just made that up. Say something bad happens to a couple guys and they survive it, and these guys are real close, and danger makes them even closer. Am I goin' too fast?"

"I think I can manage, if I concentrate real hard."

"This scary business is over, these two guys, they kind of divorce each other, find reasons not to be together, blame each other, outside sources, 'cause when the two them get together, they connect with a bad memory."

"You trying to say something about me and Leonard, Charlie?"

"I'm sayin' maybe you and Leonard have seen something in each other or yourselves you didn't know was there. It's like them movie star marriages."

"Now there's a jump."

"Woman marries some guy wants to be an actor, big star. She knows him when he's down and out, crying at night 'cause he can't make it in the industry, or maybe he can't get a hard-on he's so depressed. She knows he cuts big ones in the toilet and fills their little two-room apartment with shit stink, and they can't even afford the goddamn matches that need to be struck to burn out the smell.

Then, this guy, who wipes his butt just like everyone else, he hits the big time. Feels he's got to get rid of the old wife on account of she knew him when he wasn't quite so glamorous. Now he's got the big house and a shitter in a room about the size of the old apartment, got some blowers, destinkers, whatever that stuff is, and he's able to separate himself from some of the human problems. Stays hard all the time 'cause he's got nothing but big-tittied young blondes coming in and out of his bed trying to see who best can grease his sausage. Everyone tells him he's wonderful, a goddamn god. So he don't want someone around who's seen him at his worst, his most human, knows what he knows—that he ain't no god. He's just a regular guy and no better than anyone else."

"I've known Leonard for years, and I know his shit stinks. I've been with him through thick and thin and neither one of us has hit the big time, so we don't have to worry about that angle. I'm just worn down, that's all. I don't feel like visiting. Fact is, I'm sort of waiting on you to leave."

"Sure you haven't got some kind of tobacco?"

"I'm sure."

Charlie nodded, scratched his temple, looked at some dandruff under his fingernail, wiped it on his pants and leaned against the sink. "Let me see now," he said. "I had some kind of point. Oh yeah. Thing is, instead of the big time, two of you thought you were invincible."

"I never said that I was invincible."

"No, but you thought it. Leonard did anyway, and I think you thought he was invincible on some level. Could take anything and come out on top. And when the two of you are together, well, you're like the biggest dogs in the junkyard. But you ain't. You're just two dogs and there's always someone bigger, smarter, and meaner."

"I owe you for this session?"

"First session's free. Maybe you've seen little shadows, chinks in your and Leonard's armor, and you don't like it. It's nothing to be ashamed of. No one is anything better than human. Just some humans are better humans than others, but the best humans are still just human. In the end, we all end up like that squirrel out there."

"Save it for the Rotary, man."

"Sometimes you got to look shadows in the eye, or see if they've got eyes. You don't, they flutter around you from then on."

"You're hittin' all over the place, and isn't any of it on target."

"Keep a gun around at night, Hap? I don't mean in the house, I mean close by. You do that, man? Something you're constantly aware of, this gun?"

"Hell no. Why would I?"

"It's just I saw one stuffed under the couch cushion. You got to not get in such a hurry, you hide somethin', Hap. Got to take your time and do it right."

"You don't know everything, Charlie."

"Yeah, you're right, I'm an asshole. I know this though, you throw a shovelful of dirt over that squirrel, when the rain stops and the wind's blowin', he won't stink so much."

There was a sudden hard wave of rain. It washed over the house in a torrent, sounded goddamn spooky. Charlie looked at the ceiling, as if he might actually see the rain pounding the roof, said, "God, it keeps coming and no end in sight. Think this rain'll ever stop?"

I shook my head. "No, Charlie. I don't."

26

I didn't call Leonard after Charlie left. I didn't call him all that day, and didn't call him the next either. I sat with my gun and went through my routine. I thought about what Charlie had said and got real mad, then realized he was closer to the truth than I wanted to believe.

It wasn't Raul that was between me and Leonard, it was us. We had not only recognized that we were not invincible, we had experienced real fear, and we each knew the other was frightened. It wasn't the first time. We've always been honest about being scared, but this time it was beyond fear in the normal way. It was helplessness. Not being anywhere near in control.

Goddamn Charlie and his Kmart shoes and his shadow fingers and his wife who wouldn't give him pussy. Goddamn everything about that sonofabitch.

Four mornings after Charlie came to visit, I went into the kitchen, purposely without my gun, took the phone off the wall, sat down at the table with it and dialed Leonard's number.

Raul answered. I asked for Leonard.

"Hap," Leonard said when he came on the line. "Good to hear from you, man."

"Have you been as fucked up as me?"

"I don't know how fucked up you've been, but I've been fucked up. Come over for lunch."

"I been wanting to see you, but . . . I haven't been . . . you know?"

"Yeah. Come over."

I heard Raul say in the background, "We got plans, Lenny. Remember?"

"Come on over," Leonard said.

★

Eleven that morning, the rain still coming down, the sky atwist with savage storm, I got all the money I had in the cookie jar—about fifty dollars—and left out of there with my revolver stuffed in the glove box of my truck. I drove to town and the hospital, went in without my revolver, found where Hanson was. I rode the elevator up, pushed open the door to his room.

It smelled bad in there. That creepy hospital smell that's somewhere between disinfectant, illness, and that funky food they serve. The two days I had been in had been bad enough, but poor Hanson. Jesus.

Hanson was hooked up like a spaceman, bristling with tubes and wires. His bed was cranked up slightly toward a television that was going, and on the other side of the bed, sitting in a chair, was a young black woman. She was lean and attractive, looked to be in her late twenties. I assumed she was his daughter, JoAnna. She lifted her head, gave a little smile.

"Hello," she said. Her voice was soft, but it had a little gravel in it. I didn't know if that was the nature of her voice, or the nature of her mood. I went on in and introduced myself. She half stood, reached across the bed, shook my hand and gave her name and relation. She was, as I thought, JoAnna.

Hanson had his eyes closed and was breathing heavily. He didn't know I was there, or that the TV was going, or that ducks quacked and dogs barked. His head was bandaged thickly and he'd lost a lot of weight and looked easily twenty years older. Had I not known it was Hanson, I wouldn't have recognized him.

"How is he?" I asked. It was stupid, but I just didn't know anything else to say.

"Not good. We're taking him home though."

"That ought to help."

"Yeah."

"I was here . . . this way, I'd want to go home."

"Yeah."

"He leaving soon?"

"Tomorrow. If the doctor says okay. They can't do anything for him here. I think they want him out, make room for another patient. I guess they're right. He's not going to get better, someone else might."

"Well, you never know. Some people, they get in a bad way like this, they come out of it. He's tough. He could do it."

"Yeah. I guess."

I looked at the television. It was a *Gunsmoke* rerun. An old one, when Dennis Weaver played Chester. I kept looking at it, 'cause I couldn't look at Hanson, and JoAnna's face, so sad, so brave, made me ache. Not just for Hanson, but for myself, Leonard, everybody.

"You live in LaBorde?" I asked.

"Tyler."

"What do you do there?"

"Teach school."

"Yeah, well, you take care."

"Sure. Thanks for coming in, Mr. Collins."

I looked at the television. "I've seen this one."

"Yeah. I never watched Westerns. Daddy loved them."

"Yeah, well, me too. You take care, now."

"I will."

"You need anything I can help with, you tell Charlie and he'll get in touch with me. Hap Collins."

"Yes sir."

"Just Hap."

"Okay, Hap."

"Bye."

"Bye."

Yeah, call ole Hap, he was sure a helper, a big fixer. I went out of there and along the hall and the smell of the hospital was stronger than ever.

I drove over to Leonard's. The crack house had not been replaced. It was just a black spot splattered by rain.

I knocked on the door and Leonard answered. He was wearing a heavy coat and his face was puffy and marked with bruises and some stitches the vet should have put in but wouldn't, but the LaBorde doctor had.

He looked better though. He walked pretty well. He said, "You ole bastard," and threw open the screen and we hugged. We hugged hard and long, patting each other on the back.

"I've missed you," he said.

"Man, I feel like a fruit, hugging a fruit."

Leonard laughed. "Come in, buddy."

I came in. Raul looked at me, tried to smile, but he wasn't glad to see me. He was also wearing a coat, which surprised me. The house was warm. Leonard didn't pay Raul any mind. He said, "I'm cooking out back, come on."

"In the rain?"

"Nope. Come on. Leave your coat on."

Leonard limped a little as he went. I followed through the kitchen, onto the back porch, or where it used to be. There was a big screened-in porch now with a concrete floor. The rain was blasting on the roof and some of it was blowing through the screen. It was cold out there. In the middle of the porch was a cooker and it was smoking with hamburgers and hot dogs.

"This is nice," I said. "I didn't know this was here."

"I started it before we went to Grovetown, before all this goddamn rain started. You spent the night here, I meant to show it to you. But my mind wasn't on it and you didn't go out the back way, so it never got mentioned. What do you think? Needs some touches yet, but I like it. It'll be nice in the summer. Wire's thick enough to keep the big bugs out. Skeeters'll get in though. They can get through anything."

"That's the truth. What about the two guys with the bowling ball heads?"

"Clinton and Leon. Guess they're all right. They were here while I was in the hospital. Those fellas are all right, provided you don't have to spend more than thirty minutes at a stretch with them."

"So no trouble while you were gone."

"Leon sat on the commode and it fell through the floor with him. I talked to him on the phone at the hospital. He and Clinton got some lumber and fixed the flooring. It was old and rotten under there. Only complaint Leon had was that when he fell through the commode overturned and he got shit on him."

Raul came out. He had his hands in his pockets and looked cold. He said, "I told Leonard this wasn't cookout weather, even on the porch, but he wouldn't listen. You don't listen to me, do you, Lenny?"

"Nope," Leonard said, and smiled.

"He doesn't listen to anybody but you, Hap. He listens to you."

"Raul," Leonard warned.

"Oh yeah, I don't want to embarrass you in front of Hap. Anybody but him."

"Let's don't start," Leonard said.

Raul turned and went back inside.

I said, "I shouldn't have come."

"Yeah, you should. Here, help me carry this stuff in."

We ate in the kitchen. Raul joined us, but he wasn't exactly talky. When Leonard paused to go to the facilities, I said, "Raul, I didn't mean to cause trouble."

"I know," he said. "It's not you. It's me and him. It's lots of things."

Leonard came back. He said to me: "I think I know why you came, Hap."

"I missed you."

"Besides that. We're going back to Grovetown, aren't we?"

"I've got to. I can't keep doing like I'm doing. I'm sleeping with a goddamn revolver, Leonard. You know me. Does that sound like me?"

"I sleep with a shotgun nearby."

"But that sounds like you."

Leonard studied my face for a moment, said, "I cry at night. I just break down crying. Does that sound like me?"

"Are vanilla cookies involved?" I said. "I can see you crying over cookies. By the way, Charlie ate the ones I keep at the house for you."

"That shit," Leonard said. "He was over here the other day, and I thought I smelled vanilla cookies on his breath. He said he'd just come from your place."

A little time floated by. Leonard said, "I get these dreams too. Mostly about that crowd of people, kickin' and hittin' on me."

"Me too," I said. "And some others."

"I wake up, I think I'm still there," Leonard said.

"I tell him to let it go," Raul said. "But he won't. I know he can't forget what happened, but he won't let go that he's done something wrong. I don't get it."

"I don't think I've done anything wrong," Leonard said. "I just don't like feeling like I'm feeling. It's like my guts have been ripped out. What's wrong is I can't just let it lay."

"It's over with," Raul said. "You did all you could. You've got this tough-guy image. It's out of date. We fags, we don't have to do that. It's not in our makeup."

"What's in my makeup is in my makeup," Leonard said. "I'm a man. I got balls. So do you. I like balls. I like your balls, but I'm still a man and I got to feel like a man. Maybe I'm some kind of anomaly or something. I don't know. I don't get it. But I like a man acts like a man without thinking it's being a bully. I can't explain it to him, Hap. Can you?"

"You know I can't," I said.

"Saying I'm too stupid to understand?" Raul said.

"No," I said. "It's just a way of living your life, and I personally don't know it's better than any other, it's just all we know."

"I don't get it," Raul said. "Why all this macho?"

"When I say act like a man," Leonard said, "I mean act honorably and with courage. Macho has been turned into a bad word by turds who act like beasts, not men."

"You acted with honor and courage," Raul said. "Look where it got you. There's nothing left for you to do. You're not cops. Or heroes. You're just a couple of fellas, and Lenny, you're my fella. I want to know you're here so I can hold you nights. Is that so wrong?"

"No," Leonard said. "But I got to go back. I turn my head now, every time someone looks tough or calls me nigger, or queer, I'm gonna turn my head. Get so I'll turn my head if I think a mechanic's bill's too high. I ain't no worm."

"I don't get it," Raul said. "Really, I don't."

"I know," Leonard said. "Sometimes, I think it's just me and Hap gets it. Maybe Charlie. And Hanson. Bless him."

"I want to go tomorrow," I said. "I don't want to plan way ahead. I want to do it quick."

"I'll be ready," Leonard said.

"We have plans for tomorrow," Raul said. He looked at me. "We had plans today."

"I'm sorry," I said.

"Don't say you're sorry, Hap," Leonard said. "Listen here, Raul. I'll make it up to you. But plans to go and do something, and me and Hap doing this, it's different. It's important. It's not just made-up shit."

"That's nice," Raul said.

"You know what I mean," Leonard said.

"No, I don't," Raul said.

"Yeah," Leonard said. "Guess you don't. Hap, come by and get me tomorrow morning."

"You go, and I'll leave for good," Raul said. "You got to decide if this stupid honor of yours—and him—are more important than me."

"It's got nothing to do with what's the most important," Leonard said.

"You go, I'll go, and this time I won't come back. I don't care they hurt you real bad, I won't come back. They kill you, I won't be there to see you buried. You go, I'm gone."

Leonard turned and studied Raul. I hated it when Leonard looked that way. It was damn scary, and considering the look was intensified by swelling, bruises, and stitches, well, I just didn't like it.

"All right," Leonard said. "I've known you for a short time, Raul. I like you. I like fuckin' you. I hate your taste in movies, TV, and books. You got good taste in men, and that's it. I might even love you, but I know I love Hap, and me and him ain't even fuckin', and if that isn't real love, I don't know what is."

"Very poetic," Raul said.

"I been living with who I am and what I believe longer than I've lived with you, much longer than you've ever given thought to who you are. You might be somebody deep down—"

"Leonard," I said.

"Shut up, Hap. You might be somebody deep down, Raul, but all you want to see in yourself and me and anyone else is surface. Me and Hap, we got history and we got connection. You can make of that what you want. And let me tell you somethin'. You hit the door this time, you damn well better not come back. I get killed, I wouldn't want you at my funeral. You're there, I'd want Hap to throw you out."

"He'll be dead too," Raul said. "You'll both be dead."

Raul got up and left the room. It was awfully quiet for about twenty seconds. Eventually, we could hear Raul moving about in the other room.

"What's that noise?" I asked.

"The ironing board. He gets upset, he sets it up, irons clothes."

We sat for another twenty seconds or so. The clock in the kitchen ticked loudly. The ironing board squeaked louder and louder. Leonard said, "Think maybe we could have a double funeral, and Charlie could throw him out?"

"Sorry, man. I think he'll get over it."

"He will or he won't, but you don't be sorry, Hap."

I got up. I pulled on my coat. "This is going to sound funny, Leonard. But is everything okay between us?"

"It always has been."

"I'll see you tomorrow."

"Bright and early," Leonard said.

27

Next morning, on the way to Leonard's, I tried to remember the first time I'd seen Florida, tried to figure if I was still in love with her, or just had my feelings hurt because she chose Hanson over me. Had I lost a love or a battle? Both?

Was I searching for her by going back to Grovetown, or searching for something of myself? Both?

I just loved it when I got all Zen and shit.

I pulled up in Leonard's drive, got out in the rain and went to the door. He opened it before I could knock. He had a twelve-gauge shotgun with him, a backpack and a sleeping bag bound up in a waterproof wrapper.

"Good to see you still got a bazooka left," I said.

"I got another one in the house, and a handgun in my coat pocket, you want it."

"I brought my snub-nose. I don't like that I brought it, but I did. I get away from it too long these days, it's like I left my dick in the other room."

"You see, your manhood is tied up in your weapons, Hap. The revolver is a phallic symbol for your repressed manhood. Your impotence."

"For the first time in my life, I believe that."

We loaded his stuff in the back of the pickup. I had my stuff there too and had fixed a tarp over it to keep out the rain. By the time we had Leonard's stuff under there, we were both soaked.

Leonard slid his shotgun into the gun rack above the seat; a baseball bat already resided in the top slot. It was a bat I'd taken off a thug once who thought he was going to break my knees, but he forgot to quit talking before he started hitting, so I'd taken it away from him, broken his nose, and kept the bat. I usually kept it in the house, but I was glad to have it now. It made me feel slightly more comfortable. Leonard's shotgun added to the comfort, as did the snub-nose in the glove box and the truck's heater.

I backed out and we started up the street. I said, "Raul all right?"

"Well, we didn't sing 'The Sound of Music' together in the shower this morning, so I don't think we're all that rosy. We've really done that, you know?"

"Showered together?"

"That and sang 'The Sound of Music.' We do it quite well, actually."

"Raul still leaving?"

"I don't know. I don't want him to. I told him if he did, to call the bowling ball head brothers to watch the place. Hell, I can't figure Raul. He's all mopey and shit. Today is the anniversary of when we met, and he wanted us to go out to dinner, go to a movie, do some serious fucking. I wanted us to do that too, but I didn't want it getting in the way of me killing somebody."

"Easy, now."

"I'm gonna do what I gotta do."

"I'm not sure we got to do that."

"Let me say this, Hap, then I'll shut up. I meant what I said yesterday. We got to do this thing because of who we are, or who we want to keep being. Whatever degree it takes, we got to go to that degree. You believe that?"

"I'm not going to kill anyone. On purpose. I'm going to find out about Florida, and if I can hook Brown up with that, and what happened to us, that'll make me extra happy."

"I don't think we can undo a beating, Hap. But I got to go back there and face that town. Find Florida. Someone gets in the way of either, I might have to put a hole in them. And by the way, I packed us a nice sack lunch for later. It's in my pack."

"Bullets and lunch," I said. "You think of everything."

"Bottom line is this, Bubba. It's you and me. Anything and everything else fucks up, it's you and me. We're gonna see each other through this, do what we got to do if the sun comes up or don't. And that's the long and the short of it."

"That's the truth," I said.

"Still," he said, "I hope Raul don't leave."

I don't remember much about the drive that morning, just the rain and the scenery being a blurry yellow line in front of my face, a few twists of dried forests, glimpses of swollen creeks and ponds. We drove by where we had gone off in the marsh, and the both of us looked, our heads turning in that direction at the same time. The marsh had expanded. The water was coming over the highway and the woods were swollen with it.

Leonard said, "They pulled my car out of there."

"I know."

"Guess what?"

"It won't run."

"The insurance ain't given me but two hundred dollars for it. Guess they think I can stick that up my ass and drive around on it."

"Personally, I don't think it's much of a loss. It was about one notch above a ten-speed, and that's because it had a roof on it."

A few more miles down the road we started kicking around game plans for what we were going to do when we got to Grovetown, but the plans didn't amount to anything. It consisted primarily of eating the sack lunch Leonard had brought.

Leonard and I were about as far from sleuths as you could get. We didn't know much besides instinct, and so far that had gotten our asses whipped, got us half drowned, shot at, in trouble with the law, and Leonard had screwed up his relationship with Raul, and we still hadn't found Florida.

We ended up driving out to see Bacon. The yard was missing some of its beer cans—washed away most likely—and the house was still a shithole, but someone had helped it along by kicking out one of the porch posts. The porch roof leaned to one side like a rake's hat. NIGGER had been spray-painted in big black letters underneath one of the windows and the window was knocked out and cardboard had been put in its place. The cardboard had taken in so much rain it was puffy and bent back and you could see into the house, and what you saw was darkness. Out to the side, the tarp had been torn off the backhoe by either wind or maliciousness. The machine was a faded yellow and it looked as if it hadn't been cleaned since used last. It was on a wheeled platform attached to an ancient but powerful-looking gray Dodge truck.

We went up on the porch, shook the rain off like dogs, and knocked. After a while a curtain moved, then the door cracked open. There was a new chain across the door. Bright and shiny. Sticking above it was a double-barrel shotgun and the shadow of a face.

"Get the hell out of here," Bacon said.

"It's us," I said.

"I know who the hell it is. Get on."

"We just want to ask a few questions."

"Not of me. Get on out of here, or I'm gonna blow your ass off. It wasn't for you, I'd be all right."

"Just a moment of your time," Leonard said. "Then we'll leave."

"I've given you all the time you're gonna get."

"It's important," I said.

"It was important last time, and look where it got me."

"Come on, Bacon," Leonard said. "Just a moment."

The door slammed. The chain rattled. The door was flung open and we went inside. Water was pouring from the kitchen roof into a big pan on the floor and the pan was full and the water was running over, running over the swollen linoleum. Wind was blowing rain through the gaps in the window with the cardboard over it, and it had been going on so long a few of the floorboards were warped.

Bacon stood in the middle of the room in his jockey shorts. He had the shotgun in his right hand and he had both arms flung wide. His scalded skin drooped over a sagging rib cage. His flesh was splotched from forehead to foot with great pink patches of rawness. It looked as if big chunks of hide had been pulled off by squid suckers.

"That tar took my meat off," he said. "You hear me! They tarred me 'cause I helped y'all. They meant for me to die. I ain't safe, now. You come around, I sure ain't safe."

"Jesus, Bacon," I said. "I'm so sorry."

"That's you white folk. You're always so sorry. So goddamn sorry. Jesus, Bacon, I'm sorry. So sorry. Well, that helps, Mr. Hap. I'm all right now."

"Let's go," I said.

"Not yet," Leonard said. "I'm sorry what happened to you, Bacon. I don't feel so good myself, and it was whites did it to me, but Hap ain't one of 'em."

"He's the one got me hurt," Bacon said. He threw the shotgun on the couch, sat down carefully. You could actually hear the skin crack when he sat. Blood beaded around some of the splotches and began to run.

Bacon's voice was venomous. "Every time I move, feel my skin crack, I think of Mr. Hap, here. I had to soak in kerosene to get that tar and feathers off. It peeled, took skin with it. Both my nuts, they're solid pink. They're ripped right down to the meat. Ain't a place on them ain't scalded by tar, burned by kerosene. I ain't slept a whole night since it happened on account of the pain and knowing they're comin' back to finish me, 'cause they will. I know they will. I'm gonna have to move off somewhere. I can't stay here. I don't know where to go, but I can't stay here . . . y'all go on."

"In a moment," Leonard said.

"You ain't nothing but an Uncle Tom, nigger-fella," Bacon said.

"It's a good thing you're old and splotched like a hound," Leonard said, "or I'd have to fix your teeth."

"Yeah, threaten me 'cause you can whip me. You couldn't whip all them others."

I heard Leonard take a deep breath, blow it out slowly through his nose.

I said, "It's all right, Leonard. Let's go."

"Not yet," Leonard said. "Bacon, they came after you day after some of them came after us. Like you, we were lucky. We want to get even. We want to find who put them up to this, and we want to find out what happened to Florida."

"Fuck Florida!" Bacon yelled and half came off the couch and screamed with pain. "Oh, God," he said, and collapsed into the worn-out cushions. "That bitch, she showed up in town, she upset the balance. Things was bad before she come, but we all knew how things was played. She come around, shakin' that pretty ass, she got things messed up. She's as much to blame for what happened to me as Mr. Hap."

We gave Bacon a moment to stew in his rancor. We listened to water pound the roof of the house, listened to it run onto the floor in the kitchen, listened to it blow past the cardboard patching in the window. Leonard said, "We're gonna do this with or without you, but we're gonna do it, and you might help us do it better. Did you recognize any of the men took you out of here, tarred and feathered you?"

"No."

"Come on, Bacon," Leonard said.

"No! I said NO! Are you deaf?"

"Just tell me if this is right," Leonard said. "You left here ahead of us, went into town, came home, and next night they came out and got you."

Bacon didn't say anything, but he didn't argue either.

"They came out and got you 'cause someone let on we were here, that you helped us," Leonard said. "Who?"

"I don't know," Bacon said. "Cantuck, maybe. It could have been him. I don't think so, but it could have been. Maybe Mrs. Rainforth, she could have said something wrong. Mr. Tim might have. It ain't no tellin'. Please go. Please. They see you here . . ."

"They're not gonna see us," Leonard said.

"They gonna find out," Bacon said. "Somehow, they'll find out. They found out last time, didn't they?"

"Sorry, Bacon," I said. "Really."

"Yeah," he said. "Okay. You're sorry. Just go on, now."

It was strange and painful driving into Grovetown. It's impossible to describe the feelings that went through me as we came to the city-limits sign, and soon to the square. The square was fairly deep in water. You could pass through it, but the water was swift and it made me nervous. Once, when I was younger, I was following a pickup truck out of a hayfield where I had been working, and we'd had to stop working because a tremendous and unbelievable rain had fallen out of the sky. It was like someone had dumped an ocean on East Texas. But I was with my boss, who had given me a ride to the field, and he was taking me home, and we got behind this pickup, and we came to a bridge and the water was just too much for the hard dry ground. It had been too hot for too long, and when it finally did rain, it wasn't absorbed. It was swelling, and water was already over the bridge, though it wasn't deep. I think had we come to the bridge first, we would have tried to drive over it too, but the pickup in front of us tried it. The water hit the pickup like a battering ram, carried it into the bridge railing and the railing broke and the truck went over.

There was nothing we could do. One instant man and truck were there, the next they were gone. The water carried the truck away and under, and it was three days later when the water went down that they found him. He was still in the truck, what was left of a cigar clamped between his teeth. That's how fast he'd gone over and drowned.

It had taught me a lesson about the power of water, and I had respected it ever since. I knew what it could do, and I was haunted by it. By the deeps. By the shallows. By water.

Across the way I could see the Grovetown Cafe. Water was lapping over the curbing, threatening to enter the place. In my head I could see inside it and I could visualize all those angry people, falling down on us like cut timbers.

We decided to start at Cantuck's office, but we couldn't get to it. The water was too high over there to park. We parked at Tim's filling station, and walked over. I tell you, outside of the truck I was a nervous wreck. I knew it wasn't wise, especially going into Cantuck's office, but I wouldn't go without the snub-nose and Leonard wouldn't go without his pistol. We hid them in our coats.

Water was seeping under the door and into the lobby when we arrived. The carpet smelled like a damp sheepdog. We were both breathing harder than either of us really should have been. Perspiration was boiling out from under my arms almost as fast as the rain was coming down. Leonard's limp was more pronounced. He had gotten the original injury saving my life, and he'd healed up good, having only occasional trouble with it, but the beating we had taken had done his leg some bad business again, reactivated the old pain.

"You all right?" I asked.

"Unless you want to have a sack race, I'm all right."

The secretary had taken down her Christmas cards and tree. She wasn't glad to see us. Reynolds was out, which was, of course, a major disappointment.

Cantuck must have heard us come in, because he came to the door of his office with a jaw full of chewing tobacco. He looked a lot less friendly than when I used to see him leaving the police station in LaBorde.

"All right," he said. "Come in."

We went into his office. Cantuck sat down, picked his spit can off the desk and pushed his chew into it with his tongue.

"We just thought we'd drop in and say hi," Leonard said, taking a chair. When he sat, water pooled beneath him.

Cantuck sighed. He rolled his one good eye to the left, then the right, perhaps looking for sanctuary. I got a dollar out of my wallet and forced it into one of the cans on his desk. He eyed that, said, "You're not thinking you're softening me up with that, are you?"

I sat down. Cantuck said, "If ever there were a couple of idiots, it's you two."

"But we're your idiots," I said.

Cantuck rubbed the back of his neck and ran a hand through his hair. "You know, you could cause some problems showin' up here. I could have you run out of town. I could lock you up."

"But you wouldn't do that," I said. "Because we're your idiots."

"Don't think 'cause you got me to a hospital I owe you some favors," Cantuck said.

"We'd never capitalize on a thing like that," Leonard said. "But we did save your life."

"I'd have been all right," Cantuck said.

"You'd have bled to death," Leonard said.

"You didn't do shit," Cantuck said. "You were in the back seat, passed out."

"Hap saved us both," Leonard said. "So you owe him."

Cantuck clasped his hands together, leaned his elbows on his desk, pushed his face against his hands. He said, "What is it you want? You want to know Brown is guilty? I can't tell you. Being how he's the Exalted Cyclops of the Klan here—or whatever they're calling themselves these days—I figure he had to have known something. No one's pinning him to it because he wasn't there, and the boys are keeping the Klan pledge of silence. Now you know what I know, unless you don't know we're having some serious bad weather here and I think I'm going to send everyone home, along with myself, before we drown."

"What about Reynolds?" I said. "He involved?"

"He's a worthless piece of shit," Cantuck said, "and I figure he'll get my job. Brown starts enough grassroots unrest, makes people feel their jobs at the lumber mill, the Christmas tree farm are in jeopardy, the Mayor might see his way to appoint Reynolds. I don't know. Maybe I want that. I'm tired of all this shit. I got one eye, a swollen nut, and more grief than I need. I been thinking about opening an antique store."

"Lots of guys with one eye and a swollen nut do that," Leonard said.

Cantuck actually grinned at him.

"We don't want any trouble," I said. "We just think we might find a lead somewhere. Something to help us figure what happened to Florida."

"Oh yeah?" Cantuck said. "Couple of detectives, just like on the TV, huh? Seen some *Matlock*, have you? A few *Perry Mason* reruns. That's good, and it's good of you two to offer your vast experience in our hour of need. Way I've seen you guys operate, I don't think you could find your dick with both hands, let alone figure out who did what to who and why."

"I just want who," I said. "I don't give a damn about why."

"And that's why you'll never figure the who," Cantuck said. "It's the why that counts."

"The why in this case is damn easy," I said. "A black man killed a white man and a black woman started messing with it."

The Chief's door opened then. I turned in my chair. It was Reynolds. He had a plastic hat cover over his hat and the water beaded on it like balls of Vaseline. From his feet to his knees was soaked. "Well," he said. "My little buddies."

Leonard stood up as if to confront Reynolds.

"Man, you look rough," Reynolds said. "What happened? Get beat up in a cafe?"

"Don't think because a roomful of people whipped my ass, you can," Leonard said.

"I don't have to think nothing," Reynolds said.

"Get started on me," Leonard said, "hope you brought yourself a sack lunch, 'cause you gonna be here all night."

Reynolds finally decided to notice me. "What about you, shithead? You want me after I finish him?"

"Naw," I said. "Actually, just seeing how tough you are is making my bowels loose. Besides, Leonard gets through with you, what's left for me?"

"That's enough," Cantuck said.

"Chief," Leonard said. "All I ask is you give us fifteen minutes. Anywhere you say. Me and him, assholes and elbows."

"You heard me," Cantuck said, "put the brakes on." He stood up from his desk and leaned his hands on it. "Reynolds. You still work for me, and you knock on my fuckin' door, you want to come in. And, I'll tell you another little thing . . . close the door."

Reynolds, who was still holding the knob in his hand, gently closed it. Cantuck said, "Quit fuckin' my secretary. She has a family."

Reynolds turned beet red. "Chief, I—"

"Just shut up," Cantuck said. "Now what the fuck did you want anyway?"

"Charlene told me they was in here," Reynolds said. "I wanted to know why."

"They come to donate a dollar to one of my charity cans," Cantuck said. "Now pack your ass on out of here. I thought it was your business, I'd leave you a note or somethin'. Go on."

Reynolds went out and started to close the door. Cantuck said, "Tell Charlene to go on home. And you go on too—but not with her. And just in case you might feel you want to talk to someone about these boys being here. Someone like Brown. Don't do it. Something happens to these pieces of shit, it might make me feel bad on account of they put money in my charity cans. Are you readin' me here, son?"

"Chief—"

"The answer's 'yes sir,'" Cantuck said.

"Yes sir," Reynolds said.

"Now go on," Cantuck said. "Day's too bad to hang out here. Word is the dam's leakin' like a goddamn sieve. Next thing you know, we'll be digging bass out of our asses. Now get."

Reynolds went out and closed the door.

"You really don't like him, do you, Chief," Leonard said.

"Nope, I don't."

I said, "Thanks, Chief."

"Don't thank me," he said. "I don't want you here neither."

"You say that," Leonard said, "but you don't mean it."

"Oh yes I do," Cantuck said.

"This sort of rejection from authority figures," Leonard said, "it's exactly what makes a fellow go bad. I read that in a book somewheres."

28

Cantuck told us to go home, but he didn't make it an official order, so we waded over to Tim's station and went inside. He was sitting behind the counter with his feet up. When he saw us come in, his eyebrows went up.

"Sort of thought I'd seen the last of you two," he said.

"You almost did," I said. I looked at the pig's feet in the jar on the counter. It looked like the same pig's feet as before. I said, "Thought you sold lots of those?"

"I lied," Tim said. "I try to sell them to the out-of-towners. What do you boys want? I mean, is this safe for you?"

"Can we sit?" Leonard asked.

"Sure," Tim said. "Go ahead. I'll get us a little coffee."

He went and got the coffee. Leonard and I sat in the same chairs we had sat in before and Tim's long coat hung on the same chair where it had hung before. I put my hand in my pocket and fondled my .38, lovingly. We listened to the rain on the roof.

When I felt sure no one was about to charge through the door in a white sheet, I looked around the store, at the new pile of wood beside the stove—without a lizard this time—the crap under the barrel stove, the shiny blue something there, the dust bunnies, and the tobacco wrapper.

Everything seemed just the way it had that Christmas we had come into Grovetown, except the aluminum Christmas tree was gone. It was hard to believe it had been nearly a month. A bit of wind rustled through the place as Tim came in with coffee. It blew dust bunnies across the floor and into the corners.

When we had our coffee and Tim was seated, Leonard said, "You think your dad was behind what was done to us?"

Tim thought a moment. "Maybe he didn't have it done, but the ones done it done it 'cause he wanted it done. I bet on that. But why are you guys back?"

"We're stupid," I said.

"I believe that," Tim said.

"What about Reynolds?" Leonard said. "He behind any of this?"

"Christ, boys, I don't know. Why the third degree?"

"Sorry," Leonard said. "We're just a little down on our social skills today."

"And nervous," I said.

"I bet," Tim said. "Hell, boys, I'm glad enough to see you, but I think you ought to leave this to out-of-town law if you're thinking of doing something yourself."

"We don't know what we're thinking," I said. "We still haven't found Florida."

"She could still be okay," Tim said. "Run off somewhere for some reason we haven't got a clue. And I tell you, I'm thinking of leaving out of here myself, for a while. That old Grovetown dam, they say it's pretty creaky, all this rain. It's got more water in it now than last time, and when it broke that time it was bad news. I want Mama out of where she is, but I haven't been able to budge her. That dam breaks, her trailer park'll be the first place to get it. There's already places out there under four or five feet of water just from the seepage. Half the town has left already. Won't come back until the rain stops or the water goes down."

"That's to our advantage," I said.

"You two are fools," Tim said. "This time, someone might succeed at what they tried last time."

"And you don't want to be in the middle of it?" Leonard said.

"Damn right," Tim said. "You heard what they did to Bacon."

"Yeah," I said. "But if it's your father behind all this, you said yourself you've got immunity."

"And what if it isn't my father?" Tim said. "Guys, I'm sorry you got beat up. I'm sorry you got run off the road and nearly killed, but you came out all right. The guys involved confessed. Maybe they'll get scared and pin my father to it in time. But why do you want to meddle anymore?"

"You're about the only one here who has really befriended us,"

I said. "Maude and her boys a little. Cantuck in his own fashion. But you know these people. You might can tell us something can help. I feel there's an equation we haven't added up. I think we look at the factors just right, we ought to be able to get a total. Know what I'm saying?"

"No," Tim said.

"Florida comes here because she thinks Soothe was murdered," I said. "She wants to prove the Chief and the town are a bunch of bigots. She wants to buy this stuff the Yankee wanted to buy from Soothe and got killed over. Stuff that might or might not exist. She asks around. Talks to you. Gets a place to stay out at your mother's, then disappears. Her car disappears. Her belongings disappear."

"That's what makes me think she may have just driven off," Tim said.

"I don't think so," I said. "Doesn't fit who she was. People can sometimes do crazy things, but by now we'd have heard from her. Something's happened to her."

"You can't be certain," Tim said.

"I've thought every angle. It looked to me at first that Cantuck might have something to do with her missing, but in light of the way things have gone, that doesn't fit as well as it first did. Reynolds is possible. He and your father could have been in cahoots. They could have hung Soothe. Perhaps Florida somehow found out, so they got rid of her. That sound far-fetched?"

"I guess not," Tim said. "I wouldn't put anything past my old man. Not after the way he's treated my mother and me. I tell you, him with all that money, and me with nothing. And owing him to boot. It gets my goat. And I hate to mention it, boys, but you owe me for some tires."

"Oh, yeah," Leonard said. "You take a check?"

"I don't like to."

"Can you wait then?"

"I'll take the check."

Leonard wrote it out. Tim took it and put it in his wallet. "There now," he said. "That's all taken care of. You were saying . . . what was it?"

"He was about to say, then we show up," Leonard said, "not only are we a nigger and a nigger lover, but we're treading on dangerous ground. Same ground Florida was on."

"So," Tim said. "What can I do?"

"What we want," I said, "is for you to let us talk to your mother. You know, set it up with her. Maybe there's something she knows that didn't seem important at the time, but is now. Perhaps Florida left her clothes in the trailer and your mother took them."

"She's not a thief," Tim said.

"He didn't say that," Leonard said. "What he wants is any bit of evidence we can find. If your mother has the clothes, then that could point to Florida being abducted, killed. Might be something in her clothes that'll give us a lead. If we could find her car. Just something to start with. Anything."

"Hell," I said. "We don't know what we want, Tim. We just want it. Understand?"

"Here's what I'll do," Tim said. "I'll ask her she knows anything. I'll call out there. I want to talk her into leaving anyway, all this water risin', but that's all I'll do. My mother is not a well woman, and I don't want you two giving her grief. Got me?"

"Fair enough," I said.

Tim went in the back and we sat by the stove and waited. Five minutes later he returned.

"She won't leave," he said, "and she doesn't know anything. She said Florida was there, then she wasn't, and she never saw her again. And she didn't leave any clothes."

We bought some gas and soft drinks from Tim. I even bought one of the pig's feet. We went out and sat in the truck. The rain rattled on the roof and flooded over the windshield so thick it was like we were underwater.

"What now?" I said.

"This hasn't worked out quite like I thought," Leonard said. "I figure I pissed Raul off for nothing. It's too wet to do a goddamn thing. No place to stay. We've got less ideas than we did before we came the first time. And that check I wrote Tim is hot, I don't get some money to cover it. Boy, he is one tight sonofabitch."

"You're right," I said. "On all accounts."

"I missed out on an anniversary dinner and Raul's ass for this, and I tell you, I ain't happy."

"Maybe you could find someone to beat up."

"Yeah. Things could get better. What would cheer me up real good is getting to hit that Reynolds fucker."

"He'll hit back. I guarantee it."

"That is a drawback. Want to eat this sack lunch?"

"I been thinking about it ever since we left your house."

We got the sack lunch and ate it. I tried to eat the pig's foot too. It smelled rank and it was like eating a piece of soggy, vinegar-soaked rubber. I rolled down the window and spat a few times, then wrapped the pig's foot up in a paper sack, double-bagged it with another.

"Maybe you ought to wrap that sack in chains," Leonard said. "Drive a stake through it so when you throw it out, it ain't gonna come back."

"What now?" I said.

"We've been avoiding the cafe," Leonard said. "Might as well go there and get a cup of coffee, warm up."

We walked over, getting drenched, the water sloshing almost to our knees. I felt sick to my stomach thinking of going into that place, but with our guns in our coat pockets we were a lot braver.

The cafe was locked. There was a sign on the inside of the glass door that said CLOSED DUE TO HIGH WATER.

We got in the truck and sat for a while. "Well, we were ready to go in there and face the devil," I said. "And had it been open, we would have too. I'm proud of us."

"Me too," Leonard said. "On the other hand, I'm kinda glad it wasn't open."

"Me too."

"Know what, Hap? We're gonna have to go back to LaBorde. Get our shit together better, have a real plan. I hate to admit it, but I couldn't wait to get here today, and now we're here, and I don't know what for. Maybe if it wasn't rainin'. Or we had a place to stay. As it is we're just running around like chickens with our heads cut off. I'm wet. I'm cold. No one is here I can be mad at, and Cantuck won't let me and Reynolds play."

"I was thinking the same thing. And feeling stupid about jumping up like a big dog, and then here we are and there's nothing for us to do."

We left Grovetown, started the way we'd come, but the weather was so bad we had to creep along at thirty miles an hour, and when we came to the marsh where Leonard's car had gone in, the marsh was over the road.

We turned around, headed back to Grovetown, then took the highway that ran out by Bacon's place, hoping to find a long way to LaBorde.

We edged along slowly. The water was starting to seep out of the woods and onto the road. The sky was a light show, and the wind was so strong it was hard to hold the truck in a lane. We passed Bacon's place, went on out a ways, finally came to a rise on the highway, and when we looked down we could see darkness, and the darkness was water.

I thought about turning back, but the rain was so severe I chose not to. Even with the lights on bright, I couldn't see much beyond the length of the truck hood, only enough to recognize a swell of water across the highway below. The truck was vibrating in the wind.

Off to our right was a short gravel road that went up a hill higher than the highway, and we took it. After a little ways, we were able to make out it was a cemetery road, and we drove inside the place and parked under a great oak near an old tomb that was swelling out of the ground, threatening to fall.

The rain pounded us so hard I thought it would come through the pickup roof, and the lightning was like luminous varicose veins across the sky. It cracked and hissed and made the darkness go daylight for full seconds at a time. I feared the tree would attract it, as trees do, so I backed out from under and tried to find a clear spot. I finally settled on a place between a row of tombstones, killed the engine, and we sat there and looked at their gray shapes through the rain, and though I've never been one to be bothered by cemeteries, I was feeling pretty blue and pretty spooky right then. Being out in the open like that made me feel worse. The tree had felt safe, though logically, I knew it was the worst place we could be in a storm. Except maybe a mobile home. Storms, especially tornadoes, dearly loved a mobile home.

"Sometimes," Leonard said, "I think when I die I'd like to end up in a place like this."

"I donated my body to science," I said. "Got it marked on my driver's license. But I don't know. I may take it off next time. Stuff I used to think was silly ain't so silly anymore. I mean, you're dead, you're dead, but it means a little something to know your name might get read off a tombstone someday. Otherwise, it's like you never lived."

"'Course, giving someone your liver or eyes and them living because of you, that's quite a legacy," Leonard said.

"Then you ought to donate yourself too."

"No, I mean it's a legacy for you. Me, I want to be buried."

We sat there for about twenty minutes, not saying anything, the interior of the truck growing colder, and then I said, "You know, I just realized, first time I met Florida was at a cemetery. I been trying to remember first time I saw her, and it finally came to me."

"My uncle's funeral."

"Yeah. I don't know why I couldn't remember that. A thing like that, think you wouldn't forget."

"Cold is making my leg ache like a sonofabitch, Hap. We got enough gas to run the heater some?"

I fired up the engine and cranked the heater on high, said, "The cemetery here. It's given me an idea. Something that's been building in my subconscious all along. We been going about this all wrong."

"I could have told you that."

"We started out right, but now we're going wrong. We came to Grovetown trying to follow what Florida would have done, but we quit doing that. We did it a little, but we quit. We started trying to figure who killed her, instead of thinking like she would think."

"And how would she think?"

"She'd go first to see Cantuck. Maybe talk to Reynolds."

"We did that."

"She'd go to the road houses, talk to people knew Soothe, saw him and this Yankee together. She'd talk to Soothe's relatives."

"Chief, Rangers, you name it, they've done that, Hap. I mean, we might ask something they didn't ask 'cause we know Florida better than them, but I don't put lots of stock in it. Ultimately, we're just amateurs, and we ain't worth a damn at it. Earnest. But stupid."

"I'll buy that. But there's another thing she'd do. She'd go see Soothe's grave."

"Why?"

"Think a minute."

Leonard did just that. He said, "All right, I thought about it and I don't get it. She might want to see where he was buried, but I don't see that matters much as far as finding her goes."

"I think she might have thought she ought to move Soothe."

"Dig him up?"

"If Florida was here to do an investigation, was convinced Soothe was murdered, she might get to thinking someone like Reynolds, or whoever, might figure an inquiry by outside authorities could result from her snooping around, doing an article, and the outside authorities would come in and want Soothe exhumed—"

"To see if he hung himself, or was hung?"

"Yep. So she dug up the body to keep it out of the hands of anyone who might spoil it, want to destroy autopsy evidence that could prove Soothe was murdered."

"She did dig him up, where'd she put him, Hap? And another thing, Florida, petite as she was, wasn't all that suited for grave digging."

"She didn't like getting dirty either. However, she wasn't above using her feminine charms when it suited her needs. What she would need was a horny sap who thought doing a favor might get him a little stinky on his dinky, even if all Florida really planned to give him was her heartfelt thanks. Get my drift?"

"Well, I'll be goddamned. You mean—"

"Yep."

29

We sat there about an hour, until the rain slacked, then we started for Grovetown. When we got there the water was running wild and deep through the streets, and we had to park up by an antique shop and wade to Tim's station.

The water pushed at us so hard it was difficult to stand, but we made it. The station was locked up. We went around to the back and beat on the door there, and after a moment Tim opened up. He didn't look that thrilled to see us. He told us to go around front, and closed the door.

He let us into the store. The room was still warm, but the heater was down to coals. We went over and sat by it anyway. I checked out the junk under the stove again. It was becoming my focus point, especially that little blue object.

Tim said, "I've closed up for the day. Weather isn't giving me any work. Unless I can do something for you guys right away, I think I'm gonna pack a few things, go out to Mom's see if I can get her to come with me, head out till all this passes. I'm not wanting to be rude, but—"

"Tim," I said, "you took Florida out to Soothe's grave, didn't you?"

"What?" he said.

I knew I was taking a hell of a flier, but the more I thought about it, considering what I knew of Florida, how she thought, I figured it was as good a flyer as I might ever take.

"She wanted to move Soothe to another place, didn't she? She asked you to take her out there and help her do it."

"Why would she do that?"

I told him what I thought. He said, "That's ridiculous," but he had a look on his face like we'd just caught him jacking off to a grainy photo of a shaved dog butt.

"You took her out there, and you helped move the body. All we want is you to show us where."

Tim studied the floor. He said, "If she did want it moved, and say I did help her, and showed you where the body is, what difference would it make now? All the time he's been in the ground, I don't know they could tell much."

"Not for us to say," Leonard said. "Forensic people can do pretty amazing things."

"And how would that help you find Florida anyway?" Tim asked. "That's what you're after, isn't it? Florida? Not this Soothe thing."

I knew I had hit pay dirt. I tried not to stare directly at Tim, lest I unnerve him. I focused on the blue object under the stove when I spoke.

"I'm not trying to say you did anything wrong, though Texas frowns on bodies being moved around after they're in the ground. But if Florida had you help move the body, and then someone, Reynolds, your father, lackeys, went out there to steal and destroy Soothe's corpse because they thought there might be an autopsy, and the body wasn't there, they might figure since Florida was asking around about Soothe, trying to prove he was murdered, well, they could put one and one together, decide she moved the body. They might not figure on you, but they'd think of her."

"Then," Leonard said, "they kidnapped her, made her tell where it was."

"Considering the boys around Grovetown can be real persuasive," I said, "I think she told, showed them where it was. And if she did, and the body was in a place where they didn't think it would be found, wouldn't cause them a problem, they left it. And they left Florida with it. That's logical. If the body wasn't in a good place, they took it off somewhere in the bottoms where it wouldn't be discovered, and probably took Florida with it."

"If it's the first thing," Leonard said, "we can find Soothe, and maybe Florida. If it's the second thing, then we . . . well, we don't have plans. We're taking it a step at a time."

"I don't know," Tim said.

"We do it this way," I said. "Me and Leonard, we'll figure a way to make it look like we put it together. We won't involve you. I promise you that. You don't help, we got to talk to Cantuck."

"Why didn't you do that anyway?" Tim asked.

"Because you and your mother befriended Florida," I said. "Because we don't want to tie you to stuff we don't have to."

"And Florida was our friend," Leonard said. "Something happens to a friend and you can do something about it, you ought to."

"But the weather," Tim said. "That's right out there by the dam, and that baby is startin' to pop."

"It floods," I said, "that grave may be worse off than it is now. If both of them are out there, the sooner we get to them, better the forensic evidence. And the sooner we get some kind of knowledge of what happened to Florida, even if it's bad, the better."

"Dirt's soft out there," Tim said, "but with all this water, it could be a mess."

"We'll chance it," Leonard said.

Tim went in the back room and put on boots, pulled on his heavy coat hanging by the stove, then we went out to the big garage and Tim loaded some shovels in his pickup along with a big tarp in case we found Soothe, or Soothe and Florida, then he drove us through the water and up the hill to my truck. Leonard and I followed Tim. We went out the highway where Bacon lived. I hoped the place we were going wasn't beyond that great hill, 'cause if it was we might not make it, and tomorrow Tim might forget he knew anything. I felt the whole situation was fragile, needed to be pushed now.

We came to the road that led out to his mother's, and though it was covered with water, we took it. The water was not deep over the road, but I was nervous as the proverbial long-tailed cat in a room full of rocking chairs. I kept thinking about that pickup I'd seen wash over the bridge.

We went down the road a ways, then took a worse road, but it went uphill some and the water disappeared. It was really a high hill for East Texas, and when we got to the top, Tim stopped and we pulled up alongside him. Down below us we could see the road was blocked by water over a narrow wooden bridge. The sky was growing dark again. The rain was coming down harder, and it was so cold the heater in the pickup sounded as if it were crying.

Leonard rolled down his window, and Tim his. Yelling across from truck to truck was difficult, the rain was coming down so hard it drowned out our voices.

"I'm afraid to drive across," Tim said.

"Me too," I said. "How far is it?"

"On the other side of the bridge, up the hill and down. To the right. It's the paupers' graveyard."

"I thought that's where he was in the first place?" Leonard said.

"And still is," Tim said. "I didn't want to do this, but now I've thought on it, I think we ought to. Get it over with. We can leave the trucks here. I don't think traffic is going to be a problem today."

When we all had a shovel and I had the rolled-up tarp under my arm and Tim had a flashlight, we started down the hill. We hadn't gone a few steps before Leonard began to limp as if his leg were made of wood. He was using the shovel to help him along. I said, "Hold up. You that bad off, brother?"

"I'm a little stiff is all," Leonard said, shivering in the cold rain.

"It's not that far," Tim said.

"Going across that bridge on that leg, I don't know," I said. Leonard's leg was so swollen it looked like ground meat pumped into a sausage casing.

"Guess all the wear and tear, the weather, it's not doing me any good," Leonard said. "But I don't like being a weak sister."

"Go to the truck," I said. "Me and Tim will take care of it."

"I can make it," Leonard said.

"It's not really that far," Tim said.

"Go on to the truck," I told Leonard. "As a favor to me."

Leonard nodded. "I guess I ought to. I don't like digging anyway. Watch that water." He limped away, tossed the shovel into the bed of Tim's truck, then got in my truck on the passenger side. Through the blurry haze of the rain on the windshield, I saw him lift a hand and wave.

Tim and I went down the hill and into the water, hanging on to the bridge railing as we went. The force of the water was terrific, and I felt tremendous panic. I lost the tarp from under my arm and the water whisked it away.

We inched our way across the bridge, and on the other side the water was barely across the road. We walked along more quickly now, and up a hill, and when we came down on the other side I could see the graveyard off to the right, about halfway down the hill, the stones and markers sloping toward the Big Thicket. Definitely a paupers' graveyard.

There was a barbed wire fence around it and an open gate, and we went through there and Tim took the lead. He led me over to where Soothe's grave was, tapped it with his shovel. The grave was covered in colored glass and the cheap gravestone that stated his name, birthdate, and death was wrapped in colored beads. There was a little doll's head in front of the stone with melted wax on top of it where a candle had burned down. Part of the doll's head had melted, and wax had run down over the painted eye.

"Empty," Tim said. "All this shit was put here after we dug the grave up officially. Me, Cantuck, Reynolds, and the Ranger. You wouldn't believe how hard it was for me to act surprised when we opened it."

"Why all this stuff?"

"Voodoo," Tim said. "It's to keep Soothe in the ground." He strolled over to the grave next to Soothe's, stuck his shovel into the dirt at its base. "Old Mrs. Burk has company."

"You put Soothe in there with her?"

"Florida's idea," he said. "Just temporary. Way the weather's been, washing the place and all, no one could tell we'd done anything when they dug up Soothe's spot."

"Clever," I said. "Let's do it."

Grave digging is not nearly as easy as you might think. It's back-breaking, and next to picking corn out of pig shit with tweezers it's the most boring thing in the world. I tried to focus on things other than my injuries, my sore muscles.

I tried not to think about Florida possibly being down there, and I began to hope I was wrong. If she was dead, I wasn't sure I wanted to find her now. I tried not to think about her being forced to bring those Klan idiots out here, show them where Soothe was buried. I tried not to think about what they did to her afterwards, before they put her down here with Soothe and Mrs. Burk.

As we dug, the water ran down the hill and tried to fill the grave. We could hear the woods crackling as the water ran over the dried branches and leaves, and in the distance I could hear a roaring, which I figured was the rush of the creek swelling. But we kept digging, slogging into the mud, and after about an hour my shovel hit something hard. We scraped it clean. A coffin. Wood.

I stood there on top of it, not knowing exactly what to do next. Tim said, "Mrs. Burk, she's under that box."

I had a sudden uncomfortable thought. I said, "What if Florida told the Klan folks you helped do this? You think your father will have you done in?"

I looked at Tim. He shrugged. "If she'd told, and they were going to do something, I reckon they would have done it already. Let's widen the grave a bit."

"It's wide enough. Let's pop the lid."

"Let's widen it so we can pull it out. I think we got to pull it out, don't you? You lost the tarp, so we have to somehow get the coffin up the hill."

We started digging again, widening the grave. That nasty snake of my subconscious began to work at me again. It was trying to tell me something, as it often did.

Tim climbed out of the grave. He got the big flashlight he had carried with him, turned it on, tilted it at the edge of the grave so that it shone down on the coffin. It had grown nearly dark as midnight in the time we had been digging. Water was nearly to my knees, and rising.

"Why don't you pop the lid now," he said. "Use your shovel."

I looked up at Tim. He was standing above me, leaning on his shovel, one hand in his pocket. The rain was so thick, it seemed to be a sheath around him. Lightning sawed across the sky in bright, crooked explosions.

"All right," I said.

I took the tip of my shovel, started forcing it under the lid of the cheap coffin. It wasn't really an official coffin, which would have taken tools to open. It was one of those cheap kind they called pressed wood, which was essentially high-caliber cardboard. It was already starting to come apart due to all the rain since Soothe had been buried. Then reburied.

It popped free, and the stench from it was horrible. Lying on top of what had to be Soothe, though there wasn't much of him to recognize—bones and skin stretched over a skull so tight it looked like a stocking mask—there was another badly decomposed body. The features were basically gone and the hair was patchy. Flesh hung from the skull like chunks of dried glue and above the right eye socket the forehead was pushed in. The rain splashed on it, made the flesh loosen and it slid off the bone as if it were alive and seeking shelter.

In spite of the damage, I recognized the short blue dress the corpse wore, and there was one blue earring dangling from a rotting lobe, and in that instant, I knew I had been a sap all along. I knew what that blue thing under Tim's stove was suddenly, and I knew why Tim wanted the grave widened.

It had to accommodate me. Then Leonard.

I dropped the shovel, reached for the gun in my coat pocket, tried to turn, but didn't make it. Tim hit me across the back of the head with his shovel, knocked me against the grave wall.

My head was splitting. I assumed I had only been out for seconds, because when I came to Tim was stepping into the grave, a foot on Florida's corpse. He reached the pistol that had fallen from my hand out of the coffin and pointed it at me. I was too dazed to do anything. There were just enough brain cells cooking to know I ought to be doing something and wasn't.

I was standing up, lodged between the coffin and the wall of the grave. There hadn't been room to fall down. Tim was squatting in the coffin now, still pointing my gun at me. If that wasn't enough, he pulled a little automatic from his coat pocket with his empty hand, aimed it at me too.

Two-Gun Tim.

"It's nothing personal," he said. "I didn't want to kill you and Leonard, but I got to now. I kept thinking you'd just go off. I mean,

I like you. I liked Florida. It was just one of those things. You knew though. Right there a while ago. You knew. How?"

It took me a second to make my mouth work, but I wanted every second I could buy. "Her earring is missing. I realized it's under your stove, at the store."

"Thanks for telling me," Tim said. "I'll get rid of it. Me and her, we struggled. I figure it got caught in my coat, and when I hung it up to dry, the earring fell out, rolled under the stove."

"You stupid sonofabitch."

"Hey, look who's on the end of the gun, pal. Ain't me."

"You're the one told the Klan me and Leonard were going home."

"You just kept pushing, Hap. I thought maybe after that beating you took, that would fix you. But hearing you talk to Cantuck . . . I don't know. I wasn't so sure, and I had to be. And I didn't mean for Bacon to get it. I made an anonymous phone call to Draighten, told him where you two would be. I said you'd be coming from Bacon's place. Everyone knows Bacon."

"Why would you do this?"

"I think I need to get this over with, Hap. I don't dislike you, it's hard enough to do, but I got to do it."

"I don't think it's that hard for you, buddy."

"Oh, you don't know. It's not easy for me at all. I don't like killing."

"But you get by."

"What I want you to do is step out of the grave. I want you to get out right now, get on your knees up at the edge."

I thought about that. I realized he didn't want to shoot me in case Leonard might hear the shot. Which in this rain wasn't likely, but I decided not to mention that. He wanted me at the edge of the grave on my knees so he could bean me with the shovel again. Bean me on the head, then roll me in between the edge of the coffin and the grave wall. The other side would fit Leonard.

"I don't think I want to climb out," I said.

"Then I shoot you here."

"Why would you kill Florida?"

"The money. That's it. I liked Florida. Really. But she talked too much. I knew she carried her savings somewhere in her car, and I got to thinking about it. She drove out here behind me and I moved the body like she wanted, and I didn't really have it planned, but I knew then I could kill her, take the money, and no one would ever know. I needed that money, Hap, and everything was right for it. Grovetown wasn't going to get too worked up about a missing black girl. Maybe Cantuck. But he ain't Sherlock Holmes, you know. It was quite a bit of money she had. And not hid all that well either. Taped under the seat. All that money and she was going to buy some stupid recording with it."

"Heaven forbid someone spend their own money the way they want."

"I didn't like the way she wanted to use me, neither. Try and make me think she might bed me, but I knew she wouldn't. I put Florida in the coffin with Soothe, put them on top of Burk.

"I drove Florida's car down the road there, off to a fishing spot I used to use. There's swampy water there so goddamn deep it might go to the center of the earth. I pushed the car off in it, walked back and drove out."

"Just for money? You killed her for that?"

"I fucked her too. I figured she was gonna die, wasn't any use in that pussy going to waste. I wouldn't have hurt her, had some fun with her, had I not meant to kill her. It's just . . . I was gonna do her in, might as well get some pleasure from her. It wasn't that good by the way. Fight like she did, it isn't that good."

Greed. Tim had killed that wonderful, beautiful woman for money and sex. I'd assigned everything that had happened to bigotry, but it was greed and lust. Two sins much older, and as basic as the instinctive mating of those two *National Geographic* bears. I felt like an idiot. I felt angry. I felt as if my heart would explode.

"Come on, Hap, get out of the hole."

"If you're gonna bang me with that shovel," I said, "I'd rather take the bullet."

"I do that, Leonard hears the shot, he might drive off, then folks would come here to investigate, figure things out. I got to get you both, Hap. You might as well come on and let me do it. I can kill you with one blow if you're out of the grave. I can make it quick. After I got some from Florida, that's what I did. One blow with a rock."

In the grave, lodged like I was, I didn't have a chance in a million. But the other way, maybe . . .

"You don't come out," Tim said, "I'll chance shooting you. I don't think Leonard can hear anyway, but I got an idea he did hear it, he'd know it was a gunshot, and it'll be tidier this way."

"All right, but promise me you'll do it right. Hard and quick. Same for Leonard."

"I'll have to shoot Leonard, most likely. He won't expect it, though, and I'll do it up close. Right in the temple, okay?"

I thought, if you get that close, and Leonard has an inkling what you're going to do, he's going to snap your arm off at the elbow and use it to swab out your asshole. I thought, Leonard, old buddy, I go down, please don't fall for this bastard. Don't fall for it.

Tim put the automatic in his pocket and kept my revolver. He said, "Get up tight against the grave wall."

I did. He climbed out carefully, keeping an eye on me. He got the flashlight and held it on my face, blinding me. The light bobbed low and came back up. I couldn't make out what he was doing behind the light, but I had an idea. He was slipping the revolver into his pocket, picking up the shovel.

I put a foot inside the coffin, between Florida's stick legs, prepared to reach for the edge of the grave. I figured soon as I did that, that's when Tim would strike. He'd get me before I got out, right in the head, then all he had to do was make sure I was pushed down between the coffin and the dirt, go up and talk to Leonard. He wouldn't have to worry about the noise of the gun then. One snap and it was all over.

In the split second before I raised my hands to take hold of the edge of the grave, I thought about trying to snatch up the shovel I dropped, but knew that wouldn't work. I wasn't quick enough for that. Not quick enough to get hold of it, come out of the grave and hit him with it.

I took hold of the edge of the grave with both hands, then the flashlight dropped, and I heard the whistling of the shovel being swung. I threw my hands up in a wide X pattern and twisted my head to the side as the shovel came down and hit my wrists and pain exploded in me, but I had twisted my body so that it carried the power of the blow to the side, and with a quick turn of my arms, I wrenched the shovel free, dropped it, seized the sides of the grave, pulled myself up into a crouch.

The flashlight still lay on the ground, and there was a dark shape behind it, and I dove for it, was rewarded by my arms encircling Tim's neck.

I dropped my grasp from his neck to his sides, pinned his arms against him just as he reached into his coat pockets to get hold of the guns. I used my right knee to strike him in the side of the leg, on the pressure point there. He sagged and I butted him in the face, and he went down. I was all over him then, but the water flowing under us made us slide and we went backwards into the grave. We hit the coffin and the sides blew out, and the bodies beneath us leaped up. I felt a bony arm clasp my face, blocking my vision, filling my head with the stink of rotting meat. I don't know if it was me or Tim that screamed, but one of us did.

The rest of the coffin came apart beneath us, and we rolled in a wreck of bones and flesh. I came up on top, driving straight punches into Tim's face, and they were good punches, but I'd forgotten about the shovel I'd left in the grave, and Tim got hold of it, and though he didn't have room to swing it, he popped it forward, banging me between the eyes with the handle, then he was on top of me, trying to strangle me. I thrashed amidst the wreckage of Soothe and Florida, brought the sides of my hands down hard behind his elbows, pushed in. He couldn't hold the choke. I was gaining control. In another second I was going to turn him over and be on top, and he knew it. He shoved to his feet, leaped for the edge of the grave.

I managed to grab his leg. He kicked back reflexively. It was a lucky shot to the jaw. In the instant I was dealing with the pain he got out of the grave. I got it together pretty quick, went after him, stumbling over the flashlight as I went. The light spun toward him, showed him in its glow, then rolled away, but not before I saw he had pulled the automatic from his coat pocket.

Then there was a sound, like a stick snapping, and Tim did a little trick with his legs, as if he were trying to bury his heels in the earth, then he sagged and fell on his side, did a few kicks that carried him around in a semicircle, then he stopped moving. I could hear his breathing. It was hard and heavy.

"Hap. You okay?"

Leonard grew out of the darkness, limped toward me. He was holding his pistol. I answered, "Just barely."

"I got to thinking about things," Leonard said. "He went from not wanting to cooperate to being awfully anxious to cooperate. He wanted me to come even when you didn't. I got to wondering why he was so eager to get us down here. I'd have been here sooner, but the leg isn't working so well."

"I'm just glad you came . . . shit!" I glanced where Tim had been lying. He was no longer there.

Leonard wheeled with the gun and I got hold of the flashlight. I shined it about the graveyard. Tim, walking as if he were imitating the scarecrow in the Oz movie, was making bad time toward the far side of the graveyard, toward the woods. He got to the barbed wire fence, fell against it and stuck there, his upper body bending over it, as if he were trying to fold in half. Then I heard a loud cracking, a roar, like the sound of a freight train magnified by ten. In the glow of the flashlight I saw a tall silver mass of flying needles coming out of the forest. Pines snapped and crackled into toothpicks. Great oaks screamed as they were pulled from the ground.

The mass of silver needles was a great wall of water. Before I could say, "I'll be a sonofabitch," the wall came down on us like a thousand pianos falling, and the great gray mountain of wetness pushed Leonard and me together and carried us away.

We held to each other and the water carried us high up, then under, and I couldn't breathe, and it was the marsh all over again, only worse, because the power of the water was so awesome there was no fighting back, no swimming. It churned us up and carried us through the heights of trees. We clung to each other and breathed again. Then it was down once more into choking darkness and confusion. A moment later, we were on top of the water again, coughing, and the next thing I knew I was hung in a tree, my body slamming against the tree trunk. There was a great weight tearing at my right shoulder, and I realized it was because I was holding on to Leonard and the water was jerking at him and trying to take him and my shoulder with it.

"Let go, Hap, you stubborn sonofabitch!"

I could see Leonard's shape now, at the end of my arm, and the bastard let go of my hand, but I held his wrist and gritted my teeth. It was like the marsh, and I hadn't let go and we had made it, and I wouldn't let go this time.

"Let go!" Leonard said, "or it'll take us both!"

"Then it will," I said.

I heard Leonard laugh. A choked water laugh. A crazy laugh. Then he snapped his wrist loose of my fingers and the dark churning water pulled him from me, washed him away.

30

A few hours before morning a hot gold corkscrew of lightning hit the top of a pine across the way and knocked it in half and caught it on fire. The rain sizzled in the flames and the tree burned out quickly and the fiery limbs that fell off of it were consumed by the flooding waters.

Then the rain stopped and the clouds split open like cotton candy being torn by greedy fingers and the wind blew their remnants away. A great gold moon rose high up and was visible through the summit of the trees—a pocked Happy Face against black velvet. I looked at the stars and thought first of my father, pointing out the shapes in the heavens, then of Florida and how we had once made love in her car and lay on her car hood afterwards looking at the stars, feeling as if they were near and belonged to us.

In time the moonlight and starlight brightened even more and I spied a strange configuration in a massive oak, as if nature had made an image of the crucified Christ out of debris and put heaven's spotlights on it. I watched it for a long time, uneasy with it, then nodded some, thinking of Leonard.

Dawn came rosy, as if it had never rained, and the moon was dissolved by sunlight and the sun itself was a bleeding red boil that did little to warm the chilled air. The water below me had dropped ten feet, but it was still a rush of mud and wreckage. A bloated cow was wedged between a pine and a sweet gum, and with the water no longer rushing, I could hear flies working the carcass, getting their breakfast. I ached all over. I was freezing. My coat and clothes crinkled and popped with ice when I moved. Ice fell out of my hair.

I tried to stretch, get positioned on the limb some way I wouldn't ache, but that wasn't possible. Nothing was comfortable. But as I moved I could see the shape in the oak clearly.

It was Florida. Her corpse, mostly devoid of flesh now, her left leg missing from the knee down, was hung up in the oak amidst a wad of limbs and vines and shattered lumber. Her stick arms were spread wide and her skull was tilted down on the neck bones, held together by peeling strips of flesh and muscle. Hungry crows were so thick on top of her skull, flapping their wings, pecking at her flesh, they looked like windblown black hair. One arm was raised slightly higher than the other, and the skeletal hand pointed to the sky.

I closed my eyes, but in time I was drawn to look again, and after an hour or so I felt so strange and disconnected with reality her corpse was no longer horrifying; it was like part of the decor.

By midday I was hungry and freezing and feverish, beginning to feel as if I was going to fall because I couldn't keep my grip anymore. My hands were like claws. My calves and thighs ached with cramps. When I stood up on the limb to shake my legs out, I could hardly keep my balance. Something was moving and rattling in my chest, and its name was pneumonia.

The sun bled out its redness and turned yellow and rose in the sky like a bright balloon full of helium, but still it gave no heat. The air was as cold as an Arctic seal's nose and there was a slight wind blowing, and that made matters worse, turned the air colder and carried the stench from Florida's corpse and that of the bloated cow—which I named Flossy—to me as a reminder of how I would soon end up.

A few mobile homes floated by, mostly in pieces. A couple of rooftops drifted into view later on. I thought I might drop down on one of the roofs as it floated by, ride it out. And I think I was weak enough and stupid enough right then that that's exactly what I would have done, but the roof I had in mind hit a mass of trees, went apart, was washed away as splintered lumber.

I had become a little delirious with fever. Sometimes I dreamed I was still holding Leonard's wrist, and I was about to pull him into the tree with me, then I'd realize where I was and what had happened, and I'd go weak and wonder how it would be to drop from my limb and let the water have me.

After a time, I heard the helicopter. At first I thought the chopping sound was in my head, but finally I looked, and high up like a dragonfly, was a National Guard helicopter.

Then it was low, skimming over the trees, beating furiously, rattling the dry limbs of winter, making me colder. My coat was so soaked in water, so caked with ice, speedy movement was difficult, but I did my best to stand on my limb and wave an arm.

The helicopter passed over, started climbing. As I watched the copter soar up and away, I felt as if the world were falling out from under me. I slowly sat down. Then the copter turned back, dropped low.

It hovered over the tree where Florida's corpse was wedged, and I realized they had spotted her, not me. I waved and screamed and jumped up and down on my limb like an excited monkey. The copter moved slowly in my direction, a few yards above my tree and beat the air. A rope with a life basket was lowered out of its door.

They couldn't get too close because of the limbs, and I couldn't get far enough out to get hold of the basket. I tore off my coat and tossed it, inched my way out on the limb, heard it crack, but kept going. The basket was six feet away and the limb was starting to sag, and I knew this was it. Die dog or eat the hatchet. I bent my knees, got a little spring like a diver about to do a double somersault, and leaped into space.

My legs didn't carry me as far as I thought they might, but I got hold of the basket, barely, and it tilted and swung and I clung. They hauled up slowly, me swinging in the air, my fingers weakening by the second. And just when I thought I couldn't hold anymore, they pulled me inside and threw a blanket around my shoulders and shoved a cup of hot soup into my bloodless hands.

"Man," said the young, uniformed Guardsman who gave me the soup, "you are one lucky sonofabitch. We been all over. We haven't found but three or four people. That flood, it took the world. You Hap Collins?"

"Yeah. How did you—"

"Fella we found, said you were out there. Wouldn't let us give up. Said he'd throw himself out of the copter, we didn't keep looking. I don't think he has the strength to roll over, but we kept looking. We saw that body in the tree, then you."

I wasn't paying attention to the Guardsman anymore. I took a better look around the chopper. I had been so preoccupied with getting inside, then with the soup, I hadn't noticed that there were three other rescued civilians inside, lying under blankets. One of them rolled over slowly and looked at me and smiled, if you could call lifting your upper lip slightly a smile. It was Leonard.

"That's the guy," Guardsman said.

"Yeah," I said. "I know that sonofabitch."

The Guardsman pulled me over by Leonard and draped a blanket around my shoulders and gave me more soup. The Guardsman said, "We haven't got a doctor on board, but we'll have you to one soon."

"Thanks," I said.

I looked at Leonard. He was trying to sit up. I set the soup down and got him under the arms and pulled him up against the wall. "Throw yourself out, huh?" I said.

"Just bullshit." His voice was like crackling cellophane.

"Want some of my soup?"

"Long as I don't drink on the side where your mouth's been."

The rain stopped the day after the flood and it hasn't come a big rain since. The flood was the worst in East Texas history. Grovetown was almost wiped off the map and was designated a Disaster Area.

Leonard and I felt like warmed-over dog shit for about three months after it all. We were both pretty much broke, having gone through our savings and owing doctor bills.

Raul didn't run off while Leonard was in Grovetown. He had a change of heart, stayed home and waited. Leonard is looking for work. I go over there most Sundays to have dinner. I still don't like Raul much.

Florida's corpse was recovered and buried in the LaBorde cemetery. I was too sick to go to the funeral. Now that spring has come, there's a hill across from my house where beautiful wildflowers grow. I pick them from time to time, drive out to the cemetery in the car Charlie loaned me, and put them on Florida's grave.

Last week I started back doing odd jobs, and at the end of the week I nailed work driving a tractor, getting the ground in shape for a sweet potato crop for Mr. Swinger. It's not good work and it doesn't pay much, and it won't last long, but it has a hypnotic quality and keeps me from thinking too much. I get so I see only the field in front of me, hear the hum of the tractor, have to think just enough to do what needs to be done.

Sometimes, though, I can't help but consider it all. I heard through Charlie that Bacon was washed away with the flood, and his body has never been found. Mrs. Garner drowned too, but they found her body way down in the Thicket, the remains of that double-wide on top of her. Tim's body was located wrapped tight in barbed wire, like a metal mummy. They didn't find him all that far from his mother.

Hanson's the same. I went to Tyler to see him a couple of times, but he didn't know me and the family hardly does. I didn't go back. I couldn't see it made a difference. Charlie, on the other hand, goes there often, holds Hanson's hand and talks to him. He thinks Hanson's doing better. But he's the only one that does.

Not so long ago, Leonard and I, like gluttons for punishment, drove over to Grovetown. I was looking for Cantuck, but couldn't find him and couldn't find anyone knew anything about him. Fact was, I could hardly find anyone at all. The place is like a soggy ghost town. Half the buildings are a wreck and stink of mud and fish. Tim's filling station, except for the pumps, is just a patch of filthy concrete with dead bass on it.

We stopped by the cafe to tell Mrs. Rainforth thanks for saving our lives and Leonard's balls, for having Bacon look after us. The cafe had stood the flood pretty well, but it was closed. There was a realty sign on the door. I put my hands against the glass and looked inside. Water damage. Everything gone. I don't know where she and her boys went.

Week ago, I was sitting at home swigging a Diet Coke, trying to read an old paperback, when the telephone rang.

It was Cantuck.

"How are you, boy?" he said.

"Good enough," I said. "I'm breathing. I didn't know for sure you were. I came looking for you."

"Me and the wife got out just ahead of the flood. Lost every goddamn thing we owned. Been livin' with my sister over in

Brownsboro. We got us a mobile home now. Moved it in next to where our house used to be. We get the 'lectricity hooked up this week, and the shitter, then things can start gettin' back to normal and I can try and get down to business. Runnin' an office from Brownsboro hasn't been worth a flying fuck in a tornado."

"I presume, by business, you mean you're still Chief?"

"Yeah. Kinda what I'm callin' about. I thought you ought to know. Might involve you again in court, little later down the road. Kevin and Ray, they decided jail wasn't all that fun. They're trying to make some deal, shorter sentences. They named Reynolds. Said he let them in the jail, them and some others, and together they killed that nigger. Kevin said Reynolds swung on Soothe's legs till he choked. Rangers picked his ass up yesterday."

"What about Brown?"

"Nope. They may come through on him later, or Reynolds might. But I don't know. One rat at a time, son. One rat at a time. How's the colored boy . . . how's Leonard?"

"He's all right. Getting along."

"Good. Glad to hear it. You know what?"

"What?"

"They dug a bullet out of Tim's body."

I paused for an instant. "No shit?"

"Looks like someone killed him. Could be, we ran some tests on that slug, we might could figure out whose gun fired it."

"That a fact?"

"Yep. But dammit, way things been goin', the flood and all, me not having a place to keep stuff good, damn thing got lost. Can you believe that?"

"With you at the helm, it's hard to accept."

"Just plain disappeared. Never happened to me before. Makes me look bad, since I was the one ended up with the bullet, but these things happen. It won't happen again, but it happened this time."

I tried not to sigh. "Well, you can't blame yourself too much."

"Nope, I can't."

"Guess it can't be proved who killed Florida either?"

"No, but you know, I got this feeling, down deep. Just a feeling mind you, that justice has been served."

"Me too."

"Listen here, y'all come back this way, and it might be best if you don't, but if you do, we get the 'lectricity and the shitter in, come see me. My wife cooks a mean meat loaf, provided there's enough oatmeal to stretch it."

"Isn't that violating your religious rules?"

"Oatmeal in the meat loaf?"

"Blacks and whites."

"Well, you can be too strict, I reckon. Take care, Hap."

"One thing. Anyone ever find any music, recordings, stuff like that Soothe could have had?"

"Nothing. 'Course, if a fella found something valuable like that hidden in Florida's car. Say she got her hands on them somehow and didn't tell no one, and this stuff was still in good enough shape, a fella could hang on to it, and in time, he could come up with it like it was found another way, couldn't he?"

I let a few seconds pass. I thought about asking how Florida might have finally come by those recordings. I thought about lots of other questions no one could answer. When I finally spoke, what I said was, "But would a man that found something like that—knowing he ought to turn it over to the authorities—do something like that?"

"I think he might. And what would those recordings have to do with the authorities? Think about it."

"Even so, would it be wise for a fella to tell other people?"

"No. But he might do it anyway. If who he told was someone he thought wouldn't mind if they popped up later and the money from them went to a pet charity."

"Like muscular dystrophy."

"Yep."

"I'll be damned," I said.

We were quiet again. Maybe for a full half minute. Then Cantuck said, "Oh, we found your pickup. You don't want it back."

"Cantuck?"

"Yeah?"

"Thanks."

"You take care, boy."

I went to bed then, without my gun. I thought I was doing better.

But for the first time in months, it began to rain. It was a gentle spring rain, and I didn't like it. It woke me up. It used to help me sleep, now it makes me nervous. Twice as nervous if I should hear thunder or see lightning.

It's a week later and it's still raining. Nothing serious. Just a steady, easy spring rain, but I still can't sleep. I wake up every night and pad to the kitchen window for a look out back. There's only the woods out there, but I can't sleep. I sit up and drink coffee till morning, watch the late movies. Sometimes I play the L.C. Soothe boxed set I borrowed from Leonard. I play it and think about how this man, long dead, got this whole thing started.

Might as well. I go back to bed, I lay there and wait for the floodwaters to come hurtling down with Florida at the crest, pinned to the top of a wave like a Christmas tree ornament for the devil.

Just lay there and listen to the beating of my heart, counting the seconds gone from my life, anticipating less of the same.

You've turned the last page.

But it doesn't have to end there . . .

If you're looking for more first-class, action-packed, nail-biting suspense, join us at **Facebook.com/ MulhollandUncovered** for news, competitions, and behind-the-scenes access to Mulholland Books.

For regular updates about our books and authors as well as what's going on in the world of crime and thrillers, follow us on **Twitter@MulhollandUK**.

There are many more twists to come.

MULHOLLAND:
You never know what's coming around the curve.

HODDER